# POWER OF PERSUASION

"Have you ever heard of something called hypnotic somnambulism?" Lord Ives asked. "I would like to see if I might help you overcome your shyness using this method."

Alissa stared at him with disbelieving eyes.

"I know it sounds strange, but permit me to try," the handsome earl continued.

Alissa gave him a dubious look, then turned away. Though she had never heard of this hypnosis business, she longed to try it. But dare she?

"If it does not have any effect, you have lost nothing," Lord Ives pressed on.

Alissa looked at him again. Her eyes met his gaze with a mixture of curiosity, fear, and hope. But already she had gone too far to withdraw. She had fallen under this man's spell at first sight—and now she was putting herself in his hands.

---

EMILY HENDRICKSON lives at Lake Tahoe, Nevada, with her retired airline pilot husband. Of all the many places she has traveled to around the world, England is her favorite and a natural choice as a setting for her novels. Although writing claims most of her time, she enjoys gardening, watercolors, and sewing for her granddaughters as well as the occasional trip with her husband.

# The Gallant Lord Ives

## Emily Hendrickson

A SIGNET BOOK

**NEW AMERICAN LIBRARY**

A DIVISION OF PENGUIN BOOKS USA INC.

Copyright © 1989 by Doris Emily Hendrickson

SIGNET, SIGNET CLASSIC, MENTOR, ONYX, PLUME, MERIDIAN
and NAL BOOKS are published by New American Library,
a division of Penguin Books USA Inc., 1633 Broadway,
New York, New York 10019

First Printing, November, 1989

1 2 3 4 5 6 7 8 9

PRINTED IN THE UNITED STATES OF AMERICA

A word fitly spoken is like apples of gold in pictures of silver.

—Proverbs 25:11

# 1

Above the Wiltshire downs a peregrine falcon ringed higher and higher in the pale blue sky, then plummeted to earth, a swift messenger of death. A shrill scream rent the air, then all was silent.

A breeze rustled through the late-summer grasses, scattering the fragile blue blossoms of cranesbill as it skimmed over the downs. It whispered long-carried secrets to the skylarks that soared overhead, their song bursting across the open meadow as Alissa extended her left arm upward to receive her falcon. She whistled to the hawk and Princess swooped through the air, landing on Alissa's outstretched, stoutly gloved hand. The kill, a nice plump partridge, was deposited and the falcon rewarded. Princess wiped her beak briskly back and forth on the glove after finishing her treat. Alissa smiled with pleasure at this sign of great confidence her falcon displayed in her.

Alissa spoke softly, soothingly to Princess, praising the bird while chucking it on the cheek. Then she tucked the partridge into her game bag and wondered if the falcon was good for another toss.

Below the rise of the hill where Alissa stood with her falcon, Lord Christopher Ivesleigh, the Earl of Ives, rode his bay stallion, hoping to catch another glimpse of the falconer somewhere ahead. Along with his friend, he picked his way with care among the lichen-spotted rocks and fallen branches that littered the earth. The breeze playfully tossed bronzed leaves, and swaying branches bowed to the uneasy quiet in the woods. The sound of their approach was muffled by the quiet rush of a nearby rill as it gurgled its way toward the stream in the valley.

His companion, Lord David Birnam, Baron of Duffus, familiarly known to Lord Ives as Duffy, frowned at the littered ground. "Are you certain this is a better way to High ffolkes than the road? I canna think it be the best."

"Shh, Duffy. Did you see that? Someone is up ahead of us with a falcon. This ought to be good country for hawking, with open space in abundance." He reined in his horse at the edge of a high meadow, watching with amazement as a tall, slender girl raised her hand to receive the peregrine as it swooped down from the sky. Lord Ives observed while she talked to the bird, her face glowing with pleasure in her falcon's skill.

Alissa decided to try once more and signaled to the English setter far down the hill. Quick to respond to her cue, Lady slowly stalked through the grasses, then froze in the characteristic position of a setter at point. Alissa tossed Princess once again, thrilling as the bird ringed higher and higher in the sky until she was barely a black speck in the blue. When Princess had flown as high as she was likely to mount, exactly over the birds, but a little upwind of them, Alissa signaled to Lady and the dog flushed the birds, turning them downwind.

Princess hung a moment. With the incredible sight of a peregrine, the hawk noted the movement of partridge below before her plunge to the downs. Then, wings closed, like a living arrow she flashed to earth. Wind whistled through her bells, creating unearthly music. A puff of feathers indicated she had made a kill.

Alissa waited patiently while Lady did her work, and Princess performed a little dance before picking up her quarry to bring to Alissa.

Ives studied the girl with curiosity. She was dressed in a habit of deep teal blue, and her unbound hair cascaded down her back, the rich, tawny color of beech leaves in autumn. Her eager face glowed with a pink to put a wild rose to shame. She gaily whistled to her bird and it rose up from where the setter watched with anxious eyes. The hawk circled briefly, showing off her dashing style of flight before returning to the outstretched glove. What a vibrantly alive young woman compared to the insipid misses found in London drawing rooms.

Lord Ives watched as the young woman deftly substituted a treat of raw meat for the partridge intended for the kitchen. The falcon accepted the treat, then turned to face the men who sat, they had thought, unobserved.

The girl's charming smile rapidly faded as she whirled about to face them. She balanced the bird with unconscious skill as she studied the intruders. Obviously she was one of the members of the ffolkes family, as this was their land. The eldest daughter, if his guess was right. At the far side of the meadow her chestnut mare nickered when the other horses drew closer.

"Mind you curb that impetuous nature of yours, Ives. I keep telling you 'twill get you in trouble one of these days," cautioned Duffy in a low voice.

Alissa stared at the two who approached, the brown-haired man seated on an enormous bay, the other, a fiery-haired man with guileless blue eyes, on a chestnut gelding. She studied the man on the bay. Her heart began pumping faster than a newborn chick's. He was known to her, not that she expected he would recall her. Her throat felt so dry she couldn't swallow. That man with haughty black eyes held far too elevated a position in the *ton* to remember the painfully shy miss who had made her come-out this past Season. Beneath her teal-blue habit her stomach lurched in a familiar, terrifying manner.

Princess shifted uneasily as she sensed her mistress's tension. The jingle of the bird's ankle bells carried across the meadow with distinct clarity. Lady barked sharply as she rushed up the hill to protect her mistress.

Alissa carefully placed the hood on her falcon, while wishing the men would go away. Could she manage to speak? At last she said, "Who are you? What are you doing here?" Her mouth dried and refused to permit another word to escape. It was best if they thought she didn't know either of them. It would mean fewer explanations that could only be difficult, if not impossible, for her.

The man on the bay vaulted from his horse with ease, bowing with practiced elegance. "Lord Christopher Ivesleigh, the Earl of Ives, at your service. My friend here is

Baron Duffus. We have an appointment with Baron ffolkes, who, I expect, is your father.'' He waited, smiling with great charm, while the young woman seemed to struggle for words.

Alissa cursed her tongue, which balked at speech. This man would be like all the others, laugh at the horridly shy woman who could not so much as respond to a simple, commonplace remark. How she longed to speak with the same ease he found so ready. Her eyes flashed a look of distress at him before returning to the distant view. It wasn't so difficult to speak if you didn't look at the other person. ''He is,'' she managed to say in a voice just barely heard.

At a signal, her mare, Fancy, walked up to her, and Alissa edged over to where she might have a chance to get up in the saddle. Lady came bounding up to them, her suspicious gaze darting from one man to the other. Silently—for she knew better than to alarm the hawk—she placed herself between the strangers and her mistress.

Lord Ives guessed the young woman was shy and wanted nothing more than to get on her horse, then head for her home. After a reassuring look at the dog, who seemed to sense his mistress was in no danger from him, Ives quickly walked to her side and, with an air of one who does that sort of thing often, tossed her to her saddle. Admiration for the grace with which she balanced the peregrine was expressed most inadequately, he felt, by his few words. ''You handle the bird very well.''

Startled eyes looked down at him, their deep blue troubled. Her gaze dropped to the hawk. Her trembling lips were silent, though a hint of her smile returned. She clasped the reins firmly in her right hand while settling the falcon on her perch. The bells on the bird's feet jingled as she moved slightly, then was still.

Raising her gaze once more to where Lord Ives watched her, Alissa managed a swallow, then softly said, ''The house is west of here. Just follow the track.''

Without so much as a farewell, she dug her foot into the mare's flank. The odd trio, girl, falcon, and horse, sped across the high meadow toward the west, teal skirts rippling as she galloped away. Behind her the two men stood in frowning silence. The dog studied the men, apparently decided they could be trusted, then tore after her mistress, her white plume of a tail waving like a flag in retreat.

"Duffy, I have seen shy young misses before, but this one surpasses them all." Lord Ives gathered his reins in one hand while he gazed after the vision in blue. In spite of her shy ways, she was a lovely woman, those deep blue eyes reaching to some emotion within him.

"Wise men lay up knowledge, but the mouth of the foolish is a present destruction," quoted Duffy in perhaps not the most apt manner. "What she dinna say canna be held against her."

"The Book of Proverbs seems to bring out the Scot in you, Duffy, my man. Perhaps what you quote may be true, but the poor girl must find life a living hell if it is that difficult for her to converse. I wonder that she was allowed out here alone." They remounted and slowly headed west, taking a slightly different direction from the young woman. Lord Ives felt the shy miss wouldn't thank them for following her.

With unseeing eyes, Alissa rode hard toward the stables, ignoring the terrain she normally noted with care. With luck she could be at High ffolkes before the guests arrived, and could take refuge in her room.

What a fool she was, to even attempt to talk to the handsome lord from London. She had watched him at those glittering London balls, cooed at by fluttering belles, fussed over by elegant ladies. He had only to appear and the party took new life.

How Alissa had hated those days spent in self-conscious wretchedness. Unable to converse, too shy to mix with others, she murmured her way through countless dances, endured painful hours with the dowagers and other misses who, like Alissa, were not "taking." She relaxed only when she and her chaperone aunt returned to her London home as soon as possible. Her aunt had despaired of her, sending her failure of a niece back to High ffolkes far earlier than the end of the Season, much to Alissa's relief.

Life in the country far from the pressures of town was infinitely more to her liking. She smiled down at the hooded bird on her perch. She had no problem talking to Princess in the least.

Unheedful—indeed, uncaring—she paid no attention to where she galloped until she glanced up to see a high fence, one she usually avoided, looming before her. Her mare shied, then gamely jumped, catching a hoof on the top rail as they sailed over. In the blink of an eye, Alissa found herself falling with the horse. ''Oh, drat!'' What a stupid thing to happen.

The sudden impact forced the air from Alissa's lungs. She hit the ground hard, unwilling to jump free while trying to protect the bird. Fancy tumbled as well, and at first failed to right herself as Alissa hoped she would.

Once Alissa found her breath, she assessed the situation. She was pinned on the ground, a rough fencepost cruelly pressing against her spine. Her mare pressed against her from her front. Had the fence not been there, chances were Fancy would have crushed Alissa completely. It was impossible for Alissa to move her legs. She was immobilized from the waist down, only her arms free. Pain cut through her with near-unbearable intensity. Nearby, Lady crouched, worried eyes on her mistress. Then Fancy struggled to her feet, flicking wary eyes toward her fallen mistress. The mare slowly walked away, shaking her head in seeming confusion.

Turning slightly, Alissa could see Princess, unharmed, shifting uneasily on the ground, uncertain what to do, the hood preventing flight. Though the bird might enjoy a bit of sun, prolonged exposure would hurt her. Princess must be set free to seek her perch in the mews.

Still unable to move her legs, with her last shred of strength Alissa reached over to pull off the bird's hood, then sank back to watch as Princess soared into the sky.

''Follow her home, Lady,'' Alissa whispered, hoping her dog could hear the command. It was the last thing she knew before lapsing into unconsciousness.

As the two riders approached the Elizabethan manor house built of red brick with mullioned windows, a dainty figure walked around the corner carrying a basket of late-summer blooms. At the sound of the horses, she stopped, turning to greet the strangers.

Both Lord Ives and Duffy inhaled with awe at the sight of her. Tripping lightly across the grass came a living china doll. Blond curls peeped from beneath her straw bonnet, contrasting exquisitely with cornflower-blue eyes and a rosebud mouth of luscious pink. Her porcelain complexion had never seen the rays of the hot summer sun: nary one freckle dared to mar that perfect skin. Her voice, when she spoke, was bell-like and sweet.

"Papa told us two gentlemen were expected. I vow I never thought to see such fashionable Londoners coming to inspect Papa's sheep." Her dulcet trill of laughter, accompanied by a flirtatious batting of lashes, charmed the two men, putting all thoughts of a tall, shy young woman and her peregrine from their minds. "I am Henrietta ffolkes. Such a silly last name, but Papa insists on clinging to the old Elizabethan spelling. Please, follow me to the salon. You must be terribly thirsty from traveling, and a cool drink would undoubtedly be most welcome."

A servant materialized from the background as they dismounted. Neither man had been aware of his approach. He took the horses in the direction of the stables.

"We would be delighted, Miss ffolkes. I'm sure it must be as charming as your lovely self." Lord Ives bowed low over the dainty hand while Duffy watched the complacent smile on the exquisite face as the young woman preened herself at Lord Ives's attentions.

Duffy trailed after the others, his keen gaze observing the almost-too-beautiful young miss and his best friend. Ives appeared to be captivated by the girl. Duffy narrowed his eyes thoughtfully, then moved his gaze around the spacious entry hall.

It appeared a well-kept home. Their footsteps echoed on the flagstones of the entry until they crossed into the drawing room. Paneled in Dutch oak, it was a dimly lit place that nonetheless gave one a feeling of warmth and welcome. Plainly furnished in simple style, it was obvious to Duffy that neither Baron nor Lady ffolkes cared for show. Yet from the soft, dull colors of the aged Aubusson on the floor, to the faded tapestry on the far wall, it was a pleasant room in which to rest and visit.

Fluttering her lashes in a demure manner, Miss ffolkes crossed to give the bell-pull a tug. When the footman entered, she issued orders for a light repast plus tankards of home-brewed ale for their guests.

"I vow you would not care for a mere cup of tea after your journey. Papa said to take care of you for him, and I am certain this is what he would offer you." She dimpled in seeming modesty as she seated herself on a chair near the fireplace, gesturing to the sofa opposite her for their repose. "I must apologize for my mother's absence. She is ever in her garden. Papa must be overseeing in the field today, though I feel he should be here shortly. My eldest sister is off hawking, as is her custom most days of decent weather. Alas, that leaves me to see to your comfort, gentlemen."

A moment's thought went to the tall miss in teal blue who had smiled so radiantly as her falcon came to rest on her glove. The diamond of the first water who faced them drove the memory from Lord Ives's mind.

Within minutes a tray holding tankards of foaming ale and plates of bread and cheese was brought to the salon. It was hearty fare to men accustomed to more dainty foods when ladies served. Ives raised his pewter tankard with appreciation. "To the fairest miss in England."

The delicate blush that spread over her porcelain face was worthy of a masterpiece of art. She glanced with curiosity as a maidservant entered the room, crossing to her side with speed. A whispered message was met with a frown. Duffy heard her quietly inform the servant that the housekeeper could properly handle the matter. The servant was not best pleased, Duffy noted. In fact, the young maid seemed downright shocked before hastily assuming a bland countenance and scurrying away. Duffy glanced at his friend to see if he had observed the scene, but Lord Ives was gazing at the fair Miss ffolkes. It would be up to himself to keep a sharp eye peeled around here, that was for certain. As impulsive as Ives was wont to be, he would bear watching.

The English setter dashed into the room, heedless of a scold from Miss ffolkes. She trotted over to Lord Ives, gave him a beseeching look, then glanced at Duffy. When neither gentleman moved, she turned and raced out once more.

"Forgive the dog, please, gentlemen. My sister *will* spoil that dog of hers." Henrietta gave another of her demure smiles, flashing dainty pearl-white teeth.

As she spoke, an older woman entered the room, her vague expression changing when she saw there were guests. "Henrietta, did I know we were to have company today?" The lady wore a strange mixture of clothing. A somewhat muddied green gown was topped with a tan cambric apron that had deep pockets overflowing with pieces of string, a long-handled clippers, and a pair of canvas gloves.

"Yes, Mama. These gentlemen are newly come from London to look at Papa's sheep. Mama—the Earl of Ives and Baron Duffus. Since you could not be found, I took it upon myself to see that they had refreshment. I was certain that was what Papa and you would wish."

Lady ffolkes nodded, looking faintly bemused. "Parsons will show you to where my husband is. You won't find any sheep in the house." She glanced at her daughter with approval, a faint smile crossing her face as she turned to leave the room. "Excuse me, gentlemen, I have things to do and I am certain you won't need my assistance."

Miss ffolkes rose from her chair and walked with the men, who had risen when Lady ffolkes entered the room, to the door, where she motioned Parsons to come closer. "They wish to see Papa. Will you take them, please?" Turning to Lord Ives, she beamed a breathtaking smile up at him, and added in a sweet, girlish voice, "You gentlemen will join us for dinner this evening?"

Lord Ives again bowed low over her hand, replying they were delighted to accept, while Duffy noted that he had not been consulted by either party.

The sheep were indeed worthy of the trip down from London. Lord Ives proved to be a shrewd bargainer, earning respect from Baron ffolkes. The good baron was rightly proud of his sheep, considering them the finest to be found on the Wiltshire downs. He remarked to Lord Ives, "I expect they will do well at the sheep fair coming up in Salisbury in a few weeks. You gentlemen plan to attend that event, do you not?''

At their hasty assurances, the baron, his mind leaping into action, genially invited them to come for a visit, stay a week or more before the fair. Henrietta badgered him continually for a London Season. Should this earl find her worthy (and who could not?), it could well save a good deal of money and that dratted Season. And *that* appealed to the baron's parsimonious nature. These lords were precisely what he wanted. His prim mouth stretched into a cunning smile. He was determined to get *all* of his girls fired off, and well. He hoped that one more Season for Alissa would do the trick for that shy miss, although he might be overly optimistic. Now, for Henrietta's future . . .

''Come, you must have a look at my hounds, gentlemen.'' The three men sauntered away from the sheep fold toward where the hounds were housed in a small building and run next to the stable bloc. ''Over there is the mews where my eldest daughter keeps her hawks. Has two now—a peregrine falcon and a goshawk tiercel. Too much for a woman, I say. But she's a surprising one, gets along with them famously.''

''I believe we saw her out on the downs. She does not require an assistant?'' There was no hint of censure in his voice, yet the listener was well aware of the implication of the words.

The baron slapped his gloves against his thigh in vexation. ''Aye, that she does. Thomas has been ill with a touch of something or other. Cannot keep her in the house, you know. Girl is out in all manner of weather. She's a handful. A mind of her own. Now, her sister is something else, indeed. My dear Henrietta is all a man could wish for, if I do say so myself.''

Lord Ives murmured an appropriate reply as he watched a slim young miss run from the west wing of the house toward the stables. Her bonnet bounced gaily on her back, dangling by its ribands as she hurried, unheedful of the pretty picture she presented. She looked to be about seventeen or so, with soft brown curls tumbling about a sweet-looking face. ''Another daughter, Baron?''

"Hmpf. That's Elizabeth, my youngest. My boy, Barrett, is off to a sale north of here at Amesbury. There's a horse he fancies. I expect he will be bringing it back with him when he comes." Baron ffolkes felt in a rare good humor.

The dogs were duly admired. It was a fine setup, with stable and dog run clean and neatly kept. Lord Ives was curious about the mews, yet something held him back from asking to see that area. If the hawking daughter was so shy, she might be displeased to see strangers intruding on her domain. Miss Elizabeth could be seen in earnest conversation with one of the grooms, who leapt on a horse and rode off pell-mell toward the downs where Ives had last seen the falconer and her proud bird.

The thought crossed Duffy's mind that there was something smoky going on about here, but he kept silent, merely watching. As it was written in Proverbs, "A man's heart deviseth his way: but the Lord directeth his steps." If he was to find out what was afoot, he would be led to the discovery. In the meantime, Duffy would investigate the young Elizabeth. There was a serene look of common sense about the girl. She might prove to be of greater interest than the beauty who had eyes for only the Earl of Ives. Though far too young, she might entertain.

On the rise of ground before the house, Henrietta stood at the edge of a fine Elizabethan knot garden. Lord Ives forgot all about sheep and hounds as well as falcons, and crossed to where she so prettily waited.

"I vow, I thought you would be with the sheep until nightfall, my lord." Henrietta giggled at the thought, then, dimpling in a coquettish manner, added, "I am certain you will wish to wash up after being out by the fold. May I offer you a room where you could refresh yourselves?"

"Kind lady, it would be most welcome." Lord Ives turned to Duffy, who had reluctantly joined the pair. "We would welcome a change. Right, my friend?"

"Aye. I canna present myself in the hall in all my dirt. I suppose your family gathers there afore the evening meal, lass?" Duffy lapsed into a touch of Scots as he searched the face of the beautiful girl standing a bit too close to his friend. There was absolutely no reason why Duffy ought to feel apprehensive. The young lady came of impeccable birth. Her father was very well-set, if somewhat absorbed with the raising of sheep. Even her peculiar mother managed a magnificent garden, if this be a sample of her art. He guessed he was accustomed to seeing Ives with more sophisticated women.

Lord Ives bent to pick a flower from the colorful array around them. "To the fairest of the fair."

Henrietta blushed becomingly. "La, sir, you are a flatterer." She turned to lead the way to the house, casting flirtatious looks at Lord Ives as they walked together.

Duffy studied the sweet, serious face of Elizabeth as she crossed the garden to join them. She curtsied properly to the gentlemen, peeping a shy look at Duffy, then turned to her sister, staying her with a slender hand.

"Please, I must talk with you, Henrietta. I wish your help."

Elizabeth gave her sister a pleading look that reminded Duffy of the setter that had raced into the drawing room earlier. Duffy's feeling of unease grew.

"Surely it can wait, Elizabeth. Can you not see we have guests? I must have Parsons show them to a room, then we can speak." Henrietta's irritation was well-concealed. Only one as acute as Duffy might have noticed it. Her voice had been gently reproving, placing the younger Elizabeth in the wrong.

Duffy extended a gallant arm. "Join me in the walk to the manor, Miss Elizabeth. Now, tell me what had you in such a flutter. I saw you hurry to the mews a bit ago."

Elizabeth gave him a confused look, then calmly replied, "Do not give it a thought, my lord. Everything shall be all right. I shall make it so." With that obscure and rather odd reply, she walked with Duffy to the house, her quaint air of maturity amusing him.

Christopher Ivesleigh was enchanted with the fair charmer who walked so daintily at his side. If ever there was a dream come true, it was this lovely blond with those pretty eyes so full of innocence and trust.

"Are you planning to attend the Sheep Fair in Salisbury,

my lord? 'Tis but a few weeks off. As well as the sheep display, there will be all manner of delights to be found.'' Henrietta dimpled prettily, and Lord Ives was certain that she would be the greatest delight to be viewed at the fair.

''Your father has invited us to stay with you during that time.'' He waited to see her response.

''Ohhh, do come early. I know life in the country must seem horridly dull to London gentlemen such as you, but I vow we can be quite gay.'' Her appealing smile was irresistible to the charmed Lord Ives.

''I cannot deny your request, fair lady. Duffy and I shall be here early on, with pleasure, I assure you.''

The young lady purred with gratification at his words. She handed the gentlemen into the butler's care with an admonition to treat their guests well.

As the trio walked up the stairs, Duffy glanced back to see Henrietta giving her sister a whispered scold.

In the privacy of their allotted room, Duffy removed his coat and limp shirt. As he splashed refreshing lavender-scented water over his chest and face, he wondered how deeply Christopher's sudden interest in the fair Henrietta went. Duffy hoped it was of brief duration.

Duffy toweled himself dry, then reached for a clean shirt suitable for wear to the dining table. ''She is a lovely lass. Miss Henrietta ought to do well when she reaches the marriage mart in London.''

Christopher gave him a startled look. ''She goes to town this next Season? You have keen ears, my friend.''

Duffy gave a shrug, then tucked his shirt in his pantaloons, while giving his dull boots a dismayed frown. ''Aye, that I have. So would you if you ceased looking at that blond miss as though she was an entire window of comfits. What has caught you, Ives? Not like you to be so bowled over by so young a country lass.''

''For that matter, you were attending to that child, Elizabeth, as though she was strolling in Hyde Park at four of the clock. I find Miss Henrietta charming—as a diversion, I assure you. And Miss Elizabeth?''

''That miss is not only comely but also interesting,'' Duffy flared back. "She has a maturity far beyond her years."

"That reminds me: I wonder if the shy one will show up for dinner." Christopher tied his cravat in a precise Mathematical that was the envy of all his friends. He stepped back to survey his appearance, then donned his coat once more, now well-brushed by the footman.

Rubbing his chin, Ives strolled to the window that looked over the rolling downs that stretched far beyond the landscaped grounds of High ffolkes. "Do not be surprised if she remains to her room. She is like a shy bird, to be tamed with patience and care."

"Who made you so suddenly the wise one? I don't see any gray beard appearing." Duffy chuckled at the look of chagrin that crossed Christopher's face.

Instead of replying, Ives stiffened with alertness, listening to a quiet commotion out in the hall. Then all was silent again. He met the puzzled expression on Duffy's face with a shrug.

When they left their room, the upper hall was empty of people. Only the English setter was to be seen, sitting anxiously outside the last door on the right. The dog pawed at the door, whining softly. Ives glanced at the dog, mildly curious, as the two gentlemen walked to the stairs.

The family gathered in the hall, the London gentlemen near the last to arrive. As they began to drift in the direction of the dining room, Lady ffolkes wandered down the stairs, an abstracted expression on her face.

"Someone has been digging in my *Chrysanthemum leucanthemum*. I do wish you could keep the dogs out of the gardens." Her gaze focused on the strangers and she sent a questioning glance to Elizabeth.

"Alissa has moved a few plants to the little garden outside the conservatory, Mama." She moved forward to slip her arm about her mother, gently guiding her toward the dining room. "You recall these are the gentlemen who came from London today? Papa suggested they join us for dinner. They will be staying with us during the Sheep Fair in Salisbury as well." She smiled, yet Duffy thought he detected a note of warning in her look.

"Of course, of course. How remiss of me, gentlemen. I ought to have thought of it earlier." She stopped by her place at the foot of the table. "Where is Alissa?"

Elizabeth gave a worried look at Henrietta, and clasped the back of her chair with anxious hands.

"La, Mama, you know how Alissa feels about company," Henrietta said. "One of the maids said Alissa will not be joining us this evening. Pray do not keep our guests waiting." She bestowed a coy look on Lord Ives and preened a bit as he gave her an answering smile.

The meal seemed normal, yet Duffy, his mind still uneasy from earlier sensations, wondered about Miss Elizabeth. She ate as quickly as seemly, then begged to be excused from the table. She gave the butler a significant look as she hurried from the room, and he most discreetly followed her out.

Duffy could only surmise, and that did little good. He watched as Christopher set out to charm the young blond, glad to know it was only a diversion. Duffy supposed little harm could come of such a thing.

As they finally left the dining room, Duffy pulled Christopher aside and said in a low voice, "I dinna wish to stay here this evening. Let us be on our way. You will see the fair Henrietta again soon enough. If we leave now, we ought to be able to make it to the Pheasant Inn."

Since Duffy rarely made such a request, Christopher was inclined to acquiesce. Besides, if he was to send his man down here to fetch the purchased sheep, it was best not to tarry. As Duffy pointed out, they would be returning shortly.

The gentlemen made the most polished of departures, leaving the ffolkes family certain the London lords were utterly devastated to depart.

All but Alissa, that is. That young woman was not to be seen. Nor was Elizabeth, much to Duffy's regret.

# 2

In the afternoon sun the warm red brick of the manor house held a welcoming glow for the two travelers who rode up to the front door. Gleaming windows winked down upon them, while the mild breeze carried the fragrance of newly cut hay across the lawns. Behind them in the distance, the coach with their valets and luggage trundled along in a cloud of dust. There was not one soul to be seen.

"Silent place," commented Duffy, giving the house an appraising look as the two men dismounted.

The well-oiled hinges of the door made no sound as it opened. Parsons quietly walked to the men, bidding them welcome in a lugubrious tone. "Please follow me, gentlemen."

Lord Ives cast a puzzled look at Duffy as they mounted the steps, then entered the hall. Whereas before, their footsteps had echoed about, now all was muffled with casually strewn carpets. No hostess or host was present to greet them, the lower area of the house seemingly vacant of people of any description.

They were about to mount the stairs to the upper floor when Lord Ives placed a hand on the butler's arm. "Tell me, is there an illness in the family? This"—he gestured to the carpets about on the slate—"must have some meaning."

"That is so, milord. Miss Alissa took a tumble from her horse—the very day you were last here, I recollect. She has not been able to walk since."

After a dismayed look at Duffy, Lord Ives turned a concerned face to the butler. "Has she broken a limb? Can nothing be done for her?"

Parsons shrugged, obviously desiring to speak, yet aware of the impropriety of doing so. Speech won. "No broken bone, milord. The doctor says there is naught amiss with her, beyond the light injury sustained when she hit that fencepost. He seems right bewildered that our Miss Alissa is unable to put a foot from her bed.''

The old man gave a discreet cough, then added, ''We fear for her, poor miss, for 'tis said she daily grows weaker. Not even her falcon draws her from her room.''

''I said there was something smoky about this place,'' murmured Duffy as they completed the walk up the stairs and down the hall to the room they had occupied before. He entered with reluctance, watching from the doorway as his friend followed the butler.

Christopher was led to the room opposite where the English setter lay before the door as she had when they were last here, her head on her paws, eyes mournfully alert.

''Is Miss Alissa in there?'' Lord Ives found he was whispering, though if there was nothing wrong with the girl, there really was no need for such.

''Indeed. Miss Alissa will not even see her dog, poor animal.''

Lord Ives shook his head, then followed the butler into the guest room. It was simply furnished, as was all the house they had observed so far. Neatly kept and polished, it was a pleasant place to stay, Ives decided, nodding to the butler in dismissal.

Once the door was shut, it didn't remain that way for long. Duffy gave a short rap, then entered.

''Well,'' he huffed. ''Now, what do you think of that? I'll warrant that was what the commotion was about afore we left. And that was the reason Miss Elizabeth rushed from her dinner.'' Though he would not admit to it, Duffy had hoped to see the fair Elizabeth before they left the manor house. It had bothered him that she had failed to at least wish them Godspeed.

Lord Ives strolled to the window looking out over the downs. ''I imagine the reason we are housed in these rooms, despite their proximity to hers, is that all the bedrooms are confined to this one floor. 'Tis far from palatial, though it does have its charm.'' He strolled to the bed, slipping off his coat and tossing it on the faded velvet covering.

Turning to face Duffy, Ives stood, hands on hips, his brow furrowed. "I do not like to consider the thoughts which flood my mind at this revelation from the butler. Do you recall that maidservant who came into the drawing room shortly after we arrived last time? She must have come with news that for some reason Miss Henrietta did not wish to disclose to us . . . and which displeased her. Could it have been news of Miss Alissa? And remember the dog? She came as well to solicit something . . . our help, perhaps? I fear that does not place Miss Henrietta in a very good light, does it, Duffy?"

"Perhaps the lass dinna wish to upset the sale of sheep for her father." Duffy was oddly pleased that Christopher would now take a second, harder look at the china doll, as he privately referred to Miss Henrietta.

"But she obviously said nothing to her mother either. Strange behavior for so sweet and beautiful a young lady. Perhaps she misunderstood the seriousness of the accident."

Ives poured lavender-scented water into the basin, then hastily splashed some on his face, drying off with a soft towel before donning his coat once more. Though his shoulders were broad and the fit of his coat snug, he managed without the two footmen so many men required.

Lord Ives walked to the door, opened it, and together the men—after a frowning study of the closed door across from Ives's room—walked down the stairs to search out their hostess . . . or someone.

Parsons was hovering in the hall when they reached the foot of the stairs. He came forward, his reserved smile welcome after his earlier gloom. "Lady ffolkes is in the garden. If you will follow me, gentlemen?"

They crossed the neatly scythed lawn, then walked down a path to where Lady ffolkes supervised the placement of a young tree. "Good afternoon, Lord Ives, Lord Duffus. Nice example of a *Carpinus betulus*, is it not? Thought I would give a hornbeam a home in this spot, where someday it can offer shade to an overwarm soul. I rather like the golden leaves they present in the autumn. Looks a bit like the birch of some people, you know. Majestic tree once 'tis full-grown. Amazing to think this slip will climb to a possible height of ninety feet.'' She turned from her task, satisfied the men were doing the job properly, and took a shrewd look at her guests. ''I trust you had a tolerable journey? Lord ffolkes ought to be around here somewhere.''

Lord Ives glanced at Duffy, then replied, ''Indeed, my lady, we had a fine trip down. We were sorry to learn that Miss Alissa is indisposed.''

Lady ffolkes's eyes narrowed; then her expression cleared. ''Difficult thing, that. Don't know what to make of the gel. Henrietta tells me not to fuss, as though I ever do. Elizabeth is the one who does all the worrying about this house. Enough for the lot of us, I daresay.''

''You do not feel a concern?'' Lord Ives wanted to shake the woman, who showed so much more interest in a sapling than in her precious daughter.

''She'll come about when she will.'' With that totally obscure remark, Lady ffolkes turned once more to check the stance of the tree, giving orders to the gardener about the watering, then strode off toward the stables, her apron flapping about her as she walked. ''Follow me, gentlemen. I believe you'll find Lord ffolkes in here, if I make no mistake.''

Leaving Lord Ives and Duffy at the door of the stables, she continued to stride toward a distant garden, her skirt swirling about her feet as she marched on her way.

''Strange, unnatural woman,'' whispered Ives to his friend. He cocked his brow, revealing by his look his opinion of the woman more than words could express.

''Aye, that she be. Strange household, if you ask me,'' muttered Duffy to the back of his friend as they sought their host in the gloom of the stables.

In the dim light they made out the figures of three men: Lord ffolkes; a younger edition of the baron, presumably his son; and a groom. They were discussing a fine young hunter that nervously edged away as the strangers approached.

Ives noted the chestnut mare ridden by the falconer the last time he had seen the tall, slender woman, and paused to look the horse over.

"Welcome. Good to see you again." The baron had quickly joined them. "Fine horse, not a scratch on her in spite of the fall." He fondly stroked Fancy's delicate head as he spoke.

Glancing first at Duffy to see if his reaction was the same, Ives turned to the baron, admirably concealing his disgust at so callous a father. "Amazing, my lord. I gather Miss Alissa did not fare as well."

"Hmpf. Takes after her mother. Never a practical bone in the girl's body. Dreaming and hawking and fiddling with her clay. No wonder she took a tumble. Most likely didn't pay any attention to where she was riding. Terrible thing to risk a fine mare like that."

Ives was beyond speech for a moment. "Would it be possible to see Miss Alissa, my lord? To offer my wishes for a speedy recovery, perhaps?"

He received an astounded look in reply. "Eh? Talk to Alissa? No one ever does, you know. Think she prefers it that way. But I see no harm in it. One moment and I will take you up myself." He spoke a few words to his son after introducing the guests, then ambled toward the doorway of the barn.

The three men quietly walked into the house, through the central hall, and up the broad stairs to the upper floor. At the far end, the English setter thumped her tail in a half-hearted greeting.

Squatting down as much as stockinette pantaloons permitted, Ives fondled her head, noting the intelligent expression in her eyes. "Hanker for your mistress, do you?"

Ives and Duffy waited politely as Baron ffolkes rapped on the door, then, hearing no response, pushed the door open and entered the darkened room.

Glaring at the figure nearly concealed beneath the blue print coverlet, he motioned Duffy and Ives to follow him.

Ives exchanged an uneasy look with Duffy as the trio crossed to the foot of the four-poster bed.

"You have company. They asked to see you." Amazement that the two guests would desire speech with his eldest daughter was evident in his tone. "Gentlemen." Lord ffolkes gestured in annoyance at the silent girl, then marched out the door. He'd better things to do than loiter in a sickroom listening to polite chitchat.

The first thing Ives did was to cross to the windows and pull open the heavy cream draperies.

A highly indignant young woman half-pushed herself up, leaning on one elbow. Hair the color of autumn beech leaves tumbled from beneath a dimity nightcap. "How . . . how dare you!" she gasped. "This is highly irregular, my lord!"

Ives wondered how far down that delicious blush covered her skin. She was an intriguing thing, those blue eyes so incensed it was almost amusing but for her tragic circumstances.

Unconcerned at her anger, Ives strolled about examining the wallpaper, a hand-painted eighteenth-century Chinese, if he wasn't mistaken. The blue-upholstered chaise longue and two cozy chairs drawn up before the marble fireplace looked most attractive. Before the window was a pretty little dressing table that showed no sign of having been used for some time. He caught sight of himself in the large mirror above the fireplace, then glanced back at the girl in the bed, whose rosy face was beginning to fade.

"Beastly place to be stuck, bed. Why are you there? I should think you'd welcome an opportunity to leave the horrid thing." He raised an elegant brow in question.

Without waiting for an answer that he suspected was being carefully formulated in her mind, he walked to her bed, tossed the covers aside, but for one thin blanket, and scooped her up in his arms. Ignoring an outraged shriek, he carried her to the chaise longue and gently deposited her with the greatest of care. Leaning back from where he perched at the edge of the chaise, he said to Duffy, "Another pillow or two, I think."

"Right," Duffy replied with a touch of concern.

"You are totally mad," Alissa insisted, her husky voice a bit smoother, though most annoyed. Still she permitted the insertion of two plump pillows behind her and settled back with a sigh of resignation. "Why are you here?"

"Your father invited us to visit while we attend the

Salisbury fair. Since you were not downstairs to greet us, we prevailed upon your father to permit us a call. We missed seeing you last time, before we left.'' Seeing she appeared reasonably comfortable, he removed himself to the nearby chair, where he continued to study her.

Alissa plucked at the blue ribbons dangling untied from the neck of her lawn nightgown. How often she had thought of this handsome lord in the long hours of the night, wondering where he was, what he might be doing. Never in those mental wanderings had she thought she might see him in her own room. ''You really ought not be in here,'' she stated in soft accents.

Ives agreed with a nod. ''I know. Duffy continually scolds me for my lack of manners. Impulsive soul that I am, I could not resist. Your friend has been waiting with great patience to see you, and I felt sorry for her.'' With that he snapped his fingers and Lady trotted forward to butt her nose against Alissa's hand, hoping for a caress.

Remorseful at her neglect of her faithful companion, Alissa stretched out her hand to stroke the silken head that moved closer. A contented sigh escaped as the white plume of a tail began to wag cautiously.

''I believe she has missed you. Your butler says you have neglected your falcon. Do you have someone to hunt her for you?'' Ives rested his elbows on the arms of the chair, then rubbed at his chin with lean, tapered fingers.

''I do.'' Her innate shyness held her from speech, though there were dozens of words longing to trip from her tongue. Yet she didn't really feel intimidated by these gentlemen. Perhaps it was those eyes. One couldn't be afraid of twinkling eyes. She settled back against the pillows, loath to return to her bed and the silence she had been subjected to for the past weeks. Had it not been for Elizabeth, she would have lost her mind. Bless the girl, she ought to be returning from her errand to check on Princess.

''I know the fundamentals of hawking, though I've not had a goshawk. I am all admiration for your ability. They are not easy birds to handle. How do you do it?''

Alissa dropped her gaze, feeling self-conscious, yet terribly pleased at the sincere interest from Lord Ives. "It is but a tiercel, my lord. Like the male falcon, the male goshawk is a third smaller, thus easier to manage than a female. You ought to see him sit astride on Lady's collar. They get along famously. The gos is a good bird, though not as affectionate as Princess." In her eagerness to explain about her beloved birds, her usual reticence dropped away. It would have been amazing, had she given it thought, this casual conversation with a normally awe-inspiring stranger.

"Princess misses you greatly," Elizabeth said from the doorway. "Bobs up and down and jingles her bells in a miff, if I make no mistake about it." She studied the trio, then gave a broad smile as she entered the room. She curtsied gracefully, displaying none of the vapors a female might be expected to exhibit at the sight of men in her sister's bedroom. "I am happy to see you, Lord Ives and Baron Duffus." Gesturing they be seated once again, she perched at the very end of the chaise longue where Alissa reclined. "I am more than pleased to see my sister out of that bed. Tell me, how did you manage it?" The quiet remark was made to Lord Ives, as though she knew he would be the one who dared disobey her sister's orders.

He shrugged lightly and replied offhandedly, "I desired to know more about her hawking, and it is a dead bore to converse with someone who is in bed. Besides, from what I can see, she doesn't need to be there." He turned to Alissa. "Why haven't you gone downstairs before this? Your father says there is naught wrong with you."

Alissa gasped and darted a look at Elizabeth. "You may not be aware that I lost the use of my, er, limbs, sir." A blush stained her cheeks most becomingly.

"That does *not* mean you must stay in bed. I have seen others who don't walk make use of a wheelchair. Duffy, remind me to send to Salisbury for one. I must get Miss Alissa to show me how she manages her falcon. By the way, my dear, you should call me Christopher. Long name, I suppose, but it is mine, and after my being here"—he gestured at the dainty, feminine room—"we can hardly be said to be strangers."

Elizabeth's youthful giggles were infectious. The others glanced at her and smiled. When she had herself in hand, Elizabeth replied, "Rightly so, my lord. It might be possible for Alissa to be in the conservatory if she had such a chair. There she could have Princess brought to her. She has in the past. Princess is usually a well-behaved hawk."

"Most highly intelligent creatures can manage to be well-behaved. Though we sometimes get confused about things." Lord Ives looked at Alissa, adding, "You are amazingly knowledgeable about birds, dogs, and horses."

"Meddle not with him that flattereth with the lips," uttered Duffy piously.

"I didn't include people, Duffy. She needs to learn more about that species, I believe." Lord Ives steepled his fingers beneath his chin and studied the slim young woman across from him for a moment, then turned his head away, lest he upset her or cause her to withdraw from them.

Amusement lurking in her eyes, Alissa daringly replied, "Do you intend to be an instructor for me?"

He gave an approving nod at her touch of wit. He wouldn't have suspected her capable of such badinage. "I might, but I'm a demanding tutor, a regular dragon. Though I do get results."

Duffy raised his eyes to the ceiling and righteously chanted, "He that hath knowledge spareth his words: and a man of understanding is of an excellent spirit. Even a fool, when he is silent, is counted wise."

Lord Ives gave a sniff, then said, "I don't know if I ought to be upset with you or not, my friend. Do I gather you think I do best when I keep silence? You rate me with the fools of this world?"

Duffy shook his head. "Not so, but I confess there are times when I wonder."

The comfortable laughter shared dissolved when a shocked gasp came from the doorway. Henrietta entered the room, her riding habit angrily swishing about her legs as she strode across to where Alissa reposed on the chaise longue not far from the bed where she had spent the past two weeks.

"I do not believe my eyes," Henrietta declared in dramatic

accents. "You are an invalid, my dear. What thoughtless person has persuaded you to hazard the chaise?"

Alissa seemed to shrink before his eyes. Lord Ives watched the confrontation with curiosity.

Elizabeth gently tugged at Henrietta's arm. "Is it not wonderful? Lord Ives was concerned with Alissa and desired to see her out of that bed which has held her captive these past days. We can only be grateful at his persistence where the rest of us have failed."

Alissa appeared to wish herself beneath a ton of covers, by the expression in her eyes. Ives noted this, and hoping to spare her more of Henrietta's ire, rose smoothly from his chair. "Perhaps she is tired and wishes to return to that bed for a bit?"

Alissa began to shake her head, then stopped. She *was* tired, she decided, and visibly drooped as Henrietta chortled, "Of course she is. Call her maid. She can tend to her. You must tell me the latest doings from town, my lord."

He glanced at the eager, very beautiful face, then to the drawn one of the patient, concealed his dismay, and calmly replied, "I've not been to town for some time, you know. But let me replace Miss Alissa and I will do my best to entertain you." Henrietta was typical of the spoiled beauties he had seen in London. With no desire to provoke Henrietta, he returned Alissa to her bed, holding her firmly to his chest, noting well her light yet supple form. He then left Elizabeth behind to flutter about her sister, tucking her under the covers, while he escorted the pacified Henrietta from the room, a disappointed Duffy trailing after them.

The oddly assorted trio sauntered down the stairs and to the drawing room, where Lord Ives noted the entrance to the conservatory off to one side. He gave Duffy a significant look, then casually wandered, Miss Henrietta's hand tucked deftly into the crook of his arm, to that door.

Henrietta bestowed a disdainful look about her. "This is Mama's domain. She puts all manner of plants in here during the winter. Says she cannot bear to be without greenery about her."

Ives ignored her cutting assessment of the charming room,

gazing about with interest. Windows on three sides brought the soft and golden autumn day into the house. At the far end of this pleasant room there was a small worktable with a clutter of small instruments and a rag-covered mound.

Miss Henrietta sniffed and simpered, "La, Alissa's little animals are still here. I made certain Mama would have thrown them out."

Lord Ives walked down to look at a number of delicately sculptured animals sitting upon a small set of shelves. Exquisitely executed, they would have been welcome in the collection of any devotee of fine art. "That would indeed be a shame, but I am certain you were teasing. No one would dream of tossing out such fine work." Seeing the flicker of displeasure in her lovely eyes, he turned to Duffy. "Perhaps we should return to our rooms to dress for dinner. I find I am eager to see what beauty Miss Henrietta will present to us this evening."

Fluttering her lashes, she turned her back on the conservatory and reentered the drawing room, casting a demure look at the man at her side. Henrietta smiled, her porcelain skin glowing with pleasure. "La, sir, how you do tease. I shall see you later. Ta ta." She floated out to the staircase, ambitions of stunning the London gentlemen with her beauty swirling about in her head.

"The way of a fool is right in his own eyes," quoted Duffy.

"Do you by any means refer to me?" snapped Lord Ives indignantly.

"Whomever it fits. That young woman is a bit pampered, unless I miss my guess. 'Tis sad Miss Alissa is so affected by her."

"I perceive what you mean. Perhaps we can find a way to change all that, Duffy. First of all, I intend to send to Salisbury for that wheelchair."

"You mean to get the thing, then? She dinna say yes." The Scot gave Ives a dubious look.

"But, Duffy, my friend, she dinna say no either." With that confident remark, Ives strode from the drawing room to locate his groom.

Duffy wandered out to the hall, wondering if Miss Elizabeth would ever come downstairs. He was staring sightlessly at the scene out the window, when footsteps echoed at the foot of the staircase. Curious, he turned to discover Miss Elizabeth aimed in the direction of the servants' wing.

"There you are." He burst into speech, then felt unaccountably foolish at his words.

The sweet young woman gave him a ready smile and extended her hand. "Come with me before it is time to dress for dinner. Henrietta is in such a taking, the meal may have to be set back before she is ready to join us. I mean to check the hawks again. You have done wonders for Alissa, but now she is more concerned for Princess and I had best see to the bird."

Duffy gladly crossed the hall to take the proferred hand, feeling as though a great treasure had been bestowed upon him. They left the house, sauntering down toward the mews in no great hurry.

From his window, Lord Ives watched his departing friend, a curious gleam in his eyes. Then he turned to greet his valet, who came with information of interest, and Duffy was forgotten for the moment.

In her bed, Alissa pressed a hand against her eyes in dismay. What had she done? What a fool, to so forget herself as to lightly talk with those men. Talk! Had she really run on like a babbling brook, little evidence of her usual caution? Slowly her hand came down to touch her breast. Lord Ives had held her so close to him that she had felt the buttons of his waistcoat. It had been an elegant one, green striped satin over buff pantaloons, looking well with his dark green coat. But his closeness had stirred all manner of feelings in her. She had best not consider such things. Henrietta had pointed out the futility of such nonsense.

Memory of the hateful words spoken in her hearing by Henrietta returned to distress Alissa once again. When she had been helpless in her bed, in pain from the accident,

Henrietta had entered the bedroom and stood at Alissa's bedside, staring down at her. Though softly spoken, those words had been distinct, perhaps meant to penetrate Alissa's mind.

"I'm glad you had this accident, dear sister. Now there will be no question as to whether I go to London for my Season. Papa said I would do well there, perhaps wed an earl at the least. He and Mama thought you ought to wed first. But who would have you now? Crippled women find no husbands. You will not be a real woman, dear sister, and I will. I shall be wed, and soon!"

The spoiled young woman gave no thought to her careless words or their effect on the hearer. Henrietta's triumphant hiss had cut to the quick of Alissa's tender heart. It had taken great willpower to pretend the words were unheard and feign sleep.

Alissa turned her head to find Lady standing there, paws on the edge of the bed. Deciding she cared more for the comfort offered by her pet than a spotless bed, Alissa invited Lady to jump up. The dog cautiously managed to clamber up without disturbing Alissa unduly. Later would come dinner; then, tomorrow, and who knew what might happen then? With her hand stroking the dog's thick coat, Alissa slowly drifted off to a troubled sleep.

Dressed in faultless attire, Lord Ives surveyed the hall. Soft sounds emerged from various rooms, but no one was to sight. A maid exited the room across the hall. Ives spoke briefly to her, then quickly walked to that door, rapped sharply, then entered, leaving the door wide open.

"Do you make a habit of this, my lord? 'Tis disgraceful behavior, you know." Alissa's eyes were guarded as she surveyed the unrepentant gentleman.

"I wanted to tell you that I have ordered that wheelchair from Salisbury. Tomorrow you shall practice, and then . . . who knows? Would you join the others in the drawing room and at dinner?" He watched her carefully to gauge her reaction.

"I could never! 'Tis impossible." She gave him a hesitant look, aware of his anger at her words.

"You can! You must! Don't you see that?" he said impulsively. "If you remain in this bed, you shall never improve. Indeed, you could very well die in no time at all," he said with deliberate brutality.

She paled, gasping at the harsh words. "What a horrid thing to say. How can you be so cruel?" Tears stung at her eyes, but she blinked them back, refusing to yield before this man.

"It is no more that the plain unvarnished truth. I will see to it the chair is brought up to your room the moment it arrives, and you can look at it. Study it. I doubt it will be a thing of great beauty . . . but it will free you from this bed. There is no place you cannot venture in it, you realize. It is liberation on wheels." He bowed with noticeable irony, then silently left her room.

Alissa had much to consider while she ate her light meal. Could she continue as she had determined? Or must she alter her plans now? Lord Ives had challenged her. Dare she meet his provocative words with action? Those black eyes saw too much, she feared. Sleep proved elusive. Sometime during the night she reached a decision.

He was as good as his word. The next afternoon the chair was carried into her room while Henrietta and Elizabeth were out riding with the guests. Alissa propped herself up, stuffed another pillow behind her, then studied the ugly chair. For it was not pretty, as he had predicted. But it offered freedom.

"Matty," she ordered softly, "get me into that thing, will you?" She would show that handsome lord her mettle.


Shortly before dinner there was a stir at the doorway to the drawing room, and the assembled family and guests turned to see what had created it. A gasp rose from one and all as a wheelchair containing a young woman dressed in a russet silk gown paused on the threshold of the room.

Triumphant and looking lovely in a rather pale, interesting

way, was Alissa. With brave defiance she signaled Matty to push her into the room. "Hello, everyone. I have come to join you this evening."

Lady ffolkes raised a gloved hand to her cheek. "Dear heavens!"

# 3

The moment of shock passed, the frozen figures turned to one another with looks of astonishment.

"Dear girl, what are you about?" began Lady ffolkes.

"But you ought to be in bed, dear Alissa," blurted an obviously annoyed Henrietta.

Elizabeth swiftly crossed to Alissa's side. "I am so very pleased and so proud of you, dear sister," she whispered. She slipped a comforting hand across her sister's shoulder, then met the combined gazes of her parents, ignoring the sputtering Henrietta for the nonce. "Is this not a wonderful surprise? Lord Ives was so kind as to send to Salisbury for the chair. I perceive he is a man of action, such as you admire, Mama. And you, as well, Papa."

Both parents had the grace to acknowledge these statements with reluctant nods.

"Although Alissa will probably not wish to travel as far as London, at least she will not be confined to her bed." Elizabeth patted Alissa, a warning touch, reminding her not to say anything regarding her wishes and London. Though Elizabeth knew full well how Alissa felt about her Season, their parents seemed never to understand—if they wished to, which Elizabeth doubted.

At these words Henrietta calmed, confidently smoothing her blue muslin dress with tiny cap sleeves and dainty rosebud trim. "Of course we are happy to see Alissa downstairs." She took another look at her sister, then added, "Though I do hope you will not overly tire yourself." She appeared to admire her beauty in the far mirror, preened a bit, then went on. "I was just talking to Mama of the entertainments we might provide for our guests. 'Tis a pity you are not able to enjoy them too."

Lord Ives, who had restrained a desire to speak so far,

entered the conversation at this point. "I see no reason why Miss Alissa could not join us for a few card games of an evening. Or, for that matter, play the pianoforte for us. I was told Miss Henrietta has a lovely voice, and I had hoped to be treated to a performance. Or does Miss Elizabeth play?"

Elizabeth laughed easily and shook her head. "Not I. My talents are elsewhere." She darted a glance at Duffy; then, catching him looking at her with an admiring gleam in his light blue eyes, she blushed a becoming pink.

Alissa was about to speak up when Parsons entered the room, a faint smile of approval flashing across his face as he saw Miss Alissa in her chair. He calmly announced that dinner was served.

Matty maneuvered the awkward chair across the threshold of the dining room with surprising skill, leading Lord Ives to believe that a certain amount of practicing had been going on that afternoon after the chair arrived. The moment he had returned from his diversionary ride with the others, his groom had sought him out, giving details of the successful expedition to Salisbury.

One of the footmen had removed a side chair from the table. Matty carefully pushed the wheelchair in place, then stood back, watching her charge with gimlet-eyed intensity. Alissa's cheeks were flushed, her eyes shyly watching the others. She was silent throughout the meal. Lord Ives watched her as well, though without seeming to, while chatting to the baron about the prospects of the coming fair.

As the dinner progressed, Henrietta's flirtation with Lord Ives became more pronounced. "La, milords, we must give a little party while you are here. Would that not be festive? Mama, say you will not mind?"

"You could have a few of my late roses," Lady ffolkes offered graciously in her vague manner. "Though not too many, mind you." She speared a piece of roasted mutton, eyeing it with disfavor before consuming it.

"Another thing we should all enjoy is the fair in Salisbury," Henrietta continued. "Although I fear Alissa would hate having people stare at her. She might seem one of the exhibits! It would make her all the more unable to speak. Poor dear, to be so afflicted. I have never had any trouble expressing what is in my heart.'' She fluttered a dainty hand across the exceedingly (for a miss still not out in society) low-cut bosom of her dress while smiling demurely at Lord Ives. Then she raised a finger as sudden inspiration struck. "We could do charades. I vow they are such delightful fun. Alissa would not have to fear speaking then.'' She bestowed a sweet look on her sister, then turned to Lord Ives once more. "Perhaps you can contribute some interesting pastimes?''

Observing that Alissa had paled and looked as though she devoutly wished she was some other place, Lord Ives pushed his chair back from the table. "I believe that since the meal is over, Miss Alissa might be happier settled elsewhere.'' He pulled her wheelchair from the table and scooped her up in his arms. Giving her a warning look which she correctly interpreted to mean to hold her tongue, he strode from the room after bowing slightly to Lady ffolkes.

Instead of the tongue-tied miss that he expected to find in his arms, Lord Ives glanced down to encounter an infectious giggle and eyes that, though tired, yet danced with amusement.

Hesitantly she voiced her thoughts. "I wish I could have seen the expression Mama's face when you picked me up and . . . and then managed to bow to her. Was she at all astonished?''

A smile softened his features as he gazed at the gallant woman he held close in his arms. "I doubt it, for she popped another morsel of mutton into her mouth and commenced chewing. Does she ever get into a pother?''

Alissa sighed and, without thinking about it, allowed her head to drop against Lord Ives's comforting shoulder. "I have never seen the day," she said quietly.

"Even when you were tossed from your mare?'' He took note of the trusting movement, and was immensely pleased. He had never been in the position to have a lady so dependent upon him, and it made him feel strangely masterful. Was this the emotion that had sent knights of old off on errands for their ladies-fair? This sensation of being the protector, acting the gallant?

"Even then. She is never at a loss, it seems." Though a pink color had crept into Alissa's cheeks, there seemed no apprehension in her eyes.

Lord Ives debated a moment. "Do you wish to remain in here with us? You must be fatigued, the first time out of bed. Or shall I carry you upstairs?" He looked down at Alissa's face, fearing for her all of a sudden. A desire to protect this brave young woman from her strange family—except for Elizabeth—grew stronger.

Alissa gave him a startled look. How could he possibly guess how she felt? "Perhaps . . ." She met his gaze with cautious assessment. She suddenly tensed.

Henrietta breezed into the drawing room, then halted, a sulky look crossing her lovely face as she viewed the slim form of her sister held so carefully in Lord Ives's manly arms.

"If you . . . place me on that backless sofa over near the fireplace, I ought to do quite well, thank you, kind sir," Alissa said, her voice dropping away to a whisper as she sensed her sister's ill humor. Alissa cast Lord Ives an uneasy glance, but she had no need to fear what he might say.

"Very well, Miss ffolkes. There you are." He gently placed her on the sofa, smiling with great charm at Henrietta as she offered two pillows.

Henrietta's irritation flew when she saw the impersonal manner Lord Ives used to handle Alissa. After all, what man could possibly be interested in a mere cripple, with a young woman of Henrietta's acknowledged fairness around? Blonds were all the thing now. Poor Alissa, with her bronzed locks, was only to be pitied.

When Lord Ives set out to charm the pouting Henrietta, he soon had her relaxed and chattering away like a magpie. The beauty had not overstated the matter when she'd told of her ability to talk with ease.

Baron ffolkes was torn. Although he liked to see his pretty Henrietta doing so well with her London beau, he didn't have the pleasure of a top-of-the-trees earl in his home all that often. His conceit won over.

"Lord Ives and Lord Duffus, perhaps you would join me in a game of billiards this evening? I am certain the ladies will excuse us. I think Alissa ought to be upstairs at any rate." He glared at the daughter who'd had the temerity to leave her bed and enter the drawing room, possibly competing with Henrietta for his lordship's attentions. Not that Baron ffolkes didn't feel Henrietta could win any competition hands down. But he was aware some men might find a helpless female appealing. Not for him. He glanced at his hardy wife, who had presented him with the necessary heir before three worthless daughters. But if Henrietta could snag this London lord, he just might forgive his wife.

Duffy paused in his quiet speech with Elizabeth, gave her a reassuring nod and a promise they would talk again on the morrow, then strolled toward the door.

Across the room Lord Ives walked behind the baron with definite relief. The prattle from Miss Henrietta had nearly numbed his ear.

As he was about to leave, he cast a look at Alissa, reassuring himself she was not overdoing. Matty waited in the hall, and he spoke softly to her before following Baron ffolkes to the billiard room.

The room originally had been in use as a second conservatory, screening the main wing of the house from the servants' section. Baron ffolkes had banished the potted plants and installed the billiard table in their place. With walls painted a dull red, trimmed with dark mahogany, and decorated in a rather Gothic style, the room had a certain appeal. He had ordered a selection of chairs far more comfortable than any other seating in the house, to create a haven where he could blow a cloud as well as visit with his friends.

Lord Ives walked over to the heavy red linen draperies

that hung by the many windows to look out into the night. A dim light near the stable area was all the life to be seen. He turned back to face Duffy and the baron.

Duffy handed Ives a cue, knowing that whichever one he used, he would probably win. The ivory balls were broken by Duffy and the game began in relative silence. Lord Ives made a particularly difficult shot, gaining a winning double hazard.

Baron ffolkes was effusive in his praise. "Fine shot, very fine shot. I can see you have some acquaintance with the game."

Ives shrugged negligently. He played fairly often, but his winning was due more to a keen eye and steady hand than practice. He stood back while the others studied the layout of the balls on the table. "Pity about your daughter's injury. You mentioned seeking a second doctor?"

Baron ffolkes looked up, for a moment perplexed; then his countenance smoothed. "Indeed we did. Dashed expensive it was, too. Looked her over from head to toe." ffolkes bent over the table, cue at the ready, then made a simple push at a ball, earning himself a single winning hazard. Pleased with the stroke, he straightened and continued. "Told me that outside of the bruise to her spine, there was nothing seriously amiss with her. Oh, he used leeches—at my insistence, mind you. Didn't do any good," ffolkes confessed gloomily.

"Tragic thing to happen to a person." Ives felt a stirring of anger. Anger at the father, anger at the incompetent doctor, anger at the helplessness that assailed him. It was cruel that the vibrantly alive woman he had first seen out on the downs with her falcon should be confined to a chair the rest of her life.

"Actually," Baron ffolkes admitted, "won't make a bean of difference. Girl didn't take during her Season. Doubt she ever would. Don't wish to send her back to town again. Felt the eldest ought to marry first, though. This way I shan't have to send her, and can send Henrietta instead." He gave a canny glance at the elegant Lord Ives, wondering how attracted the wealthy earl was to the beauty of the family.

"Your daughter must have been very upset at finding herself confined to bed," Duffy ventured to say. He made an elegant shot, then stood back to watch Ives demolish them all.

" 'Tis plain you don't know the girl. Hates to be around people. Can't talk, you know. Shy. Spends all her time with those hawks of hers and fiddling about with clay. Demmed lot of nonsense. Ought to toss the lot out."

"Do you really think so?" The earl's voice was dangerously smooth. "I quite admired the little sculptures. She seems quite talented, to my eyes. What think you, Duffy? You saw them."

Duffy shivered at the silken tone of Ives's voice. It was not wise to cross his friend when in this mood. "Aye. The lass is skilled with her fingers. My mother would say they're enchanted."

"But of course," continued Ives serenely. "And the work is enchanting as well. She has promised to do one for me to give the Prince Regent. He is quite the connoisseur, as you must know. I feel he will be delighted with the gift."

Duffy choked on the wine he'd been sipping, and required a hearty slap on the back to restore him. "She's that talented, for certain. 'Tis no doubt her sculpture would be well-received." He glanced at Ives, wondering what possessed the man to make such a claim. Gift to the Regent, indeed.

Alissa had promised no such thing. But Christopher was so angry with this thoughtless father that he decided to impress upon the man the worth of his daughter's talent in the most awesome way possible. What better means than a gift to the Prince? He made a mental note to warn her of the fact later.

"I was surprised that she would be hawking without an assistant. You permitted her to go alone?" The smooth voice intoned the question most carefully, yet there was that hint of a storm brewing in the distance that Duffy did not miss.

Baron ffolkes thought he detected a faint criticism in the words and bridled at the very thought that he was not the best of parents. "She never needed one after she trained that dog of hers. Asides, who would bother her? It ain't as though she was Henrietta.'' At this very obvious point, the baron chuckled. ''Though Alissa does have a helper, you know. Matter of fact, she has all the servants wrapped around her finger.'' He shook his head as though amazed that Alissa could command such loyalty.

Duffy, hoping that Ives would manage to extricate them from this unpleasant interlude, placed his cue in the rack.

''Now, were my Henrietta out on a horse, I'd have to send along a groom to keep a watch out. A beauty like Henrietta must be guarded with care, gentlemen. Why, I remember when some Frenchie came to the manor. Claimed he wanted to know more about my sheep. 'Twas plain as your nose he wanted my girl. A dandified thing of a man, him with his fine ways and fancy clothes. Didn't like my hounds, either. I'll have no traffic with foreigners.''

Lord Ives permitted a ghost of a smile at the thought of any man who might not enjoy the pack of hounds over whom Baron ffolkes lavished his attention. ''Gentlemen,'' he inserted before the baron could take off once again on his favorite subjects—Henrietta and the hounds—''I suggest we rejoin the ladies in the drawing room. That is, if they are still there.''

''Told Alissa to go up to her room.'' The baron was obviously torn between the courtesies due and his feelings, or lack of them, for his daughter. ''Not that I don't thank you for your help, my lord, but it might have been better for her if she had stayed in bed.''

Lord Ives paused in the hall beneath the painting of the third Baron ffolkes and turned to stare at the present holder of the title. ''Stayed in bed?'' he echoed, wondering what mental gymnastics the baron would perform to justify that statement.

''Cripple, you know. No one wants a cripple around. A burden. Though I admit the girl has done her share in the past. Ran the house. Won't live long, at any rate. Better if she went simply and quickly than linger.''

Duffy noted the clenching of Ives's hands and inwardly agreed with his undoubted assessment of the baron. He coughed and suggested, "I believe we were on our way to join the ladies, were we not?"

Ives strode on ahead, ignoring his host, his anger with the man visible in eyes that burned with a dark fire.

The men found the room quiet. Lady ffolkes sat looking over a large volume on flowers. Henrietta and Elizabeth played a desultory game of cards, while Alissa dozed on the sofa. Matty stood guard not far away. She had gently placed a coverlet over her mistress, then stood by. As long as her dear Miss Alissa seemed in good twig, she did nothing, as the London lord had urged.

"Ellen, my dear, Lord Ives trounced us soundly," the baron said in his hearty voice. "Fine player. Says he intends to present one of Alissa's little things to the Prince. Did you know that?"

Alissa had opened her eyes at the sound of their entry, and her gaze flew to Lord Ives at this bald statement.

His mouth twisted in a rueful grin as he unflinchingly returned the look. "I believe she mentioned a hedgehog, if I remember correctly." His look became a challenge.

Amusement lit her lovely eyes. "I did. It may take some time, you know. A day or two at the least." An eyebrow raised slightly. "But I shall be happy to make anything you wish."

A glow warmed the chill from his heart as Ives noted she hadn't seemed self-conscious when she talked to him. Retaining her gaze, he added, "I shall look forward to watching her enchanted fingers at work. Duffy proclaimed them so. Said his mother would have as well. Isn't that right, Duffy?"

"Aye, 'tis so." Duffy turned his gaze from Alissa to the young Elizabeth demurely at her cards.

Henrietta rose from the card table, her game with Elizabeth ignored. Her china-blue eyes flashed with pettishness that her cripple sister could command so much attention. As she was about to speak, Lord Ives turned to give her his most charming smile. Her sulks faded as she succumbed to his attention.

"Could you give me a song, Miss Henrietta? I have heard you have a lovely voice." He was most persuasive, though to tell the truth, no coaxing was needed.

Henrietta looked to where Alissa reclined on the sofa. If she was to sing her best, she would need her sister's talent at the pianoforte. And Alissa looked tired. Drat. How bothersome to be so inconvenienced.

Alissa pulled off the coverlet and looked to Lord Ives. "I shall need assistance if I am to play for her."

He was at her side in a moment. Gathering her in his arms, he gently placed her on the red-upholstered stool, then stood behind her so she might lean against him as a buttress. She found she had limited strength, yet she knew the awesome tantrum Henrietta would throw if not able to perform for these handsome lords.

Henrietta frowned at the sight of Lord Ives standing behind Alissa, then realized her sister could not support herself. At the reassuring smile from his lordship, she relaxed and nodded to Alissa to begin.

Henrietta's voice rang sweet and clear, as lovely and charming as Lord Ives had been told. Yet he felt a lack of depth in her rendition of the simple tale of two lovers parted forever. Her emotion was all surface, words and music, nothing more.

His applause was not as enthusiastic as it might have been, but it seemed to please the singer and her parents. He glanced slyly at Duffy, then announced, "Duffy has a fine voice. I am certain he would be happy to sing for us. How about the ballad in Scott's book—'The Gay Goshawk,' in honor of our falconer at the pianoforte?"

Duffy darted a rather dark look at his friend, then graciously walked to stand by where Alissa was seated. "Do you know the music, lass?" When she shook her head, he shrugged and began to sing a haunting little tune.

O well's me o my gay goss-hawk,
That he can speak and flee;
He'll carry a letter to my love,
Bring back another to me.

He continued on with all of the twenty-eight short verses, his tenor clear and true. The ballad of the fairest flower in England and the trick she played on her harsh father to gain her true love far away in Scotland was eloquently sung and the humor appreciated by all.

During the song Ives had felt Alissa sagging against him, and when Duffy had sung his last note, Ives smiled approvingly at his friend, then said, "I'd best take Miss Alissa up to her maid if she is not to feign a deep sleep on us like the lass in your song. Except in this case I fear it might be real." He carefully picked Alissa up in strong arms, then marched from the room, Matty trailing behind him.

Elizabeth crossed over to compliment Duffy on his fine voice, while Lady ffolkes wandered from the room, a night candle in one hand, her book on flowers in the other.

In the hall Henrietta bestowed a thoughtful look up the stairs, where the handsome lord carried the invalid, and pouted to her father. "He could have ordered a footman to do the task. Papa, do make Alissa keep out of his way."

Wondering just how he was to contrive this feat when the young earl seemed to have an uncanny way of managing affairs to his own liking, the baron shifted from foot to foot, then mumbled, "Now, m'dear, you have nothing to fret about. He is merely being kind to the girl. Think of the glorious future ahead of you and have a bit of pity for her in your lovely heart."

"You are right, Papa." Henrietta beamed. "I cannot think why I worried. May I proceed with plans for a little party? We must entertain our guests or they will have a dim view of our Wiltshire hospitality."

"I daresay you have the right of it, m'dear. Do as you wish." But then, the girl always did. Never could deny her a thing.

Duffy walked Elizabeth to the foot of the stairs, then handed her a night candle. "Tomorrow, fair lady."

His regard sent the practical Elizabeth's heart soaring, and she floated up the stairs to her sister's room with a dreamy-eyed expression in her soft blue eyes. Of course he was too old and her parents would doubtless forbid an interest, but his attentions had quite turned her head.

Lord Ives had left the room, and Matty bustled about to prepare Alissa for the night. Elizabeth drifted across to stand at the foot of the bed, and gazed at her sister with misty eyes. "He is that fine, is he not?"

"Papa? Or Lord Ives?" Alissa asked with a feigned look of innocence on her face. Only the mischievous light in her eyes gave a clue to her inner delight.

"You tease!" Elizabeth picked up a small pillow to toss at her now grinning sister. "You know full well I mean Lord Duffus. 'Duffy' is a rather appealing name, I think."

"I suspect you find him a rather appealing person, as well. I understand Lord Duffus has a drafty old castle up in Scotland. Would you like to live thus, my dear? He has a nice Christian name—David."

Elizabeth glowed with youthful optimism. "My guardian angel is watching over me, Alissa. I know it. She will see to it that all goes well."

A bitter note crept into Alissa's voice as she queried, "Where was my angel the day of the accident? I fear angels are not always so vigilant as one feels."

Elizabeth walked around the bed to take hold of Alissa's hand, giving it an earnest squeeze. "All things happen for a reason, Alissa. You know that. Your angel allowed the accident because she knew something good would come of it. And it has. You have a wondrous lord virtually at your feet."

Her ingenuous trust was too sweet for an older, wiser heart to crush. Yet Elizabeth must be made to see reason. Shaking her head, Alissa disagreed. "Not so. Right after the fall, while I was drifting, Henrietta came in here to see me. She said that no man would look at a cripple. She also reminded me that I am not a whole woman. All men desire heirs, my dear. Lord Ives might pity me, even enjoy my company, but marry me—no. I fear I cannot bear children. I could never think of marrying. But you can and will. I also saw the light in the baron's eyes. I suspect he admires you. What think you of that?" Alissa hoped she concealed her distress. The dim candlelight helped to obscure any revealing facial expression.

" 'Tis a lovely notion. Yet he is too old for me, I fear. I had not thought to wed a graybeard,'' Her girlish pleasure at the idea of an older man—he must be all of seven-and-twenty—interested in her gleamed from Elizabeth's eyes. "I do not believe what you say about yourself is true. Surely if a man loved . . .'' She gave her sister a hopeful look.

Alissa shook her head. "Not for me.''

Across the hall Duffy rapped on the oak door, then slipped into Ives's room. "Well, my friend, you certainly like to set the cat among the pigeons.''

"I don't have the faintest idea what you mean, Duffy.'' He spoiled his pose with a devilish grin. "Miss Alissa did rather well, don't you think?'' Ives pulled off his cravat and dropped it on the dressing table beside the stickpin and fob he had worn. He glanced up at his friend as the silence grew.

Duffy nodded thoughtfully. "Miss Henrietta looks to have a bit of a temper. I hope she does not do anything to hurt Miss Alissa. I have observed how simple it is for Miss Henrietta to wound the sweet Alissa with those nasty little barbs. She does not have to actually injure the girl. 'Tis enough to damage the heart.''

Ives pulled his shirt over his head, then tossed it on the chair. He sighed as he glanced at the best friend a man could want. "Duffy . . . do you have an encouraging word among all those proverbs you quote?''

"Aye.'' Duffy thought a few moments, then said, "Keep thy heart with all diligence; for out of it are the issues of life.' ''

Ives held out his foot so his valet could remove the polished boot. "In that case we had best separate them if we can. Though I vow my ear shall become numb if I must listen to more of Henrietta's prattle. For if, as you say, the issues of life come from the heart, we must not permit Henrietta to destroy Alissa's.''

"I will find it no problem to accompany the sweet Elizabeth, young though she might be. But you . . . you seem a mite concerned with the shy Alissa."

"Have you not observed, O wise one? She is losing her reserve with me." Christopher glanced proudly at his friend. "She trusts me. I cannot begin to tell you how that makes me feel. I have a theory—one of your everlasting proverbs made me think of it. Remember? I recollect it goes something like this: 'As he thinketh in his heart, so is he.' And that is what I believe it is with Alissa. I mean to find out. Somehow. There has to be a reason why she cannot walk. I intend to solve the mystery. I mean to have her walk again!"

# 4

"**D**id you *have* to choose a hedgehog?" Alissa rested her hands on the wooden surface of her worktable and tried to glare at the man who grinned down at her so amiably. A powder-blue muslin dress, its high neck edged in cream lace, was freshly becoming, reflecting the blue of her impish gaze.

"First thing that popped into my mind. I shan't explain how it all came about, however." He didn't care to further disillusion her about her father.

Her parents made an odd pair. Baron ffolkes was lean and on the short side, with vague blue eyes and a prim mouth. His milksoppish appearance seemed at total variance with his interest in sheep and love for hounds and hunting. Lady ffolkes was tall and sturdy, long-nosed and sharp of eye, and looked to be a true countrywoman with her skirts flapping about her while she briskly supervised the gardening. How this modest creature with her whimsical charm came to be in such a household was a mystery. Perhaps it all went back to the "impractical" grandmother?

"Never mind as to that. I daresay I can manage well enough." Alissa threw a small hunk of clay on the table and began to work it, preparing it for her sculpture of the hedgehog. A hedgehog? She shook her head slightly as she considered the subject.

She was grateful Lord Ives couldn't possibly know how his closeness affected her. It had taken a long time to drift off to sleep last night after he had carried her up the flight of stairs and down the hall to her room. Never mind that Matty was right there and nothing improper occurred. Alissa had been far too aware of Lord Ives as a man. She had trembled in those strong arms, closer to a man than she had ever been, except for that brief trip from her bed to the chaise longue and back.

She had felt his breath stir her tumbled curls, known a warmth from his hands as it seeped through the fine silk of her gown. Best dismiss it all from her mind. Thoughts like that could only lead to heartbreak. Henrietta's whining demand of her father had reached Alissa's sensitive ears and that hadn't helped in the least. A true gentleman, Lord Ives had given no inkling he had heard a word from below.

She glanced at him, wondering why he had come in here after breakfast. Though if he had eaten with Barrett, he'd have had little company, for Barrett was as silent as her father was talkative. Though Barrett resembled her father in looks, he took after her mother in the area of speech.

Lord Ives wandered about the cheerful room, admiring the collection of plants that grew there. Early-morning sunlight streamed across the flagstones and highlighted the rich green of each leaf it touched. There were no dust-streaked plants or half-dead and withered specimens found in here. Attention lavished upon each plant resulted in rich rewards. Then he paused in his stroll to glance outside. Beyond the windows he could see a small flower garden.

"Your mother's garden?" he asked in surprise, for it didn't seem to fit the image of a garden arranged by Lady ffolkes. Oxeye daisies nodded their heads in the delicate breeze and clustered bellflowers and harebells clung to the last of summer warmth in the sheltered spot. To one side of the dainty plot were fading blooms of white campion.

"Ah, no." She chuckled softly. " 'Tis mine. My mother despairs of me as a gardener, in spite of thrusting Abercrombie's gardening book in my face. I like the simple, the wildflowers, not her fancy hybrids." She looked at the flowers and thought a moment. "I am like the daisy, I suppose, and likely to remain so." Her voice trailed off as she turned back to the task at hand. Daisies stood for innocence, or so went the old belief. With her difficulties, it was more than likely that her short life would remain as it began, untouched.

Christopher gave her a quizzical look. He searched his memory, trying to recall what his sister had chattered on about in her talk of flowers. From some dim recess of his mind the association of the daisy with innocence emerged. So Alissa expected to remain in that pathetic state, did she? He leaned against the frame of one tall window, crossing his arms before him, while he unabashedly studied her under the guise of watching her hands at work.

She had clever hands, long and shapely, supple and very, very soft, as he recalled. A cunning little hedgehog was beginning to take shape beneath those skilled fingers. The dark red clay was moist, and she kept a damp cloth to hand while she worked. He frowned as she stuck a small stick into the center to hollow out the wee animal from the underside.

"Why do you do that?" All thought of merely watching her was gone. His curiosity nudged him.

"In order for it to dry properly, it cannot be more than an inch in thickness or it will crack—or even break. The thicker it is, the more slowly it dries."

Christopher found a plain wooden side chair not far away and set it in place by the worktable. He straddled the chair and rested his chin on the back. "Explain. I want to understand." His gaze met hers, disconcertingly direct.

Quite taken aback at this show of interest, Alissa was for a moment at a total loss for words. Not even her dearest Elizabeth cared to ask such questions. "I, er, surely it would be of no import to you, milord."

"Christopher. I would have you call me by my name, at least while we are by ourselves. I get rather tired of being held at a distance all the time." He actually had never thought one way or the other about it. But he hoped that using his given name might make her feel more at ease with him, and that was important.

"And, yes, I want the explanation. If you please," he added with exaggerated politeness.

Alissa laughed, a sweet bell-like sound that rang across the room with delicate clarity. "It really is very simple."

Her reserve, which he had first noted when he was more of a stranger, had faded some. She seemed to come alive as she spoke, her face glowing with enthusiasm, eyes shining with sparkles of deep blue shimmering in their depths. He listened carefully to her description of the process of shaping, then drying the little creatures she created, before placing them in the small kiln that had been built for her use. Yet another part of his mind noted the charming countenance, the becoming flush on her cheeks. Admittedly she was not a great beauty like Henrietta, but Alissa had something more rare. The precise quality eluded him. He intended to observe her until he found the answer.

"I shall make one or two more animals as well as a mug or two. They break so easily, you know." Deftly she continued to work until she had the shape well-defined. Then she picked up the little stick and began to incise a texture into the body, bringing points of clay to stand out to resemble the spiny coat of the hedgehog.

Christopher was no longer watching the nimble hands as they worked so cleverly. His gaze had shifted to her hair, noting each bronzed curl, the golden riband threaded through the locks. He then admired her pretty nose, and last, the sweet curve of her mouth. He recalled her vitality when she had been on the downs with her bird that first day. How slim, graceful, and yet abominably shy she'd been then. A kind of anger gripped him. It was unthinkable that she would never walk again. She was such a glowing young woman. Sitting like this, it was impossible to believe she could not simply rise and walk.

"I believe nuncheon will be ready shortly, my . . . er, Christopher. Cook will be in a dither if we are late." She placed the stick neatly next to other tools on the table, then tossed the damp cloth over the hedgehog, carefully tucking it about the sculpture as she spoke.

"What if you wanted to do a large piece, say, a head? How would you do it?" Christopher found he wanted to delay joining the family. The longer he could keep her talking, the longer he could keep her like this, open, friendly, and all to himself.

She had begun to push her chair away from the table, and paused at his words. She thought a moment, then replied, "I would make a sketch first, then model from the bottom up—begin at the neck and carefully work up the head, using circles upon circles of clay, shaping and molding the clay in the manner I wished it to take. It would have to have a sort of honeycomb structure inside to help support the sculpture.'' She smiled as she waved her hands about in the air while she spoke, gesturing so he might better understand.

Alissa was totally unaware of the charming air she possessed when she spoke so earnestly to him, nor did she seem conscious that she held a fresh appeal of her very own for the London sophisticate. Christopher determined at that moment that he would in some manner get her away from her family, or at least her sister Henrietta. Perhaps his Aunt Catherine might have need of a companion? Alissa continued to speak while he studied her—not too intently. He didn't wish to upset her, to cause a retreat into that shyness he had observed before.

Alissa lightly touched a small bust of Elizabeth. It held a delicate charm, capturing the common sense that young lady so often revealed, with another essence of the girl—her considerate nature. ''It has that form to permit air to circulate. Otherwise it would crack or break. Remember what I said about thickness and uneven drying.''

''You make it sound so simple.'' He yielded to her desire to leave. As he walked around to move the cumbersome chair with its large rear wheels, Duffy and a pink-cheeked Elizabeth entered the room from the terrace, bringing a gust of fresh air with them. She was dressed in palest yellow muslin trimmed in pretty embroidery across the stomacher. Long loose sleeves fluttered as she gestured with animation.

'' 'Tis a beautiful day. You must come outside with us after our meal. Perhaps you could show Lord Ives and Duffy the trick Princess does with Lady?'' Elizabeth beamed another grin their way even as the pink in her cheeks deepened when she realized how she had spoken. She threw an anguished look at Alissa, then gave Lord Ives a sheepish smile.

''Now, dinna fret yourself, Miss Elizabeth.'' To the others he added, ''I told the girl I answer better to 'Duffy.' 'Baron Duffus' sounds a bit pompous and not at all like my modest self.'' He bowed to the others, who laughed at his drollery.

Christopher could sense Alissa stiffen up as Henrietta was

heard in the central hall, inquiring as to their where-abouts.

Alissa studied her hands as Lord Ives wheeled her slowly into the hall area toward the dining room. The tips of her pale-blue-and-brown-printed shoes peeked from beneath her neat round gown, shifting slightly with unease as Henrietta flashed a look of displeasure at her.

"There you are, you naughty man," she simpered to Ives, totally ignoring Duffy and her sisters. "I fear I slept late—all that excitement, you know. A woman cannot rush about her preparation for the day, either. I vow it is all such a bother." She waited, one delicate, perfect brow raised for the inevitable tribute to her beauty she fully expected to receive. She was not disappointed.

"But it is well worth your effort, Miss Henrietta. We would be desolate without your charm and grace to adorn the day." Ives reluctantly relinquished his helm at the chair to the dexterous Matty. He joined the coquette elaborately dressed in delicate white tucked-muslin sashed in pink silk with pink kid shoes that could be glimpsed when she walked. The group entered the dining room with Henrietta's chatter as an accompaniment.

A sound from Duffy suspiciously like a snort was stifled as Elizabeth held up an autumn rose for him to smell and he sneezed. He gave her a surprised look.

"Take care," she whispered. "Henrietta is as ill-tempered as she is beautiful."

"I had suspected that might be the case of it," he replied sagely. "We shall take care not to upset yon miss." He gave Elizabeth a solemn wink the others could not see before taking his own place next to her.

"Elizabeth, it is not proper to giggle at the table," intoned Henrietta as Lady ffolkes drifted in from the garden, judging by the condition of her green gown.

Before her was held the latest issue of Curtis' *Botanical Magazine*. She murmured a vague reprimand in the general direction of both her daughters, then seated herself, glancing to see if Lord ffolkes had come in before nodding to the butler to begin serving the light meal.

Lord Ives wondered that two of the girls had managed to grow up so sweet and genteel. Not that Henrietta was not ladylike. But hints of pettishness crept out from time to time that ill became her.

He smiled at her latest witticism and continued eating the food before him, scarcely paying attention to what he was served or consumed.

"I do hope we can enjoy a ride this afternoon," Henrietta said, fluttering her lashes at Lord Ives. "There are any number of lovely places to see hereabouts. Perhaps you and Lord Duffus will enjoy going up to Stonehenge? Elizabeth too, of course. 'Tis a pity Alissa cannot join us in the outing."

"That is a longish trip best left to a day when you do not sleep half of it away," inserted Lady ffolkes from behind her magazine. That Henrietta was amazed at this offering from her mother was amusingly plain to see.

"But, Mama, 'tis a most interesting place to view." The pout forming on those delicate pink lips hinted of severe displeasure.

"Actually Duffy and Elizabeth suggested we stay here and observe Alissa's pets." Ives knew the fat would be in the fire with this statement, but he had no desire at the moment to traipse off across the countryside with the fair Henrietta.

It was Duffy who saved the afternoon for the group. He directed a look across to the storm-threatened face and smiled. " 'Tis a fair treat to see a beautiful lady who has such concern for her friends. Your regard for your sister's comfort is the mark of a true noblewoman."

Thus caught, Henrietta could only pause and reflect. The war that waged within the lovely head of blond hair and behind those incredible china-blue eyes was obvious. Though the lady obviously desired to spirit Lord Ives away from her less beautiful sister, the praise heaped on her head by Duffy was intoxicating. Should she encourage them to remain, she would appear the heroine. That was the course to take, most assuredly. A slow smile crossed those delicately carved lips.

"Most kind," she murmured. "Alissa needs comfort now, I fear. No more riding across the downs with her bird. Poor dear girl."

Alissa glanced away from her sister, firming her lips lest she utter something she might regret later. True sympathy from Henrietta was as likely as a bright sun at midnight.

At the far end of the table Barrett was in conversation with his father. Or rather Barrett listened while Lord ffolkes lectured on the latest innovation in sheep shearing. No comment regarding an outing came from those two.

Christopher didn't think that Barrett was shy like his sister. Rather, the younger man seemed to be reluctant to voice an opinion. In spite of those vague-appearing eyes, the baron carried strong notions that his son dared not contradict.

Christopher's ear caught a word from Henrietta. What now? He chided himself for failing to attend.

"If we have all finished our meal, we can adjourn to the garden to watch Alissa's little pets. I am certain you will find them most amusing." She spoke with a regal authority that was almost annoying.

Christopher wondered how Alissa managed to hold her tongue, given such abundance of provocation.

Matty maneuvered the awkward chair while Lord Ives escorted Henrietta to the sheltered garden terrace. Duffy and Elizabeth slowly followed in their wake. At the door of the dining room, Lady ffolkes paused on her way to the Lily Terrace, where she intended to plant a new variety. She noted the attention bestowed on Elizabeth by Lord Duffus and gave them a vaguely displeased look.

Out on the lower terrace, the sun shown brightly on the reluctantly assembled group. Alissa had sent word to Thomas, her trusted assistant, to bring up Princess from the mews. With a melodic whistle, she called Lady to her side.

"Really, Alissa, whistling ought never be done by a lady." Henrietta reproved her sister with one eye on Lord Ives to see if he noted how concerned she was for her sister's reputation.

"Then buy me a silver whistle and I shan't need to be unladylike." The reply was not only daring but also rather amusing. Since Henrietta never spent a farthing on anyone save herself, it was a pointless demand to make.

Thomas handed a glove to Alissa so she might handle the

hawk. Alissa drew on the heavy leather and took a calming breath. It had been weeks since she had been with her bird. And to have Henrietta here distracted her. While Lord Ives and Duffy respected the quiet that ought to be maintained, Henrietta could very well shriek with laughter or fear, or do heaven knew what. Though Princess was manned, that is, accustomed to people, she was not proof against the likes of Henrietta.

Alissa accepted the hawk from the cadge where she sat when she traveled any distance, careful to keep the jesses free. Speaking in a soft, soothing tone, she stroked the bright cream-colored breast, then chucked the side of the nearly black head. Princess settled on her new perch with pleasure. She waited docilely as Alissa removed the hood, holding it by the topknot of feathers.

Lady sat close to the wheelchair, eager to be with her beloved mistress. Shifting in the chair slightly, Alissa bent over to very carefully place Princess on Lady's collar. The collar was especially wide and padded so that the bird could not dig her talons into the dog's neck. Alissa nudged the soft underbreast of the bird, encouraging it to settle on the collar, then, once the transfer was completed, sat back in the wheelchair, a pleased smile on her face.

Gently she urged, "Go for a walk, Lady."

The dog walked along the terrace toward Lord Ives with an amusing dignity. Upon Lady's back, Princess sat with regal aplomb, looking about her with those sharp eyes that never missed a thing.

"Marvelous," breathed Ives. "I cannot believe such an independent creature would so tamely be friends with a dog. Yet I notice you pick Princess up almost as you might a pet duck." His voice was full of admiration for the amazing hawk with her delightful mistress.

"She is a good bird," said Alissa, her full attention on the pair. One never knew what the falcon might do. Curiosity remained one of her strongest traits.

Henrietta exhaled a bored sigh. "Shall we go now?"

Annoyed with so little patience and dismayed at the sudden shadow that crossed Alissa's face, Lord Ives shook his head.

"Let's wait a bit longer. I doubt Astley's has any performances more unusual than this."

Head cocked to one side as though in speculation, Princess gazed down at the dog's head, then leaned forward and tweaked her ear. Lady let out an indignant yowl and took off in a dash across the terrace, Princess hanging tenaciously to the collar, her wings at near-stretch to retain her balance. Lady, in an effort to get rid of her unappreciative rider, made an alarming swerve right under a bush. Princess let go, casting herself up on a branch to wait for Lady, for all the world as though she fully expected the dog to meekly return so she could really tweak those ears that flopped about in such an intriguing manner.

Alissa had stretched in her chair, as though she would dearly like to run after the two. Pushing herself up on her arms, she called, "Lady, come here!" Then she settled back in place while keeping careful watch on the hawk.

The dark-ringed yellow eyes gave Alissa a baleful glare, as though somehow fixing the blame for the disaster all on the falcon's mistress. Princess then settled on the branch, smoothed down a few ruffled feathers, and offered Alissa a quaint nod of her head, as though to indicate to Alissa that all was forgiven.

Duffy and Ives exchanged startled looks, then, after noting that no danger seemed apparent, gave themselves up to laughter. Elizabeth joined in while Alissa fumed from her chair. She stirred in restless concern. Best get Princess hooded before she caught sight of a potential meal. Alissa could just imagine Henrietta's swoon should the falcon take off after a tasty rabbit, tearing into it, fur and all.

A shrill whistle rent the air and the bird obediently flew to Alissa's outstretched arm. Her feathers settled down and any sense of pique was done away with as Alissa gently scratched the bird's head. Princess turned this way and that, seeking an as-yet-unreached spot.

"Well, I believe we have had enough excitement for an afternoon," muttered Henrietta.

Taking a glance at Lord Ives's amused face, Alissa grinned and quietly added, "If you should like a bit more entertainment, we could always take the goshawk out to the haystacks and have him hunt for rats. With the two terriers and a ferrent to help as well, of course.''

"Of course." Lord Ives walked over to where Alissa sat with the now docile and hooded falcon on her hand. "I think we will reserve that treat for another day, thank you."

Smiling with a triumphant gleam in her eyes, Henrietta drew Lord Ives toward the house, her voice drifting back to the four who remained. "Do come with me, milord. I believe we can have a tolerable ride across the downs before dinner." She turned halfway to add, "Elizabeth and Lord Duffus, why not join us?"

"Go with them, Elizabeth. Who knows what Henrietta might do if alone?" Alissa frowned at the departing Henrietta, who might be younger in years but seemed ages older in her handling of men.

Elizabeth nodded agreement. "You can manage?"

"Matty is never far away. Go." With a jaunty smile on her face, Alissa watched the four stroll to the house and disappear. Left alone, she stroked the naughty Princess, not liking her own thoughts very much.

Thomas approached, picked up the bird, setting her carefully on the cadge, he headed off to the mews once again.

Shifting about in her chair, Alissa steadied herself with her toe as she motioned to Matty.

"Time to return to the house, I suppose."

"The garden is right nice now, Miss Alissa. Why not sit there awhile afore the others return."

"I would work on the sculpture, I believe." She had given the heavy glove to Thomas to take back to the mews. Now she looked at her hand. Slim yet powerful. And she would very much have liked to spank Henrietta, she thought with a shock. That young miss was becoming altogether too forward. Couldn't Lord Ives see what a spoiled flirt Henrietta was? His elegant lordship had ventured off with Henrietta with never a backward glance.

Alissa knew a pang of regret that she probably couldn't compete with Henrietta even if she could dance and walk with ease. The only reason Lord Ives took an interest in her, she was certain, was pity. He seemed a kind man, essentially good in nature . . . and ought not fall prey to the snares of her sister.

Suffering Matty to wheel her to the conservatory, Alissa settled down to her work, with only one small sigh to indicate she wished things were otherwise. She was able to move around with relative ease, and discovered the chair actually had a few points in its favor. It was possible to glide across to fetch something she wanted without rising.

"I am getting slothful, Lady," she confessed to the dog. Alissa placed the little hedgehog, now nearly ready for the kiln, on a tray, then picked up an exquisitely sculptured sparrow hawk she had begun weeks ago. Thanks to the moist cloth Matty kept over it, the little bird was no worse for the time elapsed.

By the time the four riders returned to the manor house, Alissa had placed the two little sculptures plus several hastily thrown mugs up on the shelf to complete their drying. Once sufficiently dry, they would be sent to the kiln. Feeling oddly out of sorts, Alissa had summoned a footman to carry her to her room, the faithful Matty trailing along behind. The house now sat in silence.


"Lovely countryside, Duffy," Lord Ives commented as they walked up the stairs. He wondered what had happened to Miss Alissa after they left. On the way from the stable he had unobtrusively checked the terrace, then the conservatory, to no avail. She was not to be seen. He had a few things to say to that young lady when he found her.

"Aye." Duffy glanced at his friend, and knowing him well, he said, "The lass dinna seem to be around. Perhaps she is in her room?" Duffy paused by his door, studying Ives. He had been introspective all during the ride, much to Henrietta's displeasure. "You can see her later."

"Of course," murmured Lord Ives, who proceeded to his own room. As Duffy's door clicked shut, Ives stopped, looked back to check the hall, seeing no one in sight, swiftly crossed to listen a moment, ear against the oaken panel. Satisfied at what he did—or didn't—hear, he flung Alissa's door open and nodded with satisfaction.

"So I was right. You *can* walk!"

# 5

Alissa clung to one of the posts of her bed, too stunned to speak at first. Two pink dots bloomed on her cheeks when she guiltily peered at him. Her gaze nervously darted away from the angry-looking man who stood just inside the doorway.

"You have no business in here," she at last managed to choke out, furious that she wasn't able to give him a round scolding. She sank onto the edge of the bed, staring at him with a great deal more defiance than she felt. The palms of her hands felt moist, and she strove for control.

"What were you going to do?" he demanded. "Did you intend to keep on with the pretense? How long have you known?"

Instead of replying, she countered, "What made you suspect? I only realized I might be able to move or stand while I was out with the bird."

He nodded. "I saw your feet shifting, noticed you used them when the bird nipped at the dog's ear." His suspicions didn't appear to have been eased. His hands still remained at his hips, his stance questioning. "Continue."

"The numb sensation in my back has slowly been leaving. I had been aware of the change," Alissa said, hoping her words would appease him. "Yet I felt unsure I would be able to actually walk again. And I have done little of that." She didn't want to explain the humiliating aspect of it, that she preferred to remain in the chair, that in one way her paralysis had made life a good deal simpler. She had hoped to stall for time. Once Henrietta was safely off, Alissa had planned a miraculous recovery.

"Why did you have to spoil things?" she demanded, her voice full of the rage that simmered within her. "I had wished to wait. Henrietta *must* go to London, not me." She took another look at the implacable countenance and shrugged. "Why bother to explain? You could never understand." The vivid memory of him at Lady Devonton's ball, ladies vying for his attention, men admiring him, his expertise on the dance floor, again flashed through her mind.

The anger seeped away from the taut figure by the door. He took a step closer as his curiosity rose. "You had but one Season in town and you do *not* wish to return?" It seemed incredible that any young woman would not desire to be in town, where all the delights of the world were to be found.

"Remember, I was but a shy daisy—a rather tall one, at that—amidst so many elegant orchids and lovely roses. I found it all terribly difficult, you see. My dear aunt despaired of me and sent me home early, much to my relief," Alissa confessed, somewhat surprised she could speak to him so openly. "I much prefer to remain here quietly. I have given my situation a good deal of thought." She decided it might be better not to reveal what conclusions she had reached.

"First of all, I do not think you are so very tall. As a matter of note, I think you are quite all right as you are, at least to my eyes. Petite dolls are not always desirable to a man. I rather enjoy a lady whose head can rest on my shoulder." He half-smiled at her startled interest. "May I say that you do not seem to have any problem speaking to me, though you profess to be most retiring? In fact, you are remarkably able to converse. How is that?"

She half-turned away, her fingers pleating the pale blue muslin coverlet with nervous intensity. "I am at home now, not in some lavishly decorated ballroom or crowded rout. 'Tis only around unfamiliar people that the room seems to close in on me and I feel as though I cannot speak." That she experienced a number of other terrifying sensations was not mentioned.

"I can see where it might be awkward to be in the midst of the *ton* if one felt like that. However, I refuse to believe you do not desire to leave your home. Surely you wish to marry." At her sudden glare, he added, "But what about your sister? As I recall, your father insists you be wed before her."

"That is why," she admonished with the air of a long-suffering teacher, "I intended to pretend just a little longer."

"A little?" His brows shot up in disbelief. "It is the early part of September. You would remain in that chair until next spring?"

"It would have been worth it," she stubbornly maintained. "I suppose you must tell everyone." Her voice held a wistful note that tugged at the previously impervious heart of the gentleman by the door.

"No. That you must do. I believe you must face this matter with your father. It will not be so very bad. I will help you all I can."

At these words, her head shot up, and she looked at him in alarm. "Help? What do you mean, help?"

He studied the nails on one hand with an air of abstraction before meeting that penetrating gaze. "If you will permit, we might try . . . an experiment. When no one else is around. No one need know about it—it would be our secret." His voice purred with his desire to convince her to allow his help.

Not trusting him at the moment, Alissa edged away, tugging at the coverlet of her bed as she shifted sideways. "I will not promise anything for now. I will consider telling Papa. Mind, I said consider." Glancing at the open door, then back to him, she said softly, "Now I think you had better disappear from here. Should anyone see you, the results could be awesome."

He nodded, peeked around the corner, then, not seeing or hearing anything, quickly stepped from the room, shutting the door behind him with a muted click.

"What did he mean . . . an experiment?" Her mind came up with a number of wildly improbable solutions, all of which were discarded most promptly. She was startled at the abrupt knock on her door. Was there to be no end to her visitors before dinner?

"One moment," she called out so she could compose herself against the pillows. If she was to continue with the ruse—no matter how long—she had best remember to be careful at all times and with everyone. Indeed, if she intended to practice walking, she had better place a chair against the door, well-hooked under the knob, before commencing such a thing. "Come in, please."

Elizabeth poked her head around the door, then slipped inside the room with the air of a conspirator. She quietly shut it, then walked across to plump herself down on the edge of the bed. "You must hear about the ride. The weather was perfect, the horses well-mannered, and the scenery superb. Henrietta will have a fit of the sullens, at the very least. My Lord Ives rather ignored her the entire time we were out. Isn't that a pity?" Elizabeth giggled, then made a supreme effort to be sober. "He seemed to be thinking very hard about something. I wonder what." She darted a glance at Alissa, then smiled with delightful mischief in her eyes. "Duffy said Lord Ives is usually the life of the group. Fancy that he should come over the thinker while here. He spent the morning with you, did he not?"

Alissa avoided direct contact with that penetrating gaze. She toyed with the edging on her comforter as her eyes sought the painting of her grandmother that hung on the far wall. "He desired that I should explain about sculpturing."

"He took your side this noon. Though I believe he truly desired to see Princess and Lady perform. If Duffy had not intervened, Henrietta would have had one of her tantrums. Actually," Elizabeth reflected, "I prefer those to a sulk. She is such a crab when she is annoyed, and that nose of hers does seem to have a tendency to get nudged out of place so easily."

"We must have patience with her, Elizabeth. Being such a great beauty places a sort of burden upon her." At Elizabeth's look of disbelief, Alissa hastily added, "She does not have to be witty, she surpasses the greatest wit just by being in the room. She can dazzle without the faintest effort on her part. She sings like an angel. She even does exquisite needlework. It would be extremely difficult to rival such."

"You have talent too, silly goose," said Elizabeth fondly, placing a comforting hand over the restless ones mangling the comforter trim. "You play the pianoforte divinely, and although your needlework looks as though the cat has been at it, you sculpture very well. And what about your hawks? Not everyone is able to tame a peregrine falcon or goshawk tiercel as you did. Certainly our sister could never do such a thing.''

Alissa bowed her head and studied her fingers as they smoothed the coverlet. It was all very well for the delightful Elizabeth to say these things so gaily. She had the interested gaze of Lord Duffus following her wherever she went. It seemed to Alissa that Lord Ives was content to spend time with her when Henrietta was not around. When she spoke, he magically turned to her to lavish his handsome attention on her. ''What you say may have an element of truth. I fear it does not make things easier to bear when every man in the room has eyes for naught but her. Except Duffy. He seems a fine man.''

Elizabeth bloomed a delicate pink. ''He is that, I suppose. I know I am the youngest of the family, but there are moments when I feel older than either of you. Do you suppose that *if* Duffy were to ask for my hand, Papa might agree? You know how Papa feels about our getting married. I cannot see what difference it makes as to the order, do you? If you like, I could join you in appealing to him to ignore what he has stated in the past.'' She looked out the window for a few moments before resuming her speech.

''But Duffy is undoubtedly being polite to a passable female while visiting here. Although he does seem to seek out my company . . . and oh, Alissa, I do so enjoy talking with him. I am looking forward to the little party Henrietta is planning. I have a feeling that Duffy is an elegant dancer.''

''That will be one time that I do not have to fear being outshone by Henrietta. She has the daintiest step of any woman I have seen—even in London.'' Alissa felt like the veriest fraud, pretending to be unable to walk when she could.

''She is not being considerate of you, love, or she would content herself with amusements in which you might join.'' Elizabeth frowned, then added, ''I have the notion she may not get her way in all things. Lord Ives seems remarkably able to protect himself from her lures.''

A ray of late-afternoon sun shot across the room, lighting up the lovely old picture on the wall, and it seemed to Alissa as though her grandmother smiled with special warmth at her.

"We ought to be getting dressed for dinner. What will you wear?" Alissa tugged the covers off, preparing for Matty.

Elizabeth sighed. "My white, I suppose. It does not do much for brown hair."

"Open the bottom drawer over there and pull out that pink shawl. I insist you wear it with your white muslin. There is a pair of matching gloves I seldom wore while in London. Use those as well. Put some pink roses in your hair, at the side, there. You will look all the crack, as Barrett says."

"No! When did our brother ever say that? I cannot recall hearing him say much of anything for a long time."

Elizabeth found the shawl, draping it about her in theatrical fashion as she walked to the door to admit Matty. The pink gloves were easily located and one tried on to check the fit. She showed it at her sister, smiling her thanks.

"Well, perhaps he did not say such a thing, but you will look quite smart, nonetheless."

The door closed behind Elizabeth, and Alissa had to face dressing for a dinner she had no wish to attend. Eating in her room would be a chickenhearted thing to do—no matter that that was how she felt. Henrietta had invited a few other young people from the neighborhood to join them this evening. Nothing fancy, she had said.

Alissa's stomach began to perform acrobatics that promised to interfere with any enjoyment of her meal.

Duffy rapped, then entered Christopher's room. "Well, are you about ready to go down for dinner? Damnably early hour, this." Then, realizing Christopher was still behind the screen, with sounds of water splashing in the copper tub, he went on, "I have never known you to dawdle at your bath, man. Are you becoming a dandy in your late age?"

The sound of someone stepping from the bath was followed by the sight of Christopher as he came around the screen, droplets still clinging to his tall, athletic form, tucking a sizable towel about him.

The glare directed at Duffy softened as Christopher

ruefully acknowledged how slow he had been. "I got to thinking about . . . things."

"What things?" Duffy settled himself on the one decent chair in the room. The other looked as though it might fall apart if one did not sit most carefully. "This is a charming house, if not the best-furnished one I have ever seen. I warrant the gardens have the latest hybrids and the most-up-to-the-minute methods, though."

Christopher nodded in total agreement. "Lord ffolkes tries to be agreeable. His interest in sheep may have stemmed from an inability to compete with a flowerbed. Although I gather that even Lady ffolkes takes to the gathering of the hunters, come late fall."

"What . . . things, Ives? You were lost in abstraction all during our ride. You have much to atone for with Miss Henrietta, you know. Poor lass was near inconsolable. Only the reminder from Miss Elizabeth that several neighboring gentlemen were to join us for dinner seemed to cheer her up. What is it?"

"I know it seems peculiar, but I can't divulge what is on my mind at the moment. Trust that you shall know all at the proper time." Christopher submitted to the ministrations of his valet, Roberts, who had silently entered the room with a fresh shirt and a collection of cravats, all starched to a nicety. Ives was dressed in an amazingly short time for a gentleman of fashion. Before long the two men, both full of curiosity, were sauntering down the stairs.

Lord ffolkes was in the central hall as they neared the ground floor, talking to the butler. "Thank you, Parsons." He waved the servant away as he came forward to greet the first of the guests for the evening. "I trust you had a pleasant ride this afternoon, gentlemen? My little Henrietta is fond of riding." He beamed a smile as the lady under discussion floated down the stairs.

Her gown of cream crepe was draped cunningly from a high bosom and vandyked around the petticoat. A demitrain trailed behind her in a most graceful manner as she slowly placed one foot before the other, waiting until all eyes were upon her before she spoke. She touched her mouth with the tip of her fan and said in a breathless voice. "La, I ought to have been here before you. What a tardy soul I am."

One slim arm reached up so that gloved fingers might pat the charming ringlets dressed in Grecian style. A few curls draped across the ivory skin revealed so abundantly by the neckline of her gown.

Lord Ives nudged an openmouthed Duffy and both gentlemen bowed low over the young lady's hand. "Our pleasure to be here to greet you, I'm sure," said Ives.

"Let us stroll into the drawing room." Henrietta turned to her father and admonished, "Do see that Mama is not late. Another book on gardening arrived today and we may not have her company until tomorrow otherwise." Thus relegating her fond papa to the rank of a servant, she tucked a dainty hand through the crook Lord Ives so obligingly formed with his arm and headed toward the drawing room with a purposeful intent. She came to an abrupt halt when she discovered Ailssa in conversation with two of the neighbors.

With a possessive hold on Lord Ives's muscular arm, Henrietta made introductions. "May I present Algernon Smythe-Pipkin and Sir William Williams, Lord Ives? Both are Salisbury men." She waved a hand at Duffy, introducing him next.

"Smythe-Pipkin, Williams." Lord Ives greeted them with nice formality. Duffy nodded with his customary geniality.

Henrietta continued to make them all feel at ease, ignoring Alissa.

Seated in her wheelchair, for she had decided to postpone the revelation of her secret a little longer, Alissa was charmingly, if plainly arrayed in a cream muslin dress with a tobacco-brown velvet tunic trimmed with pearl beads. She fingered the dainty pearl necklace around her slim neck with nervous fingers, and her eyes held apprehension as she slowly raised them to meet the stern gaze from Lord Ives. Then he smiled. Alissa almost sagged with relief. He would not tell.

The two younger men nearly expired with the thrill of meeting top-of-the-trees London lords. Conversation was enthusiastic and rapid, with Henrietta being disregarded for the moment while they spoke of horses and other things of fascination.

A sulky expression briefly touched her face at the lack of attention. Henrietta edged closer to where Alissa sat some feet behind the men, content to simply watch. "I deemed Algernon would make a good table partner for you, dear. Selina Hardwick ought to arrive any moment, and she will partner Sir William."

Before Alissa could comment on the interesting fact that Henrietta had appropriated Ives for herself, Elizabeth entered the room with Selina Hardwick by her side.

The pink shawl and gloves had transformed Elizabeth's old white muslin dress into something quite special. One short puffed sleeve peeped out from beneath the shawl, the modestly low-cut neckline was edged with fine lace, and pink riband crisscrossed the bosom above the high-waisted gown. She looked most pleased with her attire and beamed with delight when she saw Duffy.

At her side, Selina, simply dressed in a pale green muslin decorated with darker green embroidered leaves, smiled as well. When Sir William deserted the London lords to join her, she extended her hand in a warm greeting.

"Well done, Henrietta," Alissa said in a soft voice. "It seems you have paired one couple well." Henrietta gave her an odd look, then set off to captivate Lord Ives.

Matty pushed Alissa to the dining room, where she sat in uncomfortable silence next to Algernon. He was one to talk about horses and ought to have been seated next to Lord ffolkes, not Alissa.

At the foot of the table Lady ffolkes did honor to the guests by appearing in a gold sarcenet gown with a delicate ruff at the neck. Her usually untidy hair had disappeared beneath a matching gold turban. Absently murmured replies to Sir William's gallant attempts at conversation were her sole contribution, the art of chitchat not considered essential to her.

Yet it went well, considering all. Lord ffolkes did not take off on his usual subject of sheep. Barrett said a few words to Selina on his right, who happily talked with Sir William whenever he was not trying to communicate with the silent Lady ffolkes.

When at last the ladies departed for the drawing room, leaving the oddly assorted gentlemen behind to discuss who-knew-what, Alissa could only give thanks. It would take no doing at all to remain in the background once Henrietta got going with her little schemes.

When the men joined the ladies, they found Alissa playing softly while Selina and Elizabeth looked at an album of sketches. Lady ffolkes sat reading contentedly by the fireplace. Henrietta stood near the glow of the low fire, which gilded the soft cream of her crepe gown. She was breath-takingly lovely.

"Shall we play charades?" Henrietta came alive and radiated good cheer to one and all.

"I should like to have Baron Duffus sing for us again, if he would be so kind," inserted Elizabeth with a polite but firm voice.

Sauntering over to the pianoforte, Duffy bent down close to Alissa's ear. "Do you know the ballad, 'The Famous Flower of Serving-men'?"

"You are a one for ballads. Hum the tune and perhaps I can play along with you." She listened carefully, recognizing it as an old folk-song melody, and began to play the music with delicate fervor.

> You beauteous ladies, great and small,
> I write unto you one and all,
> Whereby that you may understand
> What I have suffered in this land.

It wasn't precisely a song for a gentleman to sing, Alissa reflected as she strove to follow Duffy's interpretation of the ballad. It was more a piece for a wistful young woman. She listened as the girl of the song was widowed, robbed, and driven from her home. Poor thing. Then the fair Elise cut her hair, changed her name to Sweet William, and turned herself into a serving-man. She ultimately attracted the eye of the king and in the twenty-eighth verse she won her reward.

> And then, for fear of further strife,

He took Sweet William for his wife;
The like before was never seen,
A serving-man to be a queen.

Sir William took much good-natured joshing at the conclusion of the singing. Selina gave him a limpid-eyed smile and said, "I do not see how the story could have been true if the servants wore those revealing hose and doublets. Sir William could never be mistaken for aught but what he is, a strong man."

Henrietta looked fit to sulk, Alissa observed from her sheltered spot by the pianoforte. She began to play a piece of lively music, a tune much enjoyed for dancing. Elizabeth clasped Duffy's hand and nodded to Selina. She in turn reached out to Sir William. Barrett took one frowning look and left the room, followed by his father.

Henrietta, thwarted in her desire to outshine the others with a display of her acting ability, curbed her desire to pout and turned to Lord Ives.

Algernon, deprived of Alissa's company, bowed to Lady ffolkes and courteously asked her to join the young people. She gave him a shrewd look and rose from her chair.

"I shall show you sprouts a thing or two," she said with more charm than anyone might have expected.

Algernon plainly hadn't expected Lady ffolkes to accept, and he looked a good deal surprised. He held out his hand with good grace and soon the eight were performing a country dance to the energetic meter thumped out by Alissa.

It was a good thing the floor was wide-planked oak with only scattered rugs to cheer the eye, Alissa thought as the couples formed an arch and were dancing through with great enthusiasm. Lady ffolkes surprised everyone with her dancing ability. Yet it was Henrietta who quite took the prize with her grace of form and dainty step. She put everyone else in the shade.

Lord Ives possessed splendid elegance of movement, as he had at those London balls. Such handsome footwork. Alissa missed a note. She chided herself for wishing she might dance like that. Why, she would likely expire on the spot. It would never do. She continued to talk herself out of the notion of participating in the social activity once her inability to walk—and dance—was no longer a problem.

Laughter and bantering conversation filled the air as another dance was demanded. Alissa quickly began another lively tune. Her mind was as active as the music. What was she to do? Since her papa was partial to Henrietta, would it take all that much persuasion to convince him that his darling girl, as he often called her, ought to go instead of Alissa?

The dancing continued until Alissa thought she would fall off her red-cushioned stool. Funny . . . tonight there had been no rush by Lord Ives to carry her to the stool, nor had he insisted upon standing behind her to provide support. He knew full well she didn't have need of it anymore.

She saw him smile at Henrietta, and saw her sister smirk and simper in return. What fools men seemed to be. If he could be taken in by that simpering sister of hers, he wasn't the astute man she had first believed.

But then, Henrietta was certainly a diamond of the first water. Once in London, she would outshine every woman in town. Perhaps it might be helpful to drop that little idea in Henrietta's shell-pink ear? The idea pleased Alissa and she finished what she intended as her last dance with a flourish. "No more."

Contrite, because she'd had such a wonderful time and she knew Alissa must be exhausted by now, Elizabeth hurried to Alissa to offer comfort. "Do you wish to go to your room? I could call a footman." Elizabeth had observed the attentions from Lord Ives toward Henrietta.

"I am fine, dear. Perhaps my chair, instead?" With the help of Matty and Elizabeth, Alissa returned to her chair in time to catch the smug expression that ill became Henrietta.

Lady ffolkes returned to her chair by the fireside, picking up her new book on gardening with silent pleasure.

Parsons entered the room with a large tray of delicacies planned to take the edge off the appetites stimulated by all the exercise, while a footman followed bearing a tray of beverages.

Duffy moved close to Ives as the two made their way to

the beverage tray. "I canna make you out. First you fuss over one, then you fuss over the other. You canna decide which you prefer? Or do you play the field with the ladies?"

"Shh, Duffy. I said I would explain when I can."

With that short reply Duffy had to be content, selecting a glass of lemonade for Elizabeth and an ale for himself.

In a sudden lull, Ives was heard to say to Henrietta, "You will outdazzle all the fair maids of London when you come to town. I suppose you are eagerly anticipating the balls and routs and all the other intoxicating entertainments offered to a young woman. You will have beaux by the dozen declaring themselves before the dust is off the door knocker. I make no doubt you will be the Season's Incomparable."

Henrietta heroically refrained from preening at this fulsome compliment and glanced to see if her mother had absorbed these wondrous words. She had.

The group shifted as Henrietta sought her mother's ear and Elizabeth wished to speak with Duffy.

Alissa sat observing everyone, her thoughts well-concealed. She was startled as Ives joined her. She looked up, puzzlement clear in her eyes.

"One way or another, you may get your wish."

She digested that statement a moment and gave him a cautious smile. "That is to be fervently hoped."

"When are you going to get out of that chair? I warn you, I shall permit you just so much time. And then we can try the experiment." With that threat dropped like a pebble in a pond, he sauntered off to join Henrietta, extolling to her avid ears the delights to be seen in town.

# 6

Elizabeth glanced around the cozy breakfast room at the assembled group. "I think it would be a fine morning to do a bit of fishing." She gave a determined look at Alissa, daring her to disagree.

Alissa choked on a bite of muffin and had to be patted on the back by her mother.

Duffy glanced at his friend, then the others. "I vow 'tis an excellent notion. Lady ffolkes, with your kind permission?"

"Fish are wondrously good for the plants, you know. What we do not eat, I can use in the garden. By all means go. What about Henrietta?"

A faint cloud drifted over the room before Elizabeth laughed. "Mama, can you see Henrietta walking down by the stream and fishing, or even watching such a thing? Permit her to sleep. We shall return by early afternoon at the very latest. May I ask Cook to pack a light snack to bring with us?"

Lady ffolkes nodded her agreement, then swept from the room, her current copy of the *Botanical Magazine* tucked under her arm.

Alissa gave Lord Ives a nervous look. Would he insist she forsake her wheelchair? Could she actually manage to walk very far? But whether she could or no, if seen, it would mean the end of her charade. She had practiced walking this morning before coming down to breakfast. Matty had left the room and Alissa took that opportunity to chance testing her feet. She had been rather shaky after so long a time and she frequently had to grab for support, but there was no doubt in her mind that she would walk again. If only she might postpone the revelation.

Lord Ives took note of the uneasy countenance across the

table from him and felt pity for Alissa. He would wait a bit longer before forcing her hand.

"What do you think, Lord Ives?" Alissa bravely met his gaze, searching for a hint of his intentions.

"Why, I believe it a fine notion. The sooner we go, the better. Does anyone have an idea how we can best transport Miss Alissa?" He gave her a steady look, so reassuring that Alissa was able to breathe a sigh of relief.

"The old dogcart, I expect. Right, Alissa? Papa will not have use for it until the hunting season is upon us."

Alissa pushed herself back from the table. "We had better depart soon or the fish will have gone into hiding for the day."

In a surprisingly short time the four were making their way down the drive toward the stream that ran through the east end of the property. Christopher handled the reins of the dogcart, insisting he would rather do that. Duffy and Elizabeth went on ahead, content to chat quietly in the early-morning sun.

"You could have ridden, my lord. I believe I could handle the ribbons." Alissa gave him a cool look, feeling he had an ulterior motive. But what it might be, she didn't know. She desired to trust him, but she feared his knowledge of her changed condition. She had to keep him silent.

"Aye, that I could. I wished to speak with you. How are you this morning?"

"Quite well, thank you," she replied with caution.

"Have you tried walking?" He wanted to approach his plan carefully, and needed to sound her out first.

"A bit this morning before I came down. It was promising." She frowned, recalling the old twinge in her left hip. That leg might not be too dependable yet.

"Good." He lapsed into silence. Alissa watched him with uneasy eyes. What was going on inside that handsome head of his?

The sound of the meadow birds and the jingle of the harness was broken by Elizabeth. She rode up to the dogcart, peering closely at her sister to see how she was progressing.

"We had best stop here and see about moving Alissa to the bank of the stream."

Elizabeth tied the horses to the low branches of a pollarded hornbeam, then watched while Duffy and Lord Ives formed a chair with their arms to carry Alissa down to the river-bank. Elizabeth ran ahead to spread out a soft rug beneath the shade of a sycamore.

"Now we shall see who catches the most fish," she challenged.

"I do not think 'tis fair if there are two of you and one of us," Alissa bantered back to her beloved Elizabeth.

"Aha!" Lord Ives produced four fishing poles from the back of the cart and handed them out. "I believe you will have to do your share, Miss Alissa."

Duffy and Elizabeth began to wander upstream, explaining that they wanted silence so that the fish might rise to the bait better. Alissa suppressed a grin, knowing full well that Elizabeth treasured every moment spent with the charming Duffy.

As their voices faded into the distance, Alissa wondered about the propriety of being here alone with this near-stranger. Of course neither of her parents seemed to care a fig for conventions. Her father had his own notions and most of them dealt with Henrietta. Apparently it was quite permissible for the four young people to spend an innocent morning along the stream, for fishing was thought to be an innocuous pastime. What lady wished to become amorous with a gentleman who reeked of fish?

Alissa cast her hook in the water, then reeled in the pretty colored fly with care, certain that it would be doubtful if she caught one thing. Lord Ives had the advantage, being able to stand and cast his bait into the swift-running stream. That he was an expert, she could see at first glance. He stood with such careless grace. His line with the fanciful fly at the end sailed to the precise spot where a fine trout might lurk. He reeled it in, twitching, pausing and jerking it gently to entice the trout to snap at the lure. The bamboo rod bent slightly as resistance was met.

"I believe you have caught one," Alissa cried, ignoring her own line, which dangled in the water not far from the end of her pole.

Lord Ives gave her a very masculine smile that made her breath catch in her throat. "That I have." He reeled in the struggling fish with skill, then placed the good-size trout into the grass-lined creel with understandable pride. "It must be all of six pounds. Not a bad catch." He glanced to where she sat. "You aren't even trying, miss. Perhaps something is on your mind?"

Alissa leaned her fishing pole against a rock next to where she sat, allowing the line to trail in the water. She looked up at this London lord, wondering why he was here with her, spending his time on a remote country estate. Was he really so interested in sheep? Courageously she faced him. "You said something about helping me. How? And why?" The last question was a daring one, for she wasn't certain she wished to know the answer if it was to hear of pity or the like.

She watched as he placed his pole against the tree. He had removed his coat, and now the sunlight cast dancing shadows of sycamore leaves over his crisp white linen shirt. It was not difficult to imagine the muscles beneath that linen, nor was it possible to ignore the physical appeal of the man. She turned her gaze to safer things, like the scene across from where she sat.

It was pleasant by the stream, with a gray wagtail busily searching for insects on the far bank and the delightful bubbling of the water over the stones making special music of its own. She tensed as Lord Ives sat down on the rug beside her. He was studying her face as though wondering what she might say to his plan.

"Will you walk for me?"

She hadn't expected that. "Perhaps. Before the others return. What did you mean by help?"

"Oh, the experiment."

The silence stretched out until Alissa wanted to crown him. "Well?"

"Have you ever heard of something called hypnotic somnambulism? It was accidentally discovered by a Frenchman, the Marquis de Puysegur. He was a follower of Mesmer, and while treating some of the peasants on his estate, he found they went into a kind of sleep. It has been possible to suggest remedies, diagnose ailments, and the like, using this approach. It is a current rage in various drawing rooms of Europe.'' He watched her carefully to gauge her reaction before delivering his final sentence. ''I would like to see if I might be able to help you overcome your shyness, using this method.''

Alissa stared at him with disbelieving eyes.

''I know it sounds strange, but I have witnessed some amazing things,'' he continued. ''You could permit me to try. I can assure you that I would never harm you.''

She gave him a dubious look, then turned away from him to stare at the water. Dared she? She really didn't believe he would hurt her in any manner. Though she had never heard of this hypnosis business, she longed to try it. Yet what if it failed? Her desire to improve warred with her feeling that there might be danger involved in so radical a treatment.

''If it does not have any effect, you have lost nothing.'' He was not precisely trying to coax her, but he felt she would be a good subject.

She looked at him again. Her eyes met his gaze with a mixture of curiosity, fear, and wistfulness. If only he could . . .

''Let me try.'' He took her hand in his, pulling her around so that he might look directly at her. ''Now, I want you to relax against the tree. Be sure you are comfortable. Are you? Good.'' His voice was gentle and soothing. He continued to speak to her, softly, smoothly, a drone of mellow sound.

She attempted to do as he wished. Leaning back against the broad trunk of the sycamore, she closed her eyes and tried to ease the tension from her body. Soon she succumbed to the gentle murmur of the water, muted cries of the birds, and the hushed flutter of the leaves in the delicate breeze— and always Lord Ives's low-pitched voice in the background.

Christopher picked up her hand and held it loosely in his own. Such a slim, yet strong hand. He studied the sweet oval face, so trusting in repose. It was as well Duffy had agreed to keep the fair Elizabeth occupied. Duffy hadn't known what Christopher planned but, like a true friend, went along with the request, asking no questions, for now.

Repeating over and over the suggestions he wished to plant in her mind, Christopher spoke to her for perhaps ten minutes. Then he said in a louder voice, "Wake up, Alissa. I want you to walk for me."

She lifted her lashes, then slowly sat up, wiping the corners of her eyes with her fingertips before looking at Christopher. "Well?"

His grin was a crooked slash in his strong face. "It takes time before we can see if my experiment shall work."

"Ha! I do not feel one bit different." She gave him a cautious look, then brushed down her skirt and got slowly, and most carefully, to her feet. Christopher rose as well, backing away from her a step or two.

"What are you going to do now?" He held his breath when she frowned as though trying to recall something.

"You asked me to walk for you." She placed one foot before the other and slowly began to move across the bank of the stream. At her side the fishing pole gave a hardy bob in the water. Alissa caught sight of it and squealed, "I do believe there is a fish on my line!" She made an ill-judged, hasty turn and fell. Right against Lord Ives. They both went down to the ground, her feet tangling in the fishing line as she tumbled, knocking the breath from him when she landed ker-thump on his chest.

"Oh, dear," was the very faint comment from the lady on the top. For the moment she was too stunned to struggle to her feet.

"Good grief," Christopher added. Her slender though well-endowed form was pressed against his body in full weight. He could feel every soft, delicious contour. Evidently Matty had prevailed against the wearing of stays today, for naught but supple feminine flesh could he detect. He knew Alissa was far too proper a young miss to go about improperly dressed.

He nobly brought his hands up to her side to assist her

to her feet, and then made the mistake of looking in her eyes. She was bemused, awakening desire flickering in those lovely blue eyes as she for the first time, undoubtedly, felt the body of a man pressed so close to her.

She was far, far too appealing to resist. That innocent beguilement was more than he could turn away from, for certain. He brought his lips to hers in a delightfully satisfying kiss.

Her arms just seemed to slip up to curve around his neck of their own accord, and she settled against him with an inward sigh of pure pleasure.

Ives slid his arms about her, shifting her slightly so he might enjoy the feel of that slim body better. His hand skimmed over her back with a sensuous movement until he realized where he was and with whom. He reluctantly drew away. His regret was obvious.

Her initial reaction was one of disappointment. Then embarrassment set in and Alissa wished she could simply disappear. She suspected his look of regret was that the kiss had occurred at all. Perhaps he had desired the beautiful Henrietta in his arms instead.

She turned her head and scrambled away from him as though he might suddenly devour her in one bite. Settling on the bank, she made a dismal scrutiny of the fishing pole.

"I fear the fish has gotten away." She refused to so much as look at him. Her attempt at nonchalance was admirable for one given to extreme shyness.

Ives gave her a look of approval. "Perhaps not." He moved to check the fishing line, realizing that that innocent kiss had affected him more than he had believed possible. Never before had a kiss stirred him so greatly. He glanced back to see her sitting on the bank, her feet drawn up slightly and her arms resting on her knees in a defensive posture.

Pulling in the line, he found a small trout still angrily hooked. He removed the near-two-pound trout and tucked it in the creel, then faced her again. "I must apologize. I took advantage of you when I promised I would not do such a thing. My only defense is that you are a very lovely woman and I could not resist you."

Alissa was saved from making any reply—not that she could have figured one out, mind you—when the voices of the others were heard in the distance.

Quickly Lord Ives took his rod and flicked the line over the stream in practiced fashion. A trout rose to the surface and was soon hooked. When Duffy and Elizabeth rounded the bend of the stream, it was to see Lord Ives busily removing a fish from his line while Alissa sat quietly on the bank watching.

Duffy glanced first at Elizabeth, then to his friend. "I believe we have you beat, Ives. We managed to catch four very nice trout. Can you top that?"

Christopher smiled, meeting Alissa's eyes in a warm gaze. "Yes and no," he murmured. Louder, he replied to the approaching Duffy, "Two big ones, and Alissa got a nice little one a bit ago."

Sensing a good deal had occurred while he and Elizabeth had been gone, Duffy inspected the catch. "Not too bad. That one is a real beauty." Turning to where Alissa sat, he bowed and inquired, "Shall we sample that snack your cook sent along?"

Rousing herself from the feeling of confusion which plagued her, Alissa nodded. Before she could say anything, Elizabeth delved into the rear compartment of the dogcart to pull out, not dogs, as might have been the case had her father been out hunting, but a large parcel of food. She brought it to the rug where Alissa waited and spread it out.

"Are you all right?" Elizabeth whispered. "You have an odd expression on your face."

Startled that her sister could so plainly see how discomposed she felt, Alissa shook her head and helped set out the light repast. "I believe it did me good to get out for a morning. Fresh air and sunshine are a restorative."

Elizabeth took another look at her sister and wondered what had happened while she and Duffy were wandering along the banks of the stream. They couldn't have been gone above thirty minutes. And Lord Ives had been involved with his rod and reel when they first espied him. Still . . . something had occurred. She knew it.

Each team was competing to tell the tallest fish tale when the sound of a horse coming rapidly their way could be heard. Alissa exchanged a look with Elizabeth, each having the same thought. Henrietta.

She galloped up near to where the four now sat in silence. Lord Ives hastily rose and went to assist Henrietta. She was full of chatter.

"La, I was so amazed to find you had gone fishing. Why, Alissa should not be so exposed. Dear girl, you must not overtire yourself. We ought to guard against chills and fevers, ought we not?" She glanced at Lord Ives, giving him a sweet, very feminine smile.

Alissa gave Henrietta a steady look, speculating as to what manner of sulk she would have if she knew about that astonishing kiss. Alissa bit into a crisp apple, wondering if the kiss had really occurred. Had she simply dreamed it? She had fallen into that peculiar sleep. Hypnosis, he had called it. What had happened then? When she awoke he had been sitting precisely the same way, in the same place. It was she who had tripped over her own feet, falling down to squash him like a pancake.

How embarrassing. Yet she had managed to speak to him in a normal manner . . . almost. She was terribly curious about his experiment. Why wouldn't he tell her what he had said? Didn't she have a right to know? Or perhaps that was a part of it? The secrecy.

"Alissa! You are not attending." Henrietta touched her shoulder. "I suggested the four of us go into Salisbury this afternoon. I simply must have some ribands and a few other trifles. You wish to remain at home, do you not? You must be exhausted."

Before Alissa could deny that she was tired—after all, she had dozed for a bit—Lord Ives smoothly interrupted. "I think there is room for us all in the carriage. After all, Miss Henrietta, you are such a tiny thing. Why, you hardly take up any space at all."

Henrietta beamed at what she perceived to be a compliment and allowed as how it might be fun to have a group. AS she was gracefully yielding, Algernon Smythe-Pipkin galloped up and jumped down from his horse. "Glad I found you before you left. Mean to go along, if it's all right?"

Looking as pleased as if she had conjured him up from a hat, Henrietta gave him a flirtatious look, then peeked to see if Lord Ives had noticed her other beau. She extended her hand to Algernon. "How lovely of you to come. They are just finished their little meal and we can go to Salisbury right away. You could take Alissa, Elizabeth, and Lord Duffus up in Papa's dogcart while I join Lord Ives in his curricle. I have always desired to have a ride in such a fashionable carriage." When she batted those remarkable lashes, which Alissa suspected were faintly brushed with burnt cork, at Algernon, he would have agreed to anything.

Lord Ives bowed and replied politely, "Nothing would give me greater pleasure, Miss Henrietta. Duffy, shall we return Miss Alissa to the cart?" Before Henrietta could interfere, the two men formed a chair with their arms once again and lifted Alissa up to place her in the cart.

The smirk on Henrietta's face (behind Lord Ives's back) disappeared when he turned around. She crossed to the side of her horse and waited with pretty patience until Lord Ives came to assist her.

So much for the magical kiss. Alissa watched with silent pique while the others mounted and rode off. She muttered, "Pity you did not bring your horse with you. You could have ridden with the others. I am quite capable of handling the ribbons from here to the stables."

"You are not happy. And I thought it would do you good to go into town for a little diverting pleasure."

She swallowed the lump that suddenly formed in her throat. He stressed the word "pleasure" too much. Why, it amounted to a near-caress. Weakly she allowed as how the trip to Salisbury might be amusing.

Lord Ives leaned back on the bench of the cart with a smug smile on his handsome face. The creel with a catch destined to satisfy Cook was safely tucked behind, and now he sat with his beaver jauntily on his head and whistled a merry tune as though the world was an exceedingly fine place.

Perhaps it seemed so to him. He would ride with Henrietta
to Salisbury.

Alissa scolded herself for a positively disgusting case of
envy. Her younger sister was high-spirited and extremely
lovely, if a bit indulged. It was only natural that she try to
attain the best marriage possible. Undoubtedly Lord Ives
would be the best candidate she might find this side of
London.

"You are very quiet." He gave her a searching look before
returning his attention to the horse and the rough track they
traversed.

"I believe that if a person has nothing to say, that person
ought to remain silent," she said in the primmest of voices.

"Don't be upset. You are doing very well, you know. And
it is possible we may discover a means whereby you will
not have to worry about a Season in London. Your sister
can go off to your aunt's after all."

Alissa gave him a highly skeptical look. The only reason
she could think of at the moment was her own marriage, and
there was no candidate to hand for such an event. She decided
to ignore the provocative subject. Instead she chose to learn
more about Lord Ives.

"You raise sheep, milord? Somehow or other, it seems
unusual."

"What you mean to say, and are too polite to do so, is
that a dandy like myself ought to have no other concern than
the cut of his coat or the polish of his boots."

"Are you a dandy? Fancy being kissed by a dandy." She
couldn't refrain from a gurgle of laughter. He really seemed
rather nice when they were alone like this.

His glance made her feel cosseted and very feminine. The
sensation faded when they rounded the corner of the stable
to find the others impatiently waiting for them.

The groom had the gleaming curricle ready to depart. A
diminutive tiger waited respectfully for his master to give
him the signal to jump up behind. Henrietta had changed to
a charming white muslin sprigged in blue. She peeped at Lord
Ives from beneath the brim of a leghorn bonnet decorated

with large blue taffeta bows. Holding out a dainty hand neatly gloved in white, she gracefully—Henrietta didn't have an awkward bone in her body—climbed into the carriage, then waited for Lord Ives to join her.

As she watched the vehicle disappear down the drive, Alissa reflected that Henrietta would never have tripped and fallen in so ungainly a manner. But then, she would have missed out on that kiss as well. Somehow the very thought cheered Alissa immensely.

Traffic into Salisbury was extremely busy. With the fair coming up next week, people were already filtering into town, the traveling merchants sizing up the populace as future customers.

The city being laid out in chequers, it was easy to travel about. Algernon turned up High Street and announced, "Miss Henrietta may have had a right notion. How are you going to manage with getting about, Alissa?"

"I suggest we proceed to the Market Square. If you jog over on Blue Boar Row, we can drop Elizabeth off at the trimmings shop, where she is certain to find Henrietta. Remember, there are some lovely trees to provide shade in the square."

It was a distinct disadvantage to be limited to the dogcart. A bookshop on Queen Street promised Alissa all manner of delights. She was stuck with her ruse, no matter that she now could walk. Until she elected to impart her secret, the cart remained her cage. Algernon looked as though he would dearly love to get out and about, but felt obligated to remain with Alissa.

"Algernon," she said with sudden inspiration, "do see if you can find the group. Perhaps we could show the cathedral to our guests . . . if they have not seen it as yet."

The young man quite happily hopped down from the cart and, after seeing to the horse, took off down Blue Boar Row to search for the others. Minutes later the tiger who had come to town with Lord Ives appeared at one side of the dogcart with a small parcel in his hands, which he respectfully offered to Alissa. "Fer you, miss. From his lordship."

Inside Alissa discovered a selection of marvelous comfits

such as she had never seen the likes of before. She bit into one and decided that remaining in the cart had certain advantages after all. She sat in reasonable comfort, enjoying the spectacle of people bustling about their business. There were maids with baskets over their arms, ladies strolling about the shops, in and out, with animated debate over purchases to be made.

"I thought you might enjoy a treat." Lord Ives walked up to stand at her side by the carriage. "Your sister is so busy figuring out which riband to purchase, I judged it quite safe to come over to check on your well-being. You appear to be getting along quite well. Are you?"

Alissa nodded, swallowing the last of a comfit with care. "That I am. I thank you for the treat, milord. 'Twas very thoughtful of you, I'm sure." She offered the parcel to him, which he declined with a smile.

"Mr. Smythe-Pipkin said you wished to visit the cathedral." There was a hint of a question in his voice, and Alissa could well imagine he was wondering how she would manage there. "You will be glad to forsake your deception."

"It never was a deception to begin with, you know. I truly could not walk at first. There was a numbness from the waist . . ." Her voice faded off as she realized she simply could not discuss the intimate details of the accident with him—a lady did not refer to her legs, nor to various difficulties—completely forgetting she had once confided in him.

"At at any rate, I have been there many times," she said. "I only thought that perhaps you might enjoy it. Duffy is so fond of quoting Proverbs, I figured he might especially appreciate it."

"We shall see," he murmured. He searched his pocket, then came up with a tiny package. He took her hand, dropped the little package into it, then grinned at her. "I hope you will enjoy this. I couldn't resist purchasing it for you when I saw it in the shop window." With that, he tipped his hat and walked toward the trimmings shop, from which Henrietta and Elizabeth were emerging burdened with a number of gaily wrapped parcels.

Her fingers trembling a little, Alissa opened the tiny

package to discover inside a delicate silver whistle, beautifully chased with a design of birds on the wing. She lifted her head to gaze thoughtfully after Lord Ives. What a strange and wonderful man. She feared she was falling more than a little in love with him.

# 7

"But you simply must see the cathedral. Churches are so inspiring." Henrietta smiled enchantingly up at Lord Ives and he nodded with well-mannered charm.

"And so they are. If you desire we should see it, see it we must." He assisted Miss Henrietta up into the curricle, then spoke briefly to his tiger, who darted off on some errand for his master.

Duffy and Algernon Smythe-Pipkin were game for any diversion, even wandering through the cavernous interior of the cathedral, if it pleased the ladies. From the looks cast in her direction, it was plain that Smythe-Pipkin was delighted to be anywhere the fair Henrietta deigned to grace with her presence.

Alissa said nothing regarding the projected visit. After all, had it not been her suggestion in the first place? Her wistful thoughts of being left alone in the cart once again while the others trouped through the interior were nudged aside with the more proper feeling that all visitors to the city should see the glorious church.

St. Mary's Cathedral was justly famous from one end of the country to the other for its beauty and artistic quality. Of course, it didn't have the historical significance of some others, nor was it rich in tombs of kings or national heroes, though King Henry III had attended its consecration. Alissa loved the graceful spire, the awesome interior arches, and the somber peace that was so conducive to worship.

After much fussing about on the part of Henrietta, who thought she had misplaced or lost one of her precious parcels, they slowly set out from the Market Square to High Street and on toward the cathedral. The curricle followed the lead of the dogcart under the proud handling of Smythe-Pipkin.

Elizabeth suddenly exclaimed, "We had better wait a bit.

I gather Henrietta has seen something she must have, for their carriage has stopped on High Street.'' Indeed the two had dropped far behind while Lord Ives had dashed into the bespoke perfumery shop to make a purchase for his passenger.

" 'Tis a fine church building,'' commented Duffy. That he was looking at Elizabeth when he made the statement was not lost on that young lady.

"So it is,'' replied Elizabeth. "A friend of ours was married there not long ago. 'Tis an inspiring place for a wedding.'' Her cheeks turned a rosy pink as she caught the gleam in Duffy's light blue eyes. Alissa had turned her head to see if Lord Ives and her sister were catching up, when she noticed the look of regard exchanged by the two sitting in the back of the cart.

"There's an old clock inside that I daresay you might find of interest,'' Smythe-Pipkin volunteered. " 'Tis in the central tower, is it not, Alissa?''

"Yes,'' she hurriedly agreed. She must not permit these pangs of envy to eat at her simply because Henrietta enjoyed the company of Lord Ives. He had given Alissa a little silver whistle. It probably amounted to nothing more than a mere trifle to him. For all she knew, Henrietta might have suggested it. The very thought curdled the pleasure of the day for Alissa.

"Magnificent view,'' called Lord Ives as the curricle joined them.

Henrietta gave Alissa a narrow, catlike smile that encompassed everything from cream cakes to strawberry tarts.

It was hard to understand why Henrietta seemed to feel the need to have every male within range under her spell, but then, she was so very beautiful, she didn't have to work at it in the least.

Outside the cathedral a couple of young lads ran forward to hold the reins, and Alissa wondered what in the world had happened to the little tiger who usually claimed that privilege.

She prepared to wait, with not a great deal of patience,

she admitted, when Lord Ives came up to the cart. She cast him a curious look, admiring his neatly dressed figure, recalling how that same figure had felt when pressed so tightly against hers. She could feel a warmth in her cheeks and prayed that the blush didn't reveal too much.

"It didn't seem right that we leave you once again, Miss Alissa. Therefore I made arrangements to borrow a chair for you, if that meets with your approval."

Behind his back, Henrietta gave Alissa a stormy glare. It served to give Alissa the boost she needed. "Thank you, Lord Ives. How thoughtful you are."

The tiger came from the shadows of the entry, wheeling a mate to the chair Lord Ives had purchased for Alissa to use. He reached out to pluck her from the cart and place her, ever so gently, in the wheelchair. Only Alissa heard his terse remark.

"You may not think so later."

She gave him a startled glance before turning her head to stare straight ahead. She knew better than to engage him in conversation when Henrietta was near. But what could he possibly mean? It had sounded almost like a threat!

Smythe-Pipkin stepped around the cart to offer his services to push Alissa in the chair. It was plain the poor young man knew he had no chance with the fair Henrietta when an earl smiled at her. Alissa's heart beat faster as they passed through the tall doors of the church. What was in store for her?

The interior was an impressive sight. Even Alissa, prejudiced though she might be, felt that the visitors would appreciate the details. Looking east along the nave, one could see the graceful arches soaring heavenward, a magnificent sight.

"Except for St. Paul's, 'tis the only English cathedral built to the design of one man and completed without a break," Elizabeth offered to Duffy, on whose arm she leaned.

"Aye, 'tis beautiful, make no mistake about that." Duffy looked about with interest, sweeping Elizabeth along as he strolled through the church.

"Come see the clock," Smythe-Pipkin demanded in his enthusiastic way. The group wandered down the aisle, Alissa was glad that Algernon pushed her chair ahead of the others. Somehow it hurt to see Henrietta batting her lashes at Lord Ives. She was so beautiful that any man could fall under her charm. She had a line of broken hearts trailing from Salisbury to the manor house. London had better beware. *If* Henrietta made it to London.

Alissa stiffened, clenching her hands together at the very thought. It would please her father no end to have his precious Henrietta marry a prize such as Lord Ives. The Earl of Ives remained a top matrimonial catch of the London *ton*. For a rural beauty to snag him would be the *on-dit* of the year. Was *this* why Papa had urged their visit?

"Here it is. 'Tis the oldest clock in England, is it not, Elizabeth?" Smythe-Pipkin looked to the one who seemed to be spouting the most historical knowledge for confirmation of his fact.

She nodded while Duffy examined the curious working of the gears and levers. A strange-looking object, no one could quite figure out how it operated. But the whirs and clicks indicated that it did indeed keep time.

A large group of visitors entered the cathedral, and Alissa gave them a dismayed look, though recognizing a few of the party. She sat straighter, raised her chin, and offered a smile.

Henrietta gave a trill of delighted laughter, somehow jarring to the ear in the sacred place. "Is it not wonderful to see you all," she exclaimed, while still managing to cling to Lord Ives's arm. "We are giving a simple little party and would be thrilled if you would join us." The gentlemen of the group were immediately agreeable. The young ladies smiled tautly, gazes straying to where Alissa sat. Algernon had deserted her for the moment, chatting with a local friend, no doubt seeking to impress him with the lofty connections he'd made.

Two of the young women spoke briefly to Alissa before the groups parted with many assurances that they would be seeing each other soon.

Alissa felt her wheelchair move and relaxed as she was pushed toward the chapel of St. Margaret, the small niche where the wife of Malcolm III was buried. Behind her she could hear the chatter of Henrietta and Elizabeth as they planned for the coming party. Henrietta wanted to arrange for a musical group to play. "We cannot expect Alissa to play for so large an assemblage. You know how she feels." The silvery laughter haunted Alissa as she moved away from them. The gentle peace of the chapel was soothing and welcome.

"You may leave me here for a bit and return to the others, Algernon."

"I fear it is not that young man. Do you mind so much? I wanted to talk with you." Lord Ives walked around to the front of the chair to face Alissa once they were screened from the others.

She glanced up at him, wordless at first. Her tongue so often deserted her when she wished to sound witty or at least not born yesterday.

"I want to thank you for the whistle," she said at last in her soft, melodious voice. "Now I will not be counted unladylike when I call for Princess or Lady." She gave him a sweet smile, acknowledging his unexpected kindness.

He studied her briefly before he spoke. Alissa shifted uneasily, growing uncomfortable as the moments passed and he said nothing. "Well?"

"Can you place your feet on the floor?"

"What an odd question. Of course I can place my feet on the floor. You above all people ought to know that. And I have been secretly practicing walking as well. But should we discuss it now?" She glanced about, hoping the others hadn't heard a thing.

"Stand. Please," he added at her stubborn expression.

"You want me to stand? Here? But what if they see me?" All manner of evasive tactics whirled through her head. Did she want to remain in seclusion? Or did she want to risk facing the others on more equal footing, so to speak? She knew how vulnerable she became around a mass of people.

"And if they do? With this dancing party coming up, you must get out of that chair. You can no longer permit the entire family to believe you are an invalid. Something will come along for Henrietta, wait and see."

The words chilled her heart for some peculiar reason. Did he intend to offer for Henrietta and thus remove the necessity for her Season? Or had he something else up that elegant sleeve?

She supposed there was little point to postponing her restoration to society. Soon he would discover just how inept and inarticulate she became when faced with a roomful of people. If he laughed at her or teased her about her difficulty, she knew she would die inside.

The last time a large group had come to the manor house, she dropped a platter of little cakes and couldn't answer the simplest question put her by that haughty Lady Cowles.

Alissa set first one slippered foot, then the other on the stones of the chapel floor. Briefly bowing her head to gather her courage, she bravely raised her gaze to meet his, then stood. She would show Lord Ives.

"Now, walk to me."

There was an echo in the area, she was sure of that. She gave him a puzzled look, then carefully stepped forward, one foot at a time, noting with care the uneven stones beneath her feet. It would not do to fall again. How embarrassing to tumble into those strong arms as she had this morning.

But that had a most pleasant side result, her traitorous mind urged. She shook her head as though to dispel all those wicked thoughts.

"A problem?"

"I can manage." If she only could. In a moment of rebellion she said, "You said you would help me. But nary a thing you do betters my lot. You have no idea what I endure. I wish you would go away and leave me alone."

By this time she stood before him, her sweetly curved mouth compressed in anger and those lovely blue eyes flashing with dark sparks of frustration. Her troubled gaze searched his, looking for she knew not what. Mockery? Triumph? She thought she saw compassion and some other unknown emotion. How she would have liked to put a name to that.

He gave a hesitant shake of his head. Placing his hands gently on her shoulders, he said, "I cannot explain, dear girl.

Someday, perhaps. Until then . . ." He bent his head to take a swift kiss.

It all happened so quickly that Alissa had no time to protest or evade him, not that she really wanted to do that, her treacherous mind again reminded her. Had her mouth actually yielded so softly to the touch of his? What a ninny she was to melt into a puddle every time he touched her. The kiss certainly had not helped her resolve to put him from her mind.

Footsteps echoed on the stone floor of the south transept, the clicks of the metal plates on the heels of the men's boots sounding like impending doom. Their voices came closer and closer. Alissa knew a minute of panic before she slowly turned to face the others joining her and Lord Ives in the chapel.

"How like Alissa, to slip away from us." Henrietta failed to recall that Alissa would have had to have someone push her.

"I hope she is all right," inserted a concerned Elizabeth. She had not failed to notice that Lord Ives was missing. No doubt that was making Henrietta a trifle waspish.

Henrietta's shriek could be heard from one end of the transept to the other. "You are standing! 'Tis a miracle!"

Lord Ives smoothly moved to her side, taking her delicate hand in his. Bending toward Henrietta, he said, with great admiration in his voice, "And it was you, dear lady, who insisted we come to this cathedral today. Just think what your nobility of purpose has accomplished!"

Henrietta glanced to where Alissa stood, now with Elizabeth close by her and Duffy offering an arm for escort. Her look of annoyance vanished and she gave an immensely pleased smile. "I did, did I not? Though I must confess I never expected such results." Then memory of her father's decree—that Alissa be the first to marry and be permitted a second Season in London in order to accomplish that event—returned. Henrietta's exquisite mouth assumed a pout and those china-blue eyes grew prodigiously stormy.

"How kind a sister you are, to want the best for Alissa," said Lord Ives in his most persuasive and admiring tone.

"Everyone must look upon you with only approval, charming lady." He signaled to his tiger, who discreetly removed the wheelchair, disappearing with it down the aisle.

This fulsome flattery fell most welcomely upon Henrietta's ears. How gratifying that at last someone should see what a worthy person she was.

"True, I do care about her very much. I fear she does not always appreciate my concern, however. I find it vexatious that she will go to London next spring after all. She does not wish to go and I do," pronounced Henrietta in a fit of total honesty.

"But London must not be denied the vision of your beauty, fair lady. It is too cruel to contemplate! I shall endeavor to assist you if I may? Perhaps I can think of some manner to remove the source of your provocation." He guided her away from the others in the general direction of the cloisters, where they might talk without fear of being overheard while strolling along the covered walkway.

It took some time before Henrietta figured out the meaning of this flowery compliment. Would he actually find a way to remove Alissa? How?

It never occurred to that vain young miss that Lord Ives, that handsome, well-set young lord from town, would have any interest in her long Meg of a sister. Why, Alissa was a tongue-tied, bashful miss who amused herself with those silly birds and fiddled with a messy lump of clay in spare moments. Henrietta smoothed her delicate blue kid gloves with a sense of anticipation.

Lord Ives led her along the walk, his easygoing manner most deceptive. "You are to plan the entertainment for the week ahead, am I correct? I picked up a copy of the *Salisbury Guide* to discover that Stonehenge is but ten miles north of the city."

"You now wish to see the place? La, I am so pleased you changed your mind. If you like, we can manage a picnic trip. I fear we will need to use your curricle. Papa is so antiquated in his notions regarding carriages." Henrietta was flattered beyond measure that Lord Ives had sought her out to consult regarding the entertainment. Usually everyone went to Alissa to plan the events for guests. She was clever when it came to planning amusements.

Standing in the chapel, Alissa had watched with mixed emotions as Lord Ives led her sister away. He had forced Alissa's hand, so to speak. And now he simply walked off to court her sister while Alissa must cope with Elizabeth's delight in her newfound ability to walk.

Alissa felt an utter fraud.

"Can you manage out to the dogcart? As Henrietta said, 'tis a miracle. Oh, how pleased our parents will be."

Alissa paused, giving Elizabeth a frank look. "And we shall catch larks if the sky falls. Do you really believe Papa will be *pleased*, dear? He has been looking forward to sending Henrietta to London next spring."

Shocked at the very idea that her parents might not be wildly happy that Alissa was restored to her feet, Elizabeth was about to scold her when she got a warning look from Duffy. She abruptly closed her mouth.

"Perhaps there is a way both of you girls can be satisfied." He met Elizabeth's frown and shake of the head with a puzzled look of his own.

Alissa stopped just outside the central entrance to the cathedral and gave a little laugh. "You cannot know the conditions. Like most girls, I was sent to London to find myself a husband. I did not achieve that high goal. Now I suppose my father will feel it necessary to send me again. Though he would prefer otherwise, he is trapped by his own words. I do not wish to go." She looked so sad that both Elizabeth and Duffy sought to comfort her.

Elizabeth had placed an arm about Alissa's shoulders when the sound of gentle laughter reached their ears. Henrietta and Lord Ives were walking in great amiability from the direction of the cloisters. That there were other people about made little difference to Alissa. She felt a knot forming in her stomach.

"Lord Ives desires we should plan an outing to Stonehenge. It would be an all-day excursion. We would have a picnic along. I think it would be great fun. Shall we?" She dared her sisters to disagree.

"I vow it seems a lovely idea," murmured Elizabeth.

Duffy gallantly offered his hand to assist the charming Elizabeth up to the rear-facing seat of the dogcart, where he fully intended to join her.

Algernon had wandered out of the cathedral and up to the cart, handing a generous coin to the boy who had so patiently looked after the horse and cart for them. He heard the proposal and invited himself along. "I say, that sounds like a capital notion. Ain't been to Stonehenge in an age. Queer place, that. Eerie sounds through those pillars, and that wind over the downs can be tricky. Very tricky." Satisfied he had planted the seeds of excitement in the hearts of his listeners, he turned so he might help Alissa up in the dogcart.

Somehow, Alissa never quite managed to figure out how, Henrietta ended up in the dogcart with Elizabeth to discuss the proposed outing to Stonehenge. The excuse that Alissa needed the comfort of the padded cushion and a rest from planning was mentioned in passing. Alissa found herself seated on soft black leather in the curricle, puzzled and not a little ruffled. The tiger dashed up to the carriage moments before they were to leave, with a cheerful nod at his master.

Henrietta was not best pleased at the sight of Alissa disappearing from view in the elegant equipage while the dogcart plodded along behind in the dust.

"Do wait just a bit, Algernon. When the dust settles it will be far less damaging to our bonnets." Henrietta placed a dainty gloved hand to pat her bewitching leghorn bonnet, making certain that the large blue ribbons were unsullied by the trip. Algernon, plainly delighted that he had the beautiful Henrietta as his companion for the drive back to the manor house, was only too happy to do as she wished.

Elizabeth decided it must have taken heroic effort on Henrietta's part not to demand that Algernon take off in a dash after the curricle. Knowing Henrietta well, she thought it unlikely that she would rest easy while Alissa rode with Lord Ives. Even if Alissa was not competition, she was another woman and not to be dismissed out of hand.

A breathless laugh escaped from Alissa as the carriage

skimmed around a turn on the road toward the manor house. "I am a little surprised, sir."

"Why? I had not finished talking with you, and this seemed like a good way to accomplish it. You do not care for the curricle? It cannot be too dashing for a woman who can train a falcon. I had hoped you might find the seat more comfortable."

"It is all that is to be desired in a carriage, and you must know it. I expected to ride back the way I came." But her heart sang with joy at the very idea of a ride with him, no matter how brief.

"The trip to Stonehenge meets with your approval?"

"Why not? It seems that now I am ambulatory I shall be expected to go everywhere." It also seemed she was to resume her place as though no accident had occurred. If her leg cooperated, that would be fine.

"You do not seem very glad at the prospect."

"I think of London." She turned her head away so he could not see her expression. "But I suppose there is not much to be done about it, so I had best get accustomed to the idea." When she again looked at him, there was a pleasant smile on her face and nothing of her inner turmoil showed in the least.

"I believe something might be done if you were willing. Would you consider living someplace else?" He had hesitated to bring up the subject, but with her reclaimed ability to walk, she might be in need of a haven. He wished to see her happy.

Her foolish spirits rose until his next words dashed them to the ground.

"I have an Aunt Catherine who is a very dear sort of person. I believe you might enjoy living with her. She is the adventurous type of woman, certainly never a dull one. She is not the kind to object to the hawks, nor would she mind your sculpture work in the least. As a matter of fact, she is quite artistic and you very well could find yourself giving her lessons." He wondered at his halfhearted recital of his plan for her. He had been so certain it was the very thing to answer her dilemma. She sat in silence. Minutes went by and he had the vague feeling that somehow he had blundered terribly.

"You are very kind, sir. It is not necessary for you to find me a refuge. I have quite made up my mind that I will speak to Papa and prevail in my desire to remain at home and send Henrietta in my place. My aunt is certain to welcome my sister with open arms."

"You found it so difficult?" He was curious as to why he couldn't have noticed this charming young lady at the parties in London. That she had attended the same balls and routs and he had missed her so completely bothered him greatly.

An enchanting chuckle slipped out. " 'Difficult' is putting it mildly." She toyed with the parcel in her hands. "Pity I forgot to stop at Fellows' Circulating Library while in town so I could pick up a book on travel. It seems I might have a need for it. 'Tis on Catherine Street—most prophetic, I suppose."

"You would consider such a move?" He found himself holding his breath, though why he should be so concerned with her future welfare, he didn't know.

"I promise to think about it. First I must persuade Papa that Henrietta is the one to send off to London. Perhaps she might even go for the Little Season?"

"The *ton* is a bit thin on the ground at that time, but I expect she would enjoy it nonetheless."

A secret smile hovered on Alissa's lips as the curricle turned the corner into the drive of the manor house. She looked up at the mullioned windows set in the warm red brick, then said, "Henrietta would adore it. I know. And now I must prepare myself to greet my parents."

"They will be quite pleased at your return to the world of locomotion, I'm sure."

"Are you, indeed, Lord Ives? Would that it were so."

She welcomed the assistance of a groom in the stables, who exclaimed over her ability to walk once more. "Have you seen my father? He ought to be nearby."

"Yes, miss. He be down by the sheepfold. They're redding the sheep for the fair."

"Fine. I shall see him there." She had begun to walk to the sheepfold by herself, a fine, brave figure, when Lord Ives decided he might as well go with her. He offered her his arm and was glad when she hesitantly placed her hand there, leaning on him just a little.

"You do not need to come, you know. I am prepared to handle this by myself." The tilt of her chin seemed to amuse him, and she turned away with annoyance.

"Don't be so independent. I said I would help and I will." It pleased him to see her assert herself in this new manner.

Alissa wondered what he would think if she revealed her wild momentary hopes before he had mentioned his Aunt Catherine.

The expression on Baron ffolkes's face was almost comical. Amazement, chagrin, pleasure, disappointment—all warred with each other as he saw Alissa coming toward him holding on to the arm of their elegant guest, the Earl of Ives.

"Papa, 'tis a miracle. I can walk again," she said calmly.

"So I can see," was the grim reply.

Alissa turned to meet Lord Ives's gaze with an expression that revealed a total lack of surprise at her father's reaction to her words.

"And I refuse to go to London, Papa. I would that Henrietta go in my place."

The baron gave her a sharp look, mindful of the elegant stranger who was at her side. "We will talk about it later." She had never spoken out like this in her life, and the baron was most taken aback.

"I have made other plans, Papa."

At these words her father was so astounded that he could not reply for the moment.

Alissa took advantage of his silence to make her escape to the house. She glanced at Lord Ives, nodding at his bemused expression. "I will not permit him to send me. I have your Aunt Catherine and will turn to her if I must. But I will not go to London.''

At her decisive words Christopher decided he had better write a letter. Aunt Catherine was in for a bit of a surprise.

# 8

When Alissa entered the dining room, albeit a trifle unsteady, her mother chanced to observe her daughter was again walking. "How nice, dear. I knew sooner or later you would." She turned her attention to seeing everyone was seated before signaling that the meal be served. A look at the reddish-colored carrots in the bowl placed before her brought forth a frown of concentration to mar her usually serene brow. "I thought I told Cook to prepare the purple carrots. They would look lovely next to the parsnips." Lady ffolkes sighed, obviously not happy with the kitchen help.

A footman had assisted Alissa to her chair. She settled down and watched as Lord Ives kindly helped Henrietta to her place. She fluttered her lashes and bestowed a dazzling smile on his lordship.

At the far end of the table Lord ffolkes sat, his prim mouth drawn into a thin line of disapproval as he glared at Alissa, quite puzzled. Never before had the girl been so disagreeable while company was present.

Significant glances passed between Lord Ives and Duffy. The two had met briefly before dinner to share impressions. Both found the elder ffolkeses beyond their comprehension.

It was a tedious meal in spite of Elizabeth's attempts to brighten the conversation. Hers was a heroic effort to no avail. Alissa was deep in possible solutions to her escape from the whirl of London. Lady ffolkes was wherever gardeners go when mentally absent.

Lord ffolkes stolidly ate what was placed before him while wondering whether he ought to chastise Alissa for her impertinence or take her seriously regarding her refusal of a second Season. He could always plead she was still too weak. Time would be on his side. If she was truly set on her course, she would find a way. She was a very resourceful girl. Always had been. Pity she had to take after her grandmother in looks and disposition.

As his expression lightened, so did Alissa's. She had decided she was going to be firm. For once in her life she had stood up to her father, and now she refused to back down.

The conclusion of the meal was met with a feeling of relief from nearly everyone. Lady ffolkes disappeared in the direction of the kitchen, muttering under her breath as she marched along the flagstone hall.

The gentlemen decied to forgo the usual post-dinner port. They joined the ladies in a general drift toward the drawing room, where Henrietta made a concerted effort to enchant Lord Ives with her sparkling personality. Alissa thought her flirting seemed more determined than ever.

Once assured the others were reasonably settled at one thing or another, Alissa slipped from the room to walk along the low brick wall at the rear of the house, which overlooked the Lily Terrace. The half-moon lit the narrow waters of the lily pond, reflecting a glimmer of light here and there amid the large pads.

She seated herself on one of the marble benches placed to view the spectacular blooms in season. It was very peaceful, and the serenity was a balm to her plagued being.

"So this is where you hide." Lord Ives softly trod the brick, his steps without a sound as he joined her on the bench.

"Can you hear? The beetles are buzzing and the partridges begin to call. 'Twill be good hawking." She sat in frozen anticipation, alert to every sound from nature.

"I expect you would rather go out with your birds than traipsing off to Stonehenge tomorrow."

"That is not so. I quite enjoy the beauties of nature, but the hawks can wait for a day. Thomas is good to take them out." She tilted her head in anticipation of what he might say.

"You promised I should see your tiercel goshawk rat-hunting in the haystacks. Did you forget?"

She darted a glance to the drawing-room door, where she could hear Henrietta giving orders to one of the footmen. "No. But I thought perhaps you had. We ought to return. Would you go first?"

"Only if you promise to join me in a game of piquet."

She smiled at the request. "You do not even know if I do well at the cards, sir."

"I thought you agreed to call me Christopher when we were alone."

She bowed her head, nodding with obvious reluctance. "So I did. 'Tis better if we forget that promise. Now, go, before . . . someone comes to find us. Please."

He did as she bade, and Alissa remained on the terrace for a few minutes longer, wondering how she was to cope with the coming party and dance. She couldn't bear it were she to make one of her foolish mistakes with Lord Ives here. Odd, how one or two people bothered her not at all. But a large group? Still . . . she had improved lately.

At last she dragged reluctant feet inside and edged around to the pianoforte. Perhaps if she took refuge at the keyboard she could avoid playing cards with his lordship. She was certain to make a botch of any game she tried to play with him, the way he disconcerted her.

She ambled through an old folk melody, hoping Duffy would entertain them with a song, but it was not to be. She sensed a presence at her side and glanced up to find Lord Ives staring at her with a knowing expression in his eyes.

"Piquet, I believe?"

With a sigh, she nodded. Actually she was rather good at the game—when she played against anyone in the family.

Seating herself at the little square table, she picked up the deck, extracting all the cards below seven, then offered the higher ones to Lord Ives. "I believe it is proper for the elder to shuffle the cards, milord." The glimmer of delight in her eyes held him a moment before he accepted the pack, skillfully shuffling with the expertise of a Captain Sharp. "The stakes?"

"If they are imaginary, I shall play for pounds. If real, pence."

"O ye of little faith." He dealt out the cards, two by two until each of them had twelve, and placed the remaining eight in the center of the table. Alissa made the first discard, concentrating on the game to the exclusion of the disturbing man across the table from her. They played in silence. He said pique first, she caught up with him, then repiqued as she jumped to ninety points in her score.

But it was Lord Ives who with quiet triumph said, "Capot," as he claimed the final trick.

He gathered up the deck and prepared to deal once more. "I thought you said you didn't play well. That was a dashed good hand. I don't believe you discarded wrong once in the whole game. I simply happened to have better cards."

She chuckled. "Too kind, Lord Ives. I do enjoy a good game of cards now and again, I will confess."

A second game brought Alissa not only a carte-blanche but a quart sequence and finally the capot. They were about to begin the tie-breaking game when Henrietta flounced over to where they sat.

"Papa said that if we intend to make a day of it at Stonehenge tomorrow, we should retire early this evening. I am truly looking forward to the excursion. Such a fascinating place." She kept up her chatter while Lord Ives dealt.

Alissa tried valiantly to concentrate on her game, but it was impossible. It seemed Lord Ives could manage to play well and still listen to Henrietta's idle small talk. Not so Alissa. She lost, and badly.

Pushing himself away from the table, Lord Ives bowed to Alissa. "Thank you, kind lady, for a most enjoyable game."

Alissa inclined her head graciously and contrived a display of gathering up the cards.

Ives walked with Henrietta to the staircase, where he made a small ceremony out of handing her a night-candle. Alissa had decided he was not truly caught in her sister's pretty web, but she wondered what his game might be.

"Cheer up, dear. Tomorrow is bound to be better." Elizabeth tucked her arm through Alissa's and handed her a night-candle before the two slowly made their way up the stairs to their rooms.

"Yet a little sleep, a little slumber, a little folding of the hands to sleep," quoted Duffy, his merry eyes dancing at the thought of the coming day, when he followed Lord ffolkes up the stairs.

Duffy waited until the hall was silent before slipping next door to Christopher's room. "Now what are you about, Ives?"

"I have a plan to help Miss Alissa tomorrow."

Duffy straddled a wooden chair and eyed Christopher in his striped satin waistcoat. Nice-looking garment, Duffy reflected. Everything Ives wore was in the best of taste. "Well, I dinna see how you will manage to help the one while you woo the other." He made a face at Christopher when the other laughed at him.

"Is that what you think I do? Not so, my good friend. Call it tossing dust in the eyes."

"Rotten sort of dust, if you ask me." Duffy gave Ives an assessing look, feeling protective toward the kind Miss Alissa.

"I can't recall doing that." Seeing a look of affront cross Duffy's face, Ives went on, "I truly intend to help the girl. I'll need your assistance. Try to keep Miss Henrietta occupied when it comes time to depart tomorrow. I want Alissa to ride with me."

"What makes you think you can do a thing for her, assuming the lass needs help? She seems well enough to me, especially when you consider those parents of hers. I still canna believe what you told me of her father's reaction when she came to him walking once again. He's a strange man."

"You cannot help but observe how she tenses up when Miss Henrietta comes around her. As lovely and talented as Alissa might be, the girl lacks confidence. I believe she expects too much of herself, tries to please those impossible parents, even Henrietta." He paced the floor by the end of the bed. "This party will be a trial for Alissa. I shall improve that."

Duffy rose from the chair, shaking his head in bemusement. Before he stepped from the room he said softly, "I will try to keep the fair Henrietta from your side, but 'twill take Elizabeth's help."

When he later settled down to sleep, Christopher went over

his plans for the morrow one more time, then, satisfied, shut his eyes.

Alissa stood near the stableyard, her eyes aglow with the wonder of the scene beyond. During the night, what seemed like millions of tiny spiders had worked their magic to spin thousands of miles of gossamer webs. She glanced up at the man by her side. How pleasant to find a man taller than herself.

"They shimmer like a rainbow, do they not? I see crimson and gold and green in that gauzy silver thread."

The rising sun struck each delicate filament with beams that brought out opalescent lights. Yet it was not the spectacular sight that riveted Lord Ives that morn. The sweet, natural charm of the young woman at his side, her unconscious grace revealed in every gesture, every movement, held his gaze. In her blue sprigged muslin and neat little chip bonnet tied with blue ribands, she was as fresh as those daisies she thought she resembled. He broke from the hold she retained over him with difficulty. Taking her by the arm, he nodded his agreement as he guided her toward the curricle.

"Your father has suggested the others use the landau. As it holds four comfortably, I thought we could use my curricle. You undoubtedly know that a carriage with footmen has gone on ahead with the provisions."

Before she knew what was about, Alissa found herself handed up into the equipage. She glanced back in a bewildered manner as her sisters rounded the corner of the stable. Henrietta's eyes narrowed with annoyance and she marched forward, only to be restrained by Elizabeth's hand.

"Papa wishes us to ride in the landau, Henrietta. Algernon is waiting for us even now." Glancing at Duffy, Elizabeth led Henrietta to the landau, then permitted Duffy to assist them both into the carriage. Algernon, while sorry he couldn't show off his skill with the ribbons, was just as glad he could sit by Miss Henrietta for the short time it took to get to Stonehenge.

Satisfied the group inside was settled, the coachman set off down the drive in a swirl of dust.

Henrietta glared at Elizabeth, blaming her for the change in plans. That those were only Henrietta's plans didn't bother the young lady. She was quite miffed.

Oddly enough, it was Algernon who jollied her from the fit of ill temper by complimenting her on her costume, then her good looks, and finally her charm. Henrietta basked in the attention, smiling serenely at Duffy and Elizabeth as though well pleased with the world. After all, Henrietta had no cause to view Alissa as a rival.


By the time the others at last departed from the manor, Lord Ives and Alissa had already passed through the village of Alderbury and were well on their way. She said nothing as Ives negotiated the roads into and out of Salisbury, permitting him to concentrate on the handling of his cattle amid the traffic. Each day more tradespeople were entering the area, heading toward the new location for the fair close by in Fugglestone.

Once headed north on Castle Road, she relaxed, sensing a similar reaction in Lord Ives.

He leaned back against the softly gleaming black leather upholstery and glanced over at his partner. "You are rather quiet this morning."

"I thought it best. My brother says a man detests a chattering female when he is busy." She clasped her hands together in her lap, thinking the blue kid gloves a happy match to the sprigged muslin.

"Really! I hadn't thought your brother ever spoke. Oh, beg pardon. I shouldn't have said that." His eyes twinkled with merriment as they briefly met her gaze.

Alissa ruefully shook her head at him. "Why ever not? It certainly is nothing but the truth." She felt so at ease with Lord Ives. It was as though he possessed a special alchemy in his nature.

"Most kind of you," he admitted. "Not that I believe that anything you might say would cause a problem. You seem remarkably levelheaded."

"For a woman," she finished the thought for him.

"I didn't say that." He gave her an amused glance as he guided the horses around a slow-moving cart.

"But you thought it. I do not mind, you know. Common sense is considered a rather dull virtue by some. I think it a compliment."

"You are singular in other ways as well, you know."

There was no humor now in his voice, and the serious tone reminded her of her problems. "I know. Papa scolds me about it often enough. If I am lucky I will manage to avoid the entire affair." Her frankness surprised both of them.

"Which is why you sought to remain in the wheelchair. You figured you could avoid all those unpleasant events?"

They sped past the village of Little Durnford as she considered his words. "I suspect you have the right of it."

"What is the very worst thing that could happen at a party?"

Clearly startled by his odd question, she laughed at first, then seriously contemplated what he'd said. "Why, I don't know . . . making a fool of myself in some way, I suppose. I frequently do," she said in a burst of candor.

A strange sort of detachment settled on her, seated at his side while racing across the country. It seemed as though the words she uttered had no reality, that she might say anything she pleased and it would not matter in the least to anyone.

"In what way?"

"Like when Papa hoped to impress Lady Cowles and I dropped the entire tray of cakes right at her feet."

"What did she do? Bite you instead?"

Alissa giggled at the very thought of the plump woman taking a bite from anything that wasn't utterly delicious. "Of course not. She simply murmured something about help being terribly hard to get these days, and that was that."

"She didn't! Tiresome old woman." He thought a moment, then asked, "What would be the nicest thing that could happen at a party, as far as you are concerned?"

She longed to say that she could ignore an entire roomful of people if he was at her side, talking his ridiculous nonsense to her and capturing her total attention. Since she could scarcely tell him such a tale, she settled for something else. "I suppose it would be if I were invisible. I could watch the others and not worry about doing something totally idiotic."

"But you must know other people have qualms about going out in public, fears and flutters." He wished he could manage to convince her that she was one of many. That was a part of her problem. The other part was her family, and little could be done about them.

The curricle picked up speed as they left the village of Salteston and the road came close to where the River Avon flowed serenely in the morning light. The carriage wound around the base of the low hills that rose from the river. Alissa found the pleasant breeze on her face most enjoyable, though she felt flushed. Whether it was from his probing questions or the proximity to the only man who had ever kissed her was a moot point.

"Undoubtedly you are right," she said at last. "I have told myself it is foolish beyond permission, but that never helps."

"What would be the least troubling thing that could happen to you?" How he wanted to place a comforting hand over that slim, capable hand in her lap. Would she shy away from his touch? She hadn't before.

She considered that a moment, then replied, "To step on the hem of my dress and tear a great rent in it. Then I could slip from the room and take ever so much time to repair the damage." She silently laughed at his expression. "Are you trying to accomplish something? If so, I fear I am not a good subject."

"But you did well at the hypnotic somnambulism." He turned his head to face her, meeting her gaze with an intensity that quite shook her to her toes.

The memory of that particular morning and the events following her awakening from the sleep brought a warm blush to her cheeks.

She grew silent as they approached Great Durnford and could see the people going about their business. A good many stares were directed at the curricle as Lord Ives briskly tooled along the main street of the small town.

"You do not have trouble speaking to me." His reminder was unnecessary.

She was well aware that she felt oddly comfortable with him. She couldn't explain it in the least. "My, you are persistent. I perceive 'tis best if we both forget this nonsense and talk about something more interesting than my silly problems." One thing that had impressed itself on her was that her worries seemed to diminish after discussing them with Lord Ives. Did the adage that a trouble shared was a trouble halved apply in this instance too?

Curiosity about the man at her side prompted a number of questions, and as he was inclined to indulge her, she soon learned a great deal about him. He desired to raise an improved strain of sheep, he enjoyed music, and detested snails as much as she did. His appreciation of hawking enchanted her. The fascinating subject kept them occupied all the way to Little Amesbury, where they crossed the bridge and turned toward the west.

"Excellent signs posted hereabouts."

"Well, Stonehenge is quite a sight to see. I daresay were you to wander in some other direction you might think differently. If little boys do not do mischief, the weather does. Signs rot and fade with disgusting regularity."

"I believe that is the site up ahead."

She agreed, but something kept her silent. The majestic stones rose, some at drunken angles, from the high Salisbury plain in barbaric splendor.

"I have never seen anything quite like it," she said in a hushed voice.

In the distance a plow cut a furrow across a chalky field. Overhead, heavy-winged midnight-black crows flew in silence. High in the broad blue of the sky a lark sang with piercing sweetness. Ives assisted her from the curricle, watching her rapt face with gentle amusement.

Suddenly shy with the man who had shown her such kindness, Alissa walked away from him, reveling in the wonderful mood of the place. She wandered across the grassy plain until she could touch one of the towering stones. They were in close pairs, worn smooth by the years, softened by weather and multicolored lichen. Around her, fallen stones lay as though abandoned by some giant after a game.

"Who built it?" she wondered aloud. "How did they manage such a feat?" A cool breeze touched her face in a caress. She found herself being led around the central pillar while her cheeks again warmed at his nearness. They were alone—almost. Off to one side two footmen arranged the repast sent ahead by the cook. Behind them the young groom tended the horses.

"Some say it was a cult of druids and this is a temple of sorts." He wrapped his fingers around the slender hand he so loosely had held. He noted her shiver and sought to reassure her. "I doubt if past sacrifices can affect us today."

The gentle wind barely ruffled the tall grasses as a haunting drone rose and fell in a spectral fashion. Tiny blue butterflies performed a pagan dance over the wild thyme and thistles. They then blended with fluffy blooms of the scabious before fluttering off in search of something new.

"Is it real, do you think? Or have we fallen into a trap of time?" Her pensive face looked up to his, searching, wondering.

He bent over her, drawing her closer to him, unable to resist her appeal.

"Yoo-hoo," came Henrietta's voice, floating over the plain from the side of the road where the landau had come to rest. She was followed by Algernon. Elizabeth and Duffy trailed behind the others, admiring the scene in their own quiet way. For some odd reason, Ives did not look particularly welcoming.

"Can you explain about any of this? I have always intended to read up on it, but reading, well, I am not a bluestocking like Alissa here." Henrietta smiled up at Lord Ives, ignoring the patient Algernon. She had darted a look of pure dislike at Alissa, but conscious that Lord Ives was so very, very close (really, what could they have been thinking of, to be so close?), she said nothing.

Casting a regretful look toward Alissa, Lord Ives graciously undertook to provide some information for the beautiful Miss Henrietta. Dressed in her many-tucked white muslin with the pink silk sash, she looked like an iced cake. Her leghorn bonnet trimmed with pink ribands and white roses completed the picture of utter loveliness. If only the girl didn't open her mouth, she would have been perfection.

"Real picture, ain't she?" murmured the admiring Algernon.

Alissa dutifully nodded, her agreement regarding her sister's charms carried away on the rising breeze. It mattered not to Algernon, so lost was he to the sight of Henrietta in her pink-and-white imcomparability.

But as time passed, not even the civilities of Lord Ives could continue to entertain Henrietta, especially since the dratted man persisted in drawing Alissa and Smythe-Pipkin into the conversation. Henrietta was becoming annoyed.

Alissa was amused. She had never seen a gentleman handle Henrietta as Lord Ives did. Other gentlemen bowed and catered to the young miss until she became quite bored with them. In treating her as though he might be indifferent to those breathtaking charms, he was captivating Henrietta completely.

"I am famished," sang out the irrepressible Elizabeth.

Enduring the scolding from Henrietta for her hoydenish manner was a welcome payment if it made possible the utterly delicious repast Cook had sent. Outdoing all previous efforts, the meal was superb.

Henrietta held her parasol to fend off the unwelcome rays of the sun. Elizabeth did the same, and Alissa wished she had remembered to bring hers. It was undoubtedly reposing on the hall table where she had set it down while tugging on her second glove.

Noticing her concern, Lord Ives motioned to one of the footmen, murmured a few words, then turned his attention to heaping more food on the china plate before each lady. Delicate portions, to be sure.

The footman hurried off to where the carriages waited, then back to his lordship, offering a blue parasol. Christopher accepted the item, then handed it to Alissa. "This was left in the carriage." His gaze met hers, promising not to reveal the truth, that she had forgotten something no lady would be without on a picnic.

Unfurling the lovely pagoda-shaped parasol with its white fringe, she held the wooden stick against her, cherishing the thought that Lord Ives had so thoughtfully remembered she would need it.

Not long after they finished the excellent meal, Henrietta demanded in her sweet way to be taken home. She quite feared the sun might find an uncovered spot and ruin her complexion.

Alissa found herself relegated to the landau on the trip home, and deemed the company and conversation sadly flat compared to the fascinating discussion while coming to Stonehenge. Algernon treated her with a nicety of attention. It wasn't Algernon's fault. It was the sight of Henrietta, the pink-and-white fringe of her parasol fluttering with the breeze as the shiny black curricle diminished into the distance.

# 9

Preparations for the dance proceeded, with Henrietta issuing orders in rapid succession, then changing her mind on each item at least a dozen times. Elizabeth tactfully tried to direct her elder sister on a path least likely to produce a storm. For the most part Alissa did the actual work of making arrangements, a talent she had developed over the years as her mother gradually shifted responsibility for entertaining onto Alissa's capable shoulders.

Henrietta ought to have assumed some of this work, and indeed perhaps the young lady thought she did so. The fact remained that she was far more given to talk than accomplishment.

Lord Ives and Duffy went out with Lord ffolkes, Smythe-Pipkin, and Sir William Williams in a round of shooting, fishing, and cross-country riding. The countryside appeared at its autumnal best for them, with little rain and unusually warm sun.

That following Thursday morning, Alissa woke early, looked out at the glorious day which beckoned to her, and rebelled. "This is the outside of enough. If I survive all this folderol, I shall be too tired to enjoy it." Not that she really expected to take pleasure in the dancing party, but she hoped. Oh, yes, she hoped.

Hastily donning her summer-weight riding habit of periwinkle blue, she tiptoed from her room, carrying her riding boots in one hand, her crop in the other. Sitting down on the next-to-bottom step, she pulled on her boots, then rose to go to the breakfast room. Upon rising, she encountered Lord Ives. He was grinning in a most ungentlemanly manner.

"A very neat ankle, as I noticed once before, I believe." His eyes twinkled with mischief.

She thought she contained her blush excessively well. "A

true gentleman would not have made that comment,'' she said with a repressive note in her voice. It was difficult to be angry with the man when he stood there looking so utterly marvelous in his tan breeches and dark blue coat. Those Hessians had not been polished with anything but the best-quality blacking. They shone like mirrors.

"Perhaps he might not say such a thing . . . but he would quite definitely think it. I imagine you have come to your senses and are about to decamp this household for some more soothing scenery? I suggest we eat first. Sustenance is always a good start to the day.'' He held out his hand, accepted the slim, capable one offered to him, and escorted her to the breakfast room. They were the only ones come down to eat at this hour of the day.

"Did I hear the word 'we' just now? While 'tis true I intend to slip away before Henrietta—bless her heart—thinks of something to change, I do not recall extending the invitation to anyone else.'' Alissa wandered along the buffet, selecting a hearty meal from the assorted foods set out, tossing her words over her shoulder. Her feelings were mixed. She liked his company, but she remained just a touch angry that he had compelled her to give up her plan to avoid London. Never mind that someone was bound to have uncovered her scheme sooner or later. He had forced the issue, and for that she nursed her displeasure.

Once seated, she studied Ives as he made his choices, then joined her at the table, taking the seat next to hers, much too close for her equanimity. "Well?''

"Ah, but you did invite me.'' He began carving up the excellent ham on his plate. "If you recall, there was some talk about seeing your tiercel goshawk chase rats around the haystack. I could use a chuckle or two this morning.''

He speared a piece of ham, thinking of the days spent mostly in the company of Duffy and Lord ffolkes. Trying days. Other than the time spent studying the sheep—and how much time could one spend doing that without turning blue—it had been hard weather to stomach the older man's conversation. If Ives had not already decided against Miss Henrietta,

Lord ffolkes's constant praise of the chit would have given
Ives an aversion to her.

"We have heard Miss Henrietta sing, admittedly in a pretty
voice," he explained. "Miss Henrietta and Duffy have even
managed a few duets. I sense that the lady does not especially
care for Duffy's sort of humor, as those were curtailed and
her solos resumed." Christopher's voice revealed more that
a trace of his irritation with the beauty.

Miss Henrietta had been the star of each evening, a jewel
set off by adoring parents (if one considered the vague Lady
ffolkes to be attentive) and equally admiring beaux. Algernon
Smythe-Pipkin hovered around her like a bee round a pollen-
laden flower.

"I am ready for a change," Ives declared, glancing over
to see what Alissa thought of his reaction to her dear sister.
He wanted her to see that not every man deemed the beautiful
Henrietta the ultimate companion. The cloying beauty had
driven Christopher to edge closer to Alissa whenever he
could. Lord ffolkes didn't like Ives to notice his eldest
daughter. Pity, that, thought Christopher while offering
Alissa some blackberry jam. Alissa was the best of the lot.

"Poor man. I confess I had forgotten all about my offer,"
Alissa prevaricated. She did not wish Lord Ives to believe
she had naught to consider other than what she had or had
not said to him. "Well, watching my goshawk chase rats
is certainly a change from the drawing-room entertainments."

He puzzled her greatly. While he was every kind of
politeness to Henrietta, he never sought her hand if another
might do so. And then, it sometimes appeared to Alissa that
he attempted to deflect Henrietta's attention or ire from
Alissa. Which must be utter nonsense. There could be no
reason for such gallant, self-sacrificing behavior. She listened
happily to his random comments, wondering if he was this
witty every morning or if he was making a special effort to
please her.

Their meal completed, the two left the house hand in hand,
with all the stealth of burglars seeking to escape detection.
By the time they reached the mews, Alissa was in helpless

laughter. There was something about trying not to laugh that made everything seem all the funnier.

She leaned against the door leading to where the goshawk was housed, to catch her breath. "Are you like this every morning, Lord Ives? 'Tis a wonder you are not sought by the Prince Regent to grace his breakfast table. I should think he might do with a bit of cheering up."

"Have mercy, kind lady. And I thought you promised I was to be Christopher. Come now," he coaxed, "you did promise."

Though it wasn't proper, strictly speaking, she could see no harm in such an innocent request. "Very well, Christopher. Follow me." They entered the well-kept mews to where the tiercel goshawk sat on his perch, greeting them with a cry of welcome, if one might call such a noise that.

Lady sat outside the door, waiting patiently for the three to emerge. The terriers had joined Lady, evidently figuring the more the merrier.

Alissa efficiently handled the goshawk, quietly informing Thomas what her intentions were for the morning. He hung up the cadge since it wasn't required, handed Alissa the falconer's bag with treats for the gos, and trailed after Lord Ives and Alissa at a respectful distance.

With Alissa on Fancy, the tiercel gos perched on her glove, Lord Ives closely following behind on his mount, and the assorted dogs running alongside, it was a frolicking group that burst into the meadow where last year's hay was stacked.

Alissa went to dismount, then found Lord Ives at her side, his strong hands sliding up around her waist, holding her tightly and slowly bringing her to the ground. Alissa looked up into his eyes and suddenly felt like a dainty, helpless, and delicate female. Very much the female. To dispel this confusing sensation, she removed the leash from the goshawk, then took off his hood. Her heavy glove protected her from the talons, so very strong and powerful. Though the tiercel goshawk was a third smaller than the female, it was not a bird to be careless around. His sharp-tipped grip might have less power than the female's, but he could do his share of providing game for the pot.

"My gos has done this before, and I believe he quite enjoyed the game. Thomas has brought along the ferret. He will set it down on the far side of the haystack. As soon as the ferret goes about his business, we ought to see action." She held the bird high so he might watch, ready to fly in a second.

The ferret did its job well, and soon a furry object dashed from the stack. The sighting by the gos was instantaneous with flight. He was off and tearing about the haystack like a demon. In seconds the hawk struck and a rat was shortly deposited for Thomas to bury later. The gos returned to Alissa to be praised and offered a tidbit of raw kidney from the leather bag. The bird ate the treat and then settled down, giving a pleased tweep. Alissa smiled at Christopher as she stroked the large bird's feathers.

The terriers remembered this game and set to barking. The ferret darted in and out, no doubt happy he was a pale color so the bird wouldn't get confused and nab him rather than the nasty rat. Lady joined in with the crowd, adding her deeper yowl to the melee. The gos took off once again as he spied another rat. Around the haystack he went, terriers dashing madly behind, with Lady bringing up the rear. The ferret poked his head out of the top of the stack to see if they were ready for another rat when he saw the gos make the kill. Down popped the ferret to scare out another rat, and on went the chase.

Christopher shook his head, thankful he had on clothes which permitted hearty laughter with no restriction. "Do you do this very often?" he said weakly as he watched the untiring terriers charge around the corner of the haystack.

"Now and again. Thomas says the reduction in the rat population is much appreciated." She chuckled as the ferret crawled out from the bottom of the stack, obviously wondering whether to make another foray.

The game went on for perhaps another twenty minutes, when Alissa ran out of raw kidney. The gos settled on a nearby bench, giving Alissa a baleful look from his orange eyes. He ruffled up his feathers, then sat scanning the grass for a movement or the sound of a rustle. All of a sudden, without a sound, he was away to pounce on a mouse. He killed and devoured it, then chortled his contentment. Alissa pulled the silver whistle from her pocket and summoned the gos to her. He promptly came, then sat looking as pleased as could be, bobbing his head once Alissa took him up.

" 'Tis enough for one day, I believe.'' She replaced the hood on the gos, then prepared to return the hawk to the mews.

"My sides ache with laughing at those antics. What a team you have.'' He placed his hands at her waist, then set her up on her saddle with great care. His eyes met hers, laughter dying as he noted how fresh and lovely she looked. She was vibrant and blooming with quiet charm, unspoiled by the false attentions of dandies. He was suddenly very glad she hadn't taken while in London. The notion of Alissa turning into one of those simpering misses without a thought to claim as their own was appalling.

He mounted his horse and they rode back to the mews in a companionable silence. She efficiently handled the bird, Thomas assisting with the minor details. Ives wondered that she didn't simply hand the hawk over to her helper. "You ought to let Thomas do that work for you.''

"That is one thing I cannot do if I am to retain the bird's affection and respect. They must look to me for most things. True, Thomas feeds them when I cannot, but I am here most days.'' She deposited the goshawk near a shallow pan, then removed his hood. Looking pleased with the sight of one of his favorite spots, he proceeded to splash about in his morning bath.

Christopher watched as she gently handled the large, powerful hawks, bringing the peregrine out for her bath, then setting her on her block above the grass. "They enjoy being out-of-doors, don't they?''

"That they do,'' she said with affection. "They each have a block upon which to survey the area. You'll note the garden birds do not seem afraid of the hawks. However, you will also observe those little birds keep their distance. One false move upon their part and all is over. The only time I have ever seen either one of the birds totally frustrated was when the gos discovered squirrels.''

Christopher looked about, found a conveniently situated log, and sat down, ignoring what damage it might do to his good tan breeches. He was quite captivated by this side of Alissa. Out here she was free of the restrictions of the drawing room, free of the fears she had of society in general. ''Tell me what happened,'' he invited.

Satisfied that the birds were happily settled, Alissa left them to join Christopher on the log. She sat with an innate grace, giving him an impish smile as she began her story.

''We were inundated with squirrels last year. The gos was out on his perch, untethered, when the darting about of the squirrels caught his eyes. They truly were having a marvelous time, flying about the tree, dashing hither and yon. Well, the gos took off after them, charging about the tree in a most undignified manner. I should think he would have become dizzy, as they led him a merry dance through the uppermost branches. Just as he was about to pounce on one particularly frisky squirrel, the scamp escaped into a hole.''

Christopher chuckled, enjoying the sight of an animated Alissa as much as her little story. It wouldn't have mattered to him what she had to say, as long as they could sit peacefully in the morning sun and he could simply watch her. ''Go on,'' he prompted. ''What happened after that?''

Turning her head to look at the goshawk where he preened his feathers, she smiled. ''He sat on a very high branch and sulked, while I did everything but stand on my head to get him down. I coaxed and wheedled forever, it seems. Perhaps if I'd had this little whistle he might have come sooner. As it was, I thought he was going to remain in a permanent pout.'' She gave the silver whistle a delighted look before shyly glancing at Christopher. ''It was an excessively kind thing for you to do. I appreciate it.''

He shrugged off his small gift with easy grace. ''It gave me pleasure. You enjoy the birds, don't you?''

'' 'Tis amazing what one can do with a lure, a whistle,

and, most of all, kindness. In a few weeks' time, with patience and a bit of guile, you can teach a wild-caught falcon to fly quite tamely, yet even more menacingly than before he was captured.''

How simply she explained what was required—yet how many women could have done the same? he wondered.

''You must have other things to occupy your time come winter. Tell me, what is the social life around these parts following the fair and the hunting season?''

Her eyes crinkled up in amusement. ''I'll have you know we have two assemblies, a theater, horse races—with a ball at the Assembly on the last day—and a musical festival near the last of November. I expect Henrietta will sing again this year. They always beg her to perform.''

''And what about you? If you succeed in convincing your father to permit you to remain at home, what will happen to you?''

''I could start a school for little girls. Children have never frightened me, you see.'' Her eyes defied him to comment on that particular item.

He held out his hand and was enormously pleased when she trustingly placed her own in his light clasp. ''Could I try my experiment once again?''

Bowing her head, Alissa considered his request. They had sat here as old friends, laughing and talking as though they had known each other forever. Raising her gaze, she bravely met his. ''I trust you.'' Even as she uttered the words, she wondered at her temerity.

Again Christopher spoke softly, compellingly. He so wished to help her from her fear of large groups. However, he would be the first to admit that he might fail in his attempt. He had tried something like this once before, and though it was successful, that didn't mean Alissa would do as well.

When Alissa woke, she still found her eyes fixed on the tall beech tree. Nothing seemed altered; not even her hands had moved. Shifting her gaze to Lord Ives, she sought an answer to her previous questions. ''What did you say to me? Why are you doing this hypnotic whatever-you-call-it?''

"Why don't we go for a ride? Perhaps I can think of a way to explain." He rose, offering his hand to help her to her feet.

With that, Alissa had to be content for the moment. Thomas assumed care of the birds. Alissa walked ahead of Ives to where the horses waited for them. Her leg gave way slightly and she stumbled.

"Beautiful day, isn't it?" she remarked with a notable lack of originality. She accepted his assistance with reluctance. She ought to dislike him, she reminded herself. Only he did have a way of making animosity difficult.

"Exceedingly."

That he was glancing her way was in no manner a compliment, she decided. He merely wished to be agreeable.

"I do like the color of the beech trees, come autumn. Such a mellow ripeness to them." Her gaze drifted across the downs, filling her senses with the familiar sight of her beloved gentle hills.

"Beech trees and beautiful scenery go together." The words recalled to mind his first sighting of Alissa. Her hair had reminded him of the rich color of beech trees in autumn. Gold, copper, brown, all threaded through the hair loosely confined by a riband at her nape. Apparently she cared little for a hat, nor did her ivory skin seem to suffer from exposure to the rays of the sun.

They rode along, enjoying the peace, when Alissa suddenly asked, "Well, Christopher, I am waiting."

"Ah, yes. I merely mean to assist you, help you rid yourself of this dread of large numbers of people. I have no idea if my attempt to plant this notion in your head will be successful. We shall see tomorrow." He continued to ride as though he had not shattered the tranquillity of the morning with his reminder of what lay ahead.

Tomorrow. She stopped her horse and gave Ives a stricken look. "For a short time I actually forgot that ordeal. Has it occurred to you that if you succeed, I might be required to return to London for that Season I wished to avoid? Henrietta would not be best pleased at that turn of events. I confess I am not thrilled."

He hardly knew what to say. He had no more desire that she return to the glittering London scene than she did. Alissa had no need of town polish. She was far superior to all of those suave beauties with her natural grace and country charm.

A flock of goldfinches darted across the hill to the bank of the road to settle down in a patch of thistles. They proceeded to feast on ripe seeds, bits of fluff floating away as they attacked with hungry vigor.

"Silly birds, are they not?" she asked fondly as she sat quietly to observe the dainty finches with the splash of red visible above their beaks while they poked into the downy thistle heads. "I expect I am equally silly, borrowing trouble when there may be none." Glancing up, she met his curious gaze. "I shall hope. 'Tis about all I can do at this point." She rode on a little more, then abruptly turned to face him. "I expect we had better resume our duties." At his questioning look she added, "I shall help with some final alteration in plans already altered uncountable times, and you shall conform to the model guest."

They shared soft laughter as the horses were turned homeward and the day seemed to dim. Clouds came up and the wind rose in fitful gusts.

"Rain before dinner, if I do not miss my guess." She touched Fancy lightly with her heel and rode pell-mell over the hills until they reached the stables, never once looking behind to see if Lord Ives followed. Somehow she knew he would.

The glow that had illuminated her face while out on the downs seemed to fade as they walked to the house. As they neared the terrace entrance, voices could be heard, peace quite definitely disturbed.

"Follow me," she whispered, then quickly walked to the conservatory, slipping through the door to the hazy warmth of the interior. "I meant to give this to you before, but it slipped my mind." From one of the shelves she took a small object, the little hedgehog. Tilting her head, she gave Ives a measuring look, then said, "I doubt you actually desired it, but here you are, whether you wish it or no." It was not her customary gracious speech, but she was nervous, fearing rejection of her work.

Ives accepted the small gift, examining it closely, marveling at the detail. There was sufficient to clearly define the wee animal, yet not so much that it was overburdened with fussy stuff. "While 'tis true I invented the tale of the gift to his royal highness, this is worthy of such a gesture. You have a great talent, Alissa." He intended to say more along this line, bolstering her confidence in her abilities, of which she seemed to possess too little. This good objective was doomed as Henrietta poked her head around the corner and saw them together.

Eyes narrowed, Henrietta stepped into the conservatory, glancing first at one, then the other. She observed wisps of straw clinging to Alissa's habit, noted a bit of thistledown on Lord Ives's natty riding coat, and reached her own conclusions. "What a lovely morning you seem to have had. 'Tis a pity we all could not have joined you on your excursion. Did that naughty sister of mine bore you with her birds again, milord? You must find the time hanging sadly if you consider such paltry amusement." She tucked her arm in his and gently but inexorably drew him from the room. Her voice floated gaily back to where Alissa stood. "Do join us for our nuncheon shortly. We shall be quite a jolly group, as others are to be here as well."

Alissa stood frozen. For the first time Henrietta had truly angered her. What right had that young woman to barge in here to drag off a man who . . . seemed perfectly willing to go, Alissa admitted. "Oh, drat!"

"Problems, Miss Alissa?" Duffy entered by the same terrace door and crossed to stand by the collection of animals.

"Do you have a sister, Lord Duffus? Duffy," she amended at his frown.

"Aye, but I dinna think it be quite the same. For she is married and settled down with two babes. My brother is a quiet lad who likes to fish and hunt. I've no doubt there are many situations such as yours, however. Jealously like hers is not a rare emotion." His light blue eyes were grave with concern for the lass he'd come to admire. "I believe she sees you as a rival."

"You must be joshing, sir." The very notion that Henrietta might be jealous was so laughable as to be beyond belief.

"I have kept my eyes open while in this house. You are beloved by all who live and serve here. Your friends are true, though perhaps not numerous. Observe Miss Selina. She is to be at lunch. They are of an age, yet Miss Selina turns to Elizabeth. So Miss Henrietta bolsters her opinion of herself by casting little slurs at you." He seemed to take no affront at Alissa's frown of disbelief.

"I cannot credit what you say, but I thank you for your efforts to cheer me up . . . if that indeed was your intent?" She replaced the ceramic hawk she had been holding in her hands and prepared to head for her room to change out of her habit for nuncheon.

Going up the back stairs, she hurried to her room, the words Duffy had said still ringing in her ears. It was not to be believed. Henrietta, the beautiful, the perfect Henrietta, could never be jealous of Alissa!

She removed her habit, tossing it on the bed instead of hanging it up as she usually did. The buttons at the neck of her cambric habit shirt were stubborn and she impatiently tugged at one, sending it flying across the room. She dropped the small fabric insert worn to fill in her neckline onto her bed in disgust.

Elizabeth rapped gently, then slipped inside the room, quickly shutting the door behind her as she saw Alissa's state of undress. "Did you have a good morning? I gather you have been out riding with Lord Ives. Henrietta was not pleased to find him gone when she at last sauntered down the stairs. What did you do?"

Alissa pulled out her sprigged muslin once again and dragged it over her head, fastening the tapes with trembling hands. "Elizabeth, help me with my hair. I will never make it down in time otherwise." She handed a comb to her deft-fingered sister, then explained the morning. "We break-fasted, then I took him to watch the goshawk chase rats. It truly seemed to amuse him, for he laughed ever so hard. Then we went for a brief ride and came home.''

Her younger sister gave her a questioning look. "I sense you have not told me all, but never mind. I had a lovely morning visiting with Duffy. He is a most entertaining man.''

"He seems to have a penchant for quoting Proverbs." Alissa glanced at her sister with curiosity. Her now brushed and prettily arranged hair was secure from harm.

"I believe he planned to enter the church before he inherited the title. He is so kind and understanding. Do you believe nine years too great a span for a good marriage between a couple?'' Elizabeth blushed, but held her ground.

Diverted completely from the business regarding Henrietta, Alissa rose from the dressing table and clasped Elizabeth's hand in hers. "I think the difference no problem at all.''

Together they walked down the stairs to the central hall, where they encountered their mother. The woman had a distinctly vexed expression on her face.

"Alissa, there is a falcon on my aspidistra!''

# 10

"The aspidistra?" echoed Alissa faintly. This exceedingly rare plant was one her mother valued highly. Why, it was probably the only one to be found in the entire country. Praying her leg would not betray her, Alissa lifted her skirts to run to the conservatory, where she found Princess sitting calmly on the plant, contemplating the one lone bud as though she might eat it. Knowing the whimsical nature of her pet, Alissa would put nothing past the hawk. She also knew how her mother looked forward to seeing the plant bloom for the first time.

"Princess . . ." Alissa said soothingly, wondering how best to persuade the bird off her newfound perch.

The falcon merely cast a baleful look at her mistress as though accusing her of neglect. Guilt nagged at Alissa as she recalled how many times she had neglected the birds the last weeks.

"May I be of assistance?" Lord Ives entered the room, drawing on his riding gloves as he neared. He slowly edged up to the bird, talking softly to it all the while. When beside it, he held out his well-covered hand, nudging the lower breast of the bird. Princess gave him a curious look, then camly stepped unto his outstretched hand as though she had done it every day.

An enormous sigh of relief escaped from Alissa as she checked the plant to see if any harm had been done. Other than a couple of bent leaves, it appeared in fine shape.

"Naughty Princess," Alissa murmured affectionately. Since the hawk had no concept of guilt, and it clearly had not been her fault that she had escaped from her block, or had found the open door intriguing, scolding would not serve.

"Shall we go, Miss Alissa?" Lord Ives glanced back to the doorway to the drawing room, noting the curious eyes

131

watching. In the distance could be heard Henrietta, sputtering about the impropriety of Alissa's behavior.

Well aware she had committed another of her infamous blunders, Alissa, pink-cheeked and head held high, nodded and marched out the terrace door with Ives and Princess right behind her.

"I am in a rare pickle now," she muttered. With no regard for the status of the man next to her, she grumbled, " 'Tis always the way. I seem to go from one disaster to another." She gave a morose little sigh.

Ives observed that she seemed more chagrined than actually embarrassed, and it gave him hope for the next evening.

Skirts slightly lifted, she marched along at Christopher's side, keeping pace until they reached the mews. Thomas was leaving the goshawk's quarters. His eyes grew wide with horror as he realized what must have happened.

"We are all in the soup this time, Thomas. Princess got into Mama's rare aspidistra plant. I nearly had a spasm when that bird eyed the bud as though it might be her newest toy. If Mama does not demand the hawks be dispatched, I shall be very much surprised."

She watched Ives transfer the falcon. He took care to see that Princess wouldn't escape again. When the bird's jesses were carefully fastened to the leash, which in turn was firmly attached to the swivel of her perch, they left.

Christopher guided Alissa back toward the manor, his brow furrowed in concern. "Can it really be that serious?" He reached out to clasp her hand lightly in his own, seeking to offer her comfort and reassurance.

" 'Tis not the first time something like this has occurred. I must express my thanks for your quick thinking, Lord Ives." She gave him a look of heartfelt gratitude, thinking he was very like a knight to the rescue in his action. He would have made a very gallant knight, she decided. His armor would have been polished to mirror finish and he would have had every maiden in the country offering her kerchief to tie about his arm during a tilting joust. What heart flutterings that handsome visage would have provoked among the court of the day. What charmed her so was that he really seemed to *care* about her dilemma.

He stopped and gave her an exasperated look. "I thought we agreed it would be 'Christopher,' Alissa. Good grief, woman! After all our mutual trials?" He gave her hand a shake as though to put some sense into her head by doing so.

She shrugged and nodded agreement. "Christopher. What if I forget myself and use your name in public? 'Twould be a scandal." She made a rueful face at him, knowing full well she could commit such an error when faced with a throng of people and her tongue get all tied in knots.

He chuckled. "I have seen worse."

"Have you really?" Intrigued with this new side of him, she was about to query as to what that scandal might be when she remembered it was not at all the thing for her to do.

"I promise to tell you all about it someday. Not at the moment. You have your mother to face first. It could not be reckoned your fault if the leash somehow got undone and the bird escaped."

Her guilty look deepened. "That is just it. I had taken her off the leash. Thomas promised to look after her, but that does not excuse me. If I tell them Thomas left her to take the gos to the mews, they will demand I dismiss him for his neglect. And I simply refuse to do that."

He gave her an approving look. "Tell them it won't happen again. I shall try to help you all I can."

"I fear there is little you can do." If her father took a notion to rid the estate of her hawks, they would be gone overnight.

"If it comes to that, I will take them rather than see such fine hawks returned to the wild. You have done an excellent job of training." He discovered he was totally sincere. He liked being with the birds, and if Thomas came with them, he would have someone to assist in handling them properly. "You could always come to visit them."

His admiration caused her cheeks to bloom a delicate rose. "I fear it probably would not be proper for me to come see them, but I thank you for the offer. You may suddenly find yourself with a pair of hawks . . . Christopher.'' She glanced shyly at him, a hint of a smile peeping forth from a previously worried countenance.

They entered the house by the terrace door, to find the luncheon party assembled in the hall. Alissa shrank back against the comforting figure of Lord Ives as she met her mother's angry stare. Lord ffolkes gave Alissa a frown which threatened to surpass all others, while Henrietta twittered on and on about the impropriety of Alissa running off with her skirts raised. Elizabeth sidled up to Alissa to offer a gentle touch on the arm.

Selina Hardwick crossed the hall to offer her hand to Lord Ives. ''I admire your cool head, Lord Ives. How happy we must all be that the bird did not damage Lady ffolkes's prize plant. 'Tis but an amusing episode now.''

Alissa shot Selina a grateful look as Lord Ives made an elegant bow over Selina's hand. ''How true. Things like this happen.''

''All too often in this house,'' muttered Lord ffolkes as he glared at Alissa.

''Courage, little one,'' murmured Lord Ives before he left Alissa to attend to the chattering Henrietta.

Alissa wanted to laugh out loud that Ives should call her little. ''Long Meg'' was what her father usually tossed at her head, making her feel about ten feet tall rather than a mere five feet and eight inches.

''I do hope our meal is not ruined,'' fretted Henrietta.

Lady fflokes had disappeared into the conservatory to reassure herself that the rare aspidistra was still in fine condition. It was almost, Alissa decided, as though she was disappointed that the plant had not suffered in the least— unless you counted two slightly bent leaves.

Duffy strolled over to her side, his light blue eyes alive with mirth. '' 'Twas a fine sight, Miss Alissa. The two of you working in concert to remove the dreaded menace from the house. A fine sight.'' He chuckled at something which he failed to reveal, then turned to watch Elizabeth cross the room to her mother's side. ''Elizabeth said your guardian angel would prevent disaster from overtaking you.''

"Duffy, I believe my guardian angel has a very difficult time of it. I seem to fall into one misfortune after another. Elizabeth has such faith."

"And yours has been greatly tried, has it not?" His sympathetic look was nearly Alissa's undoing.

Parsons entered and spoke briefly to Lady ffolkes. She turned to nudge Elizabeth.

Elizabeth walked to where Duffy and Alissa stood near the door. "Come, Parsons said our meal has been rescued from disaster and we are at last to eat." She threw an apologetic look at Alissa before drifting from the room on Duffy's arm.

Alissa reflected that she would be lucky not to commit some horrible faux pas before the meal was over, feeling as uncomfortable as she did. At least Lord Ives had managed to silence Henrietta. That young miss beamed with delight at the fulsome compliments being showered on her by Ives and Smythe-Pipkin. Sir William Williams escorted Selina to the dining room with evident pleasure. Alissa hoped Henrietta didn't notice the defection of one of her court.

Actually it turned out to be a rather gay party. Alissa tried to ignore the knowledge that it was but a prelude to the dance the following evening. Friday loomed as the greatest menace she could imagine.

Smythe-Pipkin partnered Alissa with great good humor and Alissa could feel a kinship to the young man. He sent yearning glances at Henrietta while Alissa cast surreptitious peeks at Lord Ives. Nothing in her short life had prepared her for this man. He so confused her that she felt as though her head whirled.

Yet they had enjoyed the morning's fun. At least she had and she truly believed Lord Ives had as well. Christopher. Dared she even think the name? She jumped slightly as Algernon addressed her.

"I say, Alissa, do pay attention. 'Tis not at all the thing to be wool-gathering at the table. I wished to know how long that lord from London will be here." Algernon sent a vexed look at Lord Ives, as though eliminating his competition of the minute might solve all his problems with the fair Henrietta.

"He will be here for the fair, and as you know, that event is but one day. They wish to check the sheep that are on display early, and of course partake in the merrymaking that goes on till late in the night. Heaven knows when our guests will depart." She omitted her suspicions that her father hoped to snare a title for Henrietta before those guests left.

"Your father sending his sheep today?" Smythe-Pipkin kept his eyes glued to the couple across the table, though he continued to speak with Alissa. Had she been a vain sort of person, she might have been miffed at such behavior. As it was, she could only sympathize.

"The men left at dawn with the animals, hoping to find the roads not too clogged," Alissa replied, wishing he would look at her. "Did you know 'tis estimated that upwards of twenty thousand sheep will pass through the gate this year? Papa is upset because they have raised the tolls again. But as the price of wool has risen and mutton commands a good sum, he is not too unhappy in general."

She also wondered how long Lord Ives would remain with them. They would all attend the fair together on Saturday, the entire family and most of the servants, using every vehicle on the estate fit to travel.

"I imagine you look forward to the entertainments to be found?" He looked as though he wished to whisk Henrietta away that very moment.

Alissa decided it really would be much nicer if Algernon would look at her when he spoke, and she nudged him gently in the ribs. "Doing it a bit too brown, Algernon. She likes the unattainable best, you know."

"I say, do you think . . . ?" Smythe-Pipkin's brown eyes grew hopeful as the germ of an idea took root. He narrowed his gaze and thoughtfully studied Henrietta.

"It might be possible." Alissa gave him an encouraging smile, then blushed as she caught the sapient eye of Lord Ives upon her.

Following the meal, the group wandered out to the terrace.

Alissa kept Henrietta within sight, figuring that if anything were to happen, it would begin with that young miss.

Henrietta explained her plans for the dance the following evening to a delighted Selina, while Elizabeth listened with resigned ire. To hear Henrietta, one would think she alone had planned and executed the preparations, when everyone in the house knew Alissa had done much of the work.

One day, thought Elizabeth, Alissa would not be around and Henrietta would discover that she had to do the planning and ordering herself.

"You have a thought which pleases you, lass?" Duffy steered Elizabeth away from the other women, ostensibly to view the lily pond, though, to be honest, there wasn't a bloom to be seen.

Delighted to get out of range of Henrietta's voice, Elizabeth nodded. "I hope that someday Alissa will be able to get away from here. Then Henrietta—"

"You had best talk to her guardian angel and pray that Alissa be spared, come the dance." Duffy leaned against one of the statues Lady ffolkes had placed to admire her pond and glanced back to where Alissa talked earnestly to Smythe-Pipkin.

"I wish I could help her," Elizabeth admired Duffy's pale green waistcoat and fawn breeches under his dark brown coat. He looked so solid, so dependable. If only Alissa had someone like Duffy to assist her.

"Aye, 'tis plain she dinna take to a mob of people. If the dance petrifies her, what will she do at the fair?" Duffy bent over to pick a strand of grass that had escaped the gardener and chewed on the end of it. His warm gaze seemed to lighten the burden Elizabeth carried.

"There will be no problem for her at the fair. No one pays any attention to her in a place like that. Have you ever seen anyone at a fair? Really seen them, I mean? There is so much going on about you, it does not matter in the least what you do. I suspect she feels oddly safe." Elizabeth gave him a speculative study that made the gentleman distinctly uneasy.

"Just what do you have on that mind of yours, lass?"

"Well . . ." Elizabeth bent closer to confide her plan, and Duffy, bless his heart, kept nodding, though his heart was full of misgivings.

On the terrace, Alissa walked with Algernon until they were a reasonable distance from the others. She was relieved that the young man was willing to forgo gazing at Henrietta like some moonling for a little while.

"Henrietta admires decisive men. Perhaps you could be more firm with her. You really ought to do *something*." She devoutly longed to tell him to stop making such a cake of himself, but good manners forbade that.

Algernon gave her a dubious look and shook his head. "I ain't so certain about being firm. She is such a fragile blossom." Yet she could tell he dwelt on her words.

"I suppose it would be too daring for anyone but a London lord to attempt," said Alissa with tongue definitely in cheek.

"Never say I am less," sniffed Algernon, and went off to consider what Alissa suggested.

"What are you up to now, Miss ffolkes? I vow I have not seen so much animation in Smythe-Pipkin since his horse tossed him coming over a fence." Lord Ives watched the departing Algernon with a sense of annoyance. What right had that coxcomb to hover around Alissa, anyway?

Alissa was saved from answering by an unexpected source. Henrietta clapped her hands together and cried in a delighted voice, "I have the most famous idea. Let us play blindman's buff!"

As the young men knew full well that the game was open to all manner of interesting situations, the might-have-been-expected groan didn't materialize. It was a popular game, with good reason.

Naturally Henrietta proclaimed herself first to be blindfolded. Lord Ives gallantly offered his snowy handkerchief, standing too close to Henrietta while tying it on, in Alissa's critical view. He turned Henrietta around three times until she pronounced herself quite dizzy, then retreated to a position behind Alissa.

There was much merriment as Henrietta stumbled about, reaching out, hoping someone would come in contact with her. They all made silly noises, slipped under her arms, and generally eluded her. The gentlemen didn't appear to try quite as hard as the ladies.

It was Algernon who at last permitted himself to be "caught." Henrietta had decided to play by indoor rules, and announced she would try to guess who had been nabbed. She felt Algernon's face, then her hands slipped to his shoulders, and much to everyone's amusement, she declared, " 'Tis Algernon!" She pulled off her blindfold, giving him a vexed look.

"Oh, I say, you are a clever puss." Algernon bestowed such an admiring smile that Alissa longed to kick him in the ankle.

Now Algernon was blindfolded and teased as to whether he could see even one peep from beneath the handkerchief. He entered into the spirit of the game with a gusto that delighted Alissa. Henrietta actually seemed impressed with his good nature.

At last a turn came to Lord Ives. He dramatically staggered about, arms waving in a threatening manner while Elizabeth giggled from behind Duffy's back and Alissa stood quietly, watching with utter fascination. It was another facet to the London lord she hadn't expected. He was quite delightful in a mad way.

As he drew near her, Alissa was aware of Henrietta's frown. Alissa knew full well that Henrietta hadn't been trying very hard to elude Christopher. Alissa debated whether she ought to retreat or stand her ground, when his hand snaked out and caught her by the shoulder. She was well and truly captured.

Strong capable hands slipped down her arms, then back up again. Alissa trembled at his caressing touch. One hand reached up to her face; his fingers explored her cheek, her eyes, gently passed over her mouth and nose. His other hand joined in the investigation, and she felt weak under the double onslaught. Her knees threatened to give out on her at this sensual probing. Every nerve quivered with heightened awareness. Then his fingers slid back to tangle in her hair, threading through the heavy mass of golden-brown strands with infinite care. She held her breath, unable to even twitch a muscle. Her eyes remained fastened on that covered face, wishing she might be drawn against him, to know again his closeness. The kiss shared by the stream still lingered vividly in her memory.

Around them the laughter died little by little as the others waited for Ives to declare Alissa's name. The silence stretched on until at last it was broken by him.

Christopher placed his hands on her shoulders and announced in a voice not quite an unshaken as one might expect from a man of the town, " 'Tis Miss Alissa."

After that the game somehow lost its appeal and the participants began talking among themselves. Henrietta claimed Lord Ives and chattered away in her charming, breathless way as she waved the handkerchief about in the air.

Alissa wandered toward the lily pond, not hearing the soft sound of thunder in the distance. Clouds had come up quite rapidly and the wind whipped her dress about her legs. She ignored the storm warnings, deep in reflection of the game just now played.

He had been able to see her. She knew he had. She had noticed the blindfold tilted a bit, so it would have been easily possible for him to detect the color of her gown. She was the only girl who had worn a leaf-green India mull print!

So—why had he pretended he didn't know who she was? Much intrigued with this curious thought, she continued to stroll along the pond toward the arched laburnum retreat her mother had created some years ago. A crimson leaf from a flowering crab flew past her. The rumble of thunder grew more menacing, yet she ignored it, rather enjoying the freshness of the wind as it tugged at her hair, the same hair he had caressed so tenderly.

Why? *That* was the question.

The first patter of drops was unnoticed due to the abundance of shelter from the laburnum. Then the rain increased, splattering around her, and she realized she must get to the house quickly to prevent a soaking. Turning, she began to run, then slipped on one of the stones on the path when her cursed leg gave way. The fall knocked the breath

from her, but she didn't think she was injured, more the pity.
Had she sustained some harm, she might have had a reason
to retreat from the dreaded party tomorrow night. It seemed
her dratted leg was not yet to be trusted.

She sat up, rubbed her bruised elbow, then attempted to
get to her feet. She was hampered by the damp fabric that
clung to her legs. About to pull it up so as to allow easier
movement, she was startled to discover a person running
through the rain to the dubious shelter of the laburnum
avenue.

"Christopher!" She gasped and wiped a straggling wisp
of hair from her face. She glared at him, still not quite
reconciled to his destruction of her scheme.

"Are you all right? I became worried when you were the
only one who didn't show up in the drawing room. I
remembered you had drifted in this direction after the game
was over."

"There does not seem to be any permanent damage, thank
you," she admitted with small grace. "My skirts are a bit
tangled, that's all." She was helped to her feet, then swept
up into his arms.

"We'll get wet, but the rain won't get any better, so we
may as well make a dash for it." He held her closely as he
began the mad run to the house. His steps were solid and
sure even on the slippery grass and paving stones of the path.
They reached the terrace and he ran to the entrance of the
conservatory.

There he paused inside the door, gazing down at the rain-
washed face, so appealing . . . and laughing at their mutual
predicament.

"We must look like drowned rats," she reluctantly
giggled. He made it so difficult to sustain her anger at him.
Laughter faded from her face as she noted the expression
in his eyes. She had seen that before. She found herself
crushed against him.

His kiss tasted fresh and sweet, like spring rain. The arm
Alissa had placed on his shoulder slipped up to his neck and
held him. Tightly. How she had yearned for this once more.

Slowly he permitted her feet to slide to the ground, his

hands settling at her shoulders when she at last stood on the floor. Her face was just at the right height, making a kiss so simple an accomplishment.

He broke away, lifting his hand to touch her chin. "I had not expected a shower bath this afternoon," he mused aloud. Nor had he dreamed he would hold her again so soon, to know that the taste of her lips was as he remembered, berry sweet and intoxicating.

Deep rose wildly flushed her cheeks, and her eyes grew troubled before her lashes swept down in modest confusion. "I had best get out of these wet things, lest I catch an inflammation of the lungs or something equally dreary." She backed away from him, her lashes lifting to reveal eyes wide with awed wonder.

She turned hastily and fled the conservatory, leaving Christopher behind to saunter up the stairs. He paused at his door, looking across at the solid panel of oak that guarded the entrance to her room. A maid hurried out with the leaf-green mull he had so carefully noted earlier in the day. As he went into his room, he glanced back to see footmen coming down the hall with pails of steaming water. He hoped a few were to be directed for his use as well. An image of Alissa, her leaf-brown hair tied up on her crown and soapy water cascading down her body, lingered in his mind as he closed his door and began to change from his dripping-wet clothes.

He had stripped down to the buff and was wrapped in a dressing gown, wondering if he would indeed get hot water, when a smart rap on the door brought a succession of footmen with the longed-for bath.

Roberts tut-tutted at the rain-soaked breeches and wondered aloud if Weston's fine coat would ever be the same again.

Remembered kisses tarried in Christopher's mind until another rap at the door brought him to his senses and he stepped from the tub as Duffy was let in by the departing Roberts, who tsk-tsked at the armload of wet clothes all the way to the laundry room.

"I wondered what happened to you," said Duffy, dropping

down on his usual chair. "Miss Henrietta is most vexed that you are not there to partner her in a game of cards."

"Pity," replied Ives, looking not the least repentant. "I was busy rescuing Miss Alissa from the possibility of serious inflammation of the lungs."

Duffy raised his expressive brows. "Who can find a virtuous woman? For her price is far above rubies."

Christopher paused in pulling the clean and blessedly dry cambric shirt over his head. "You occasionally find a very apt quote in that favorite book of yours."

"Well, it can apply to more than one particular lady, you know." Duffy grinned at the disappearing head of dark hair, then continued. "Elizabeth spoke to me earlier. The lass wants me to rescue her sister Alissa tomorrow night. For some peculiar reason, I suspected I ought to consult with you regarding that matter. You seem to have developed a proprietary interest in the lady." It was amazing how Christopher could whip up an incredible cravat in such a short time.

Tugging on a pair of biscuit-colored breeches, Ives tucked in his shirt before selecting a waistcoat of fine marcella in the same shade. Christopher agreed. "You did well to come to me with the information." He slipped into a corbeau jacket of finest Bath cloth, adding, "There will be no need for anyone else to worry about her. I intend to take care of Alissa tomorrow night. Of course, it is merely because I desire to help her. I feel sorry for her."

"Aye." Duffy concealed a broad grin behind his hand.

# 11

"I wish I had a new dress," Alissa fretted as she studied the contents of her wardrobe. She knew concern for her dress was a frivolous matter. Doubtless the man she found so fascinating would pay little head to the fabric or design. Yet she longed to shine for the evening.

Elizabeth watched her sister from the comfort of the chaise longue. Alissa had inherited this elegant piece of furniture from the same grandmother whose picture hung on the wall. That lady had been so delighted to find a grandchild who looked so like herself that she willed everything she possessed in her own right to Alissa.

"Why not your Clarence-blue lutestring with the pretty embroidery on it? I do think it is vastly becoming to you."

"You do not feel the bodice is cut too low?" Alissa gave the dress in question a dubious look, remembering just how tightly the bodice molded to her bosom, the square cut seeming to expose far more than she felt modest. The sleeves were almost nonexistent, leaving her with the sensation of being half-undressed.

"No," Elizabeth said firmly. She had such high hopes, and wanted Alissa to shine this evening. Elizabeth's own simple gown of white muslin over a pretty blue slip and sashed with blue had been worn to several parties, but Duffy had not seen it and it was a favorite of hers.

Alissa held out her dress, remembering the unhappiness she had known the last time she wore it. It had been to one of the balls where she had seen Lord Ives. Would he recall? She very much doubted it. Too many people, especially beautiful young women, had clustered about him. Yet he did seem a kind man, a paradox, really. On one hand he was the polished London gallant at ease on the dance floor, courteously attentive to the ladies. On the other, a thoughtful,

144

friendly man, one who delighted in the simple pleasures of the country. She could not think of one other man she had observed while in London who would have sat on a log while watching her gos chase rats around a haystack! Nor one who would have laughed quite so heartily.

A wistful smile hovered about her mouth as she recalled other, more intimate moments. He had kissed her again. Since she'd not had other kisses with which to compare them, she didn't know how these might rank. But she was sure they were exceptional. She had trembled right down to her toes at his touch. Highly improper of him, of course. He seemed to have a penchant for doing things that were improper from time to time. He also seemed to delight in carrying her about, for he had done it often enough. How she wished . . . But how foolish. Guardian angels aside, her wishes were like so much tissue, to dissolve at the first sign of wet. Yet the dratted man had spoiled her plan, forcing her to seek another. For that, she could not thank him.

"You care for him, do you not?" asked Elizabeth in her soft, sweet voice. "He seems a fine man."

Alissa gave her sister a dismayed look and shook her head. "I do not want to care for him. After the fair he must leave here, and all my feelings will go with him."

"It is possible he might seek your hand." Elizabeth was an incurable optimist. Her view was that nothing was to be considered out of the question until proven so.

Returning her pretty gown to the wardrobe, Alissa walked over to sit on the end of the lovely old chaise longue. "You do not know what you say. Lord Ives is an active member of Parliament. He associates with very elevated, important people. He would be giving dinners that the Prince Regent himself might attend. Can you see me in that milieu? And he would entertain lavishly. I would be paralyzed with fright." She stared out the window for a moment, seeing not the soft clouds and pale early-autumn sky, but the dear face of the man she loved. "Aye, 'tis impossible." She patted Elizabeth on the arm, knowing her sister meant the very best.

"Perhaps if all things go well this evening, you may hold things in a different light? You are a bit shy, but that is no crime. 'Tis only Henrietta who makes it seem so, by her ease of conversation.''

"If my leg will behave and not give out on me, I shall do well enough. 'Tis most unsettling, never knowing when it will fail to support me. It has not been right since the accident.'' She gave Elizabeth an anxious look. Though not much had been said about her troublesome leg, it worried her not a little. She had not confided about the fall beneath the laburnum arch. Nor what followed.

Elizabeth longed to give Alissa some of her own resolution. Not that Alissa lacked courage. She had so much to offer a husband; her ability to manage the house matched many a matron's. And her loving care for her hawks foretold the attitude she would have toward children. If only she could overcome this cursed shyness of hers. Well, Duffy had promised to help, and Elizabeth would hold him to that. "We shall hope for the best.'' Elizabeth rose and returned to her room to dress for the party.

There would be a dinner, to be followed by dancing in the drawing room. Henrietta had twisted her father around her finger and persuaded him to permit not only a musical group imported from Salisbury but also the partial clearing of the hall so that the guests might congregate in there as well. As there was no sign of rain, couples were certain to drift out to the terrace.

Alissa leaned against a windowpane, staring out at the gardens, contemplating what might happen. What was it Lord Ives had said? To consider what the worst might be? Well, what could happen? She could trip and tear her dress. Not too bad. Though she would feel dreadful to ruin her pretty gown.

She might spill food on someone dressed in the finest of clothes. Now, that truly would be a disaster. Or . . . she might say something utterly stupid, embarrassing everyone around.

Impatient with her silly mental wanderings, she tried to concentrate on positive things. If Lord Ives kept his word and stood at her side, she knew nothing would happen.

Although her feelings regarding him were like a shuttlecock in a game of battledore—badly tossed.

She clung to that thought as she rubbed a scented lotion into her skin before donning her fine India cotton chemise and drawers, then her stays and delicate petticoat. She then pulled on the Clarence-blue gown, taking care to smooth the dress down over her petticoat with its pretty embroidered hem. It was a good thing the dress fastened up with concealed hooks and tapes in the front so she need not fuss about the lack of a maid.

Henrietta had managed to snare Matty, while her mother naturally had her personal maid. Elizabeth never fussed about anything and always looked lovely. But then, she was barely out of the schoolroom and not eligible for special attention. In many households, Elizabeth would have been held back from such entertainments as this country dance. At High ffolkes, conventions like that didn't seem to matter. Alissa sometimes wondered if her mother paid all that much attention to what went on in the house. It seemed that as long as things flowed smoothly, she allowed each girl to do as she pleased.

Before leaving the security of her room, Alissa checked to see that nothing showed that was not supposed to show, and that her abundance of hair remained in place. The candlelight shimmering in her mirror sent flashes of light from the delicate white-and-gold embroidery on her gown. Gold riband threaded through her hair in what she felt was a rather fetching manner, thanks to Elizabeth.

What would Alissa do if Duffy actually asked for Elizabeth's hand? Judging from the look in his eyes, it was a definite possibility. But would Papa consent to the marriage of his youngest? Allow her to be the first to wed?

There was no putting it off any longer: she must go downstairs. Taking a determined breath, she opened the door and stepped into the hall just as Henrietta was about to leave her room.

Alissa drew in an awed breath. Never had she seen her sister look more beautiful. Dressed in a pale blue taffeta gown trimmed in silver embroidery, she looked like an angel. Alissa had glimpsed the dress when it was delivered only a week ago, but Henrietta had been secretive about it. It was daring for a miss who had not yet made her come-out. Yet Alissa knew there would not be one word said to Henrietta. She looked ethereal and very, very lovely. Her blond curls tumbled about her head in an intricate style, with silver ribands and tiny blue silk flowers woven through. Around her neck the simple strand of pearls had silver riband twined about it, a charming confection.

Alissa wouldn't have to worry about anyone looking at her. Who could notice her when Henrietta was around? If Lord Ives didn't succumb to this beauty, he was blind.

Henrietta smiled graciously. "You look very nice, Alissa. Indeed, almost pretty." Thus she effectively ruined all the pleasure Alissa had known before she left her room.

Elizabeth left her room just then and exclaimed over Henrietta's gown with genuine delight. "How lovely, Henrietta! We can all go down together like three blue flowers. Mama ought to be pleased." Elizabeth was happy, for she knew that after Henrietta wore the dress three times it would come to her. One did not argue at getting beautiful dresses when nearly new.

"Oh, dear, I seem to have forgotten my handkerchief. You go ahead. I shall come down as soon as I find the one I especially want." Henrietta smiled prettily at her sisters and left their side with a flutter of silver riband.

Alissa took courage from Elizabeth's gentle touch on her hand and they walked down together. Duffy beamed a delighted look at Elizabeth and whisked her aside the moment she reached the foot of the stairs.

"I hope all goes well this evening, Alissa." Lady ffolkes—garbed in a pomona-green silk, her hair nicely done up beneath a simple evening cap—admonished her daughter simply by the tone of her voice. "Lord Ives has graciously explained what occurred with your falcon, and I forgive you the lapse. I realize that having guests about the house can be disconcerting for you. However, I expect you to help with the entertaining this evening. Henrietta has worked so hard to make this little party a success. The least you can do is exert yourself on her behalf. Ah,'' Lady ffolkes exclaimed with pleasure, ''here is the dear girl now. If you expended half the effort she does at placing people at ease, you would be married by now, Alissa.''

Alissa turned dutifully to watch her younger sister float down the stairs in the most regal of manners. Duffy and Elizabeth stood off to the right of Lady ffolkes, Lord Ives near the foot of the stairs, his hand extended toward the incomparable beauty who smiled so enchantingly at them all. He was dressed all in black but for his snowy cravat and an elegant white waistcoat delicately embroidered with a very subtle design. His stunning good looks and refined taste quite impressed Alissa.

The dinner guests had gathered in the hall, making a sizable group to watch Henrietta's breathtaking descent. Only Barrett frowned, looking like a thundercloud at a summer picnic.

''You are a fairy princess come to life, Miss Henrietta. We are at your feet, yours to command.'' Ives made an elegant leg, then tucked her hand into the crook of his arm. Henrietta cast a benevolent smile on the assembled party, took one assessing glance at her mother, and led the way in to dinner.

Alissa gave her mother a worried look. Although she might be absentminded at times, she ought not to take kindly to Henrietta usurping her rightful place. But protocol seemed to be suspended for the evening, as Lady ffolkes merely nodded graciously and the other guests trouped in without ceremony.

Algernon frowned gloomily at Alissa as he ambled into the dining room at her side. ''Hullo.''

''I am delighted to see you too, Algernon. And how well you are looking,'' Alissa said with an asperity quite unlike her usual calm self.

''You don't understand. She is so beautiful she will never look at me.'' Algernon gave a mournful sigh.

''Especially if you continue to wear that Friday face. If you want my advice, you will pay attention to someone else this evening, or at least show some spirit.'' Alissa gave her suggestion with little hope he might actually listen to her. Smythe-Pipkin tended to be a bit blind when it came to anything concerning Henrietta. Deaf, too, come to think on it. Alissa was becoming most impatient with the young man at her side.

Algernon gave Alissa a considering look but said nothing.

The soup was served and consumed with no disasters, and Alissa breathed a sigh of relief as the meal progressed smoothly. It seemed her guardian angel was actually at work. Since she sat between Algernon and Sir William Williams, there was no problem with conversation. She simply listened. Algernon extolled the beauties of Henrietta while Sir William asked questions regarding Selina. For a few moments Alissa considered the wisdom of setting up a matrimonial bureau much like the employment agencies in London, then realized it would require meeting all sorts of strangers, and promptly abandoned the notion.

Lady ffolkes led the ladies from the dinner table to the drawing room, leaving the gentlemen to their port and storytelling. Alissa kept a cautious eye out for Henrietta. However, there seemed no danger of playing the pianoforte for a singing concert this evening, as the musical group was even now tuning up. Shortly afterward, Alissa wandered into the shadows of the terrace to listen to the delightful strains of a familiar country dance.

"So . . . this is where you conceal yourself."

"Lord Ives. The stories must have been dull this evening to release you so quickly." Alissa smiled at him in spite of her resolution to have nothing to do with the man.

She had ached with envy at the sight of him next to Henrietta. The glimpse of that exquisite blond head next to the tall dark man with the black eyes unsettled her. Silly girl, she chided herself, he is merely doing the civil. Another peek had convinced her she wanted to be elsewhere. Wretch. Whatever made her think she loved him?

"You promised me a dance." He held out his hand and Alissa gave him a guarded smile.

"Delighted." She hoped her unpredictable leg would not fail her at this moment. It was something quite difficult to talk about—impossible with a gentleman. Her misgivings were well-concealed as he led her to the drawing room and into the dance.

If she had admired his dancing ability before, it was nothing compared to his grace as a partner. She was twirled and dipped with consummate ease, as though she managed to comport herself with this sort of flair all the time. She normally did not do all that badly. When she forgot herself, she was as nimble on her feet as anyone could wish. And tonight her leg supported her just as it ought.

Concentrating on Lord Ives, she didn't see anyone else, not Henrietta or her mother, not anyone. Alissa allowed her gaze to roam over his face, absorb the magnificence of that exquisite waistcoat, and simply enjoyed herself.

"Tell me, what magical words did you say to my mother regarding the falcon? She has dropped all complaints."

He gave Alissa a wicked little smile and said, "I praised her gardens and noted how the hawks kept unwanted little pests from damaging her plants."

Alissa shook her head in delight at his audacity while he twirled her about in a delicate movement of the dance.

Elizabeth watched her and beamed with pleasure at the elegant manner with which Alissa danced. "See," she confided to Duffy when the pattern of the dance brought them together, "she can do well when she is with Lord Ives. If only she will manage to keep this up."

Duffy had remained silent regarding Ives's scheme for Alissa. For one, he knew full well that plans often collapsed. As well, he surmised that dear Miss Henrietta took a dim view of any of her court paying attention for long to another lady—especially a sister.

People continued to enter the manor house, more than had attended at any time in the past. The hall overflowed with chattering, laughing guests. Henrietta had been lavish with the invitations she addressed.

Alissa was whirled about in the final pattern of her dance, then walked to the side. She gave a demure smile to her partner before they parted, then watched as Lord Ives crossed the drawing room to seek Henrietta's hand. It was then that

Alissa became aware of the excessive number of people.

Lord Ives cast a worried glance about him, wondering how Alissa might react to this crush. Still, he had caught sight of Henrietta's angry glare during his dance with Alissa and he decided he had better placate the young miss before she took offense. In his experience, spoiled beauties were wont to do irrational things.

Taking a distressed look around her, Alissa felt as though the walls were closing in on her, and she edged toward the hall, hoping to find more space there.

Elizabeth noted the haunted expression on Alissa's face and signaled Duffy. However, Duffy didn't catch the gesture, as a lady wearing an impressive number of plumes in her hair passed between them at that moment. When Elizabeth next viewed him, he had bowed politely to Miss Selina and was escorting her into the next country dance.

Elizabeth was approached by Algernon for a dance, and, not wishing to hurt the dear young man for the world, she accepted. Frustrated in her desire to help Alissa, she hoped that the guardian angels were working extra hard tonight.

The crowding didn't prove to be any less in the hall, and Alissa could feel the palms of her hands getting sweaty. She placed one trembling finger at her throat and noted how rapidly her pulse was racing. It beat rather fast when she was with Lord Ives, but that was quite different.

At first a dismal feeling that she wouldn't be able to cope assailed her. Then she took a deep breath, telling herself these people wouldn't eat her. She began to make her way to the less-crowded terrace. Someone stepped on Alissa's toe, then another jostled her about, pushing her from behind, and she wondered how her gown would fare. How odd, she mused; in the past she would have fled by now.

"Dance with me, Alissa," commanded her brother in a determined voice. He had come up to her after seeing her frightened expression when nudged by a plump lady in a purple gown.

Alissa agreed, thinking things actually were going far better than she'd expected. That Barrett was as quiet as she didn't seem to bother him in the least. He just ignored the people.

So far Alissa had not managed to accomplish that trick. Usually the people seemed to close in on her, and she was sure they were bound to be as critical as her father or Henrietta. But tonight she was determined to enjoy herself.

"Nice party." For Barrett, that constituted conversation.

Alissa gave him a soft laugh. "You know you would rather be out riding."

"True." He grinned down at her as he escorted her to the terrace and then proceeded to lead her through a sprightly dance. Alissa raised her feet quite prettily and managed the turns very well.

"You really are rather good at this dancing, dear brother. When did you practice?" In her curiosity she momentarily forgot her anxieties.

"Selina Hardwick has a cousin who visits her from time to time. She taught me." He walked Alissa through a clever maneuver, then grinned at her surprise.

Alissa was quite impressed at that speech. It was the longest she had heard from Barrett in ages. "You quite outshine me this evening."

The dance ended. Barrett spied Selina's cousin and took himself off. Alissa stood watching after him, lost in wonder. Could it be possible she might not be required as a house-keeper for Barrett after all?

She remained on the terrace, feeling comfortable in the shadows. Out here her palms grew dry, she was able to swallow with ease, and her heart beat at a near-normal rate. The party was going beautifully. Scent from the perfumed wax candles floated to tease her nose with a delightful fragrance, like her mother's garden in May.

Lost in her reflections, she almost missed hearing her name. Henrietta called sweetly, demanding Alissa's presence in a polite but insistent manner. Reluctantly Alissa walked to her sister.

"Mama said you are to help me, Alissa. I simply cannot do everything. I have had to promise every dance. You will have to see to it that our guests are given refreshments."

Alissa frowned at the odd request. Parsons was more than capable of overseeing the serving. Certainly Alissa had never

before been asked to perform this task. Still, it could be she
was needed. Parsons might have been called to do something
else. Alissa gave a reluctant nod. "Very well. Though you
know full well I dread doing this."

An airy wave of the hand was followed by curt words.
"It will do you good. Mama and I agree it is time and more
that you got over this nonsense. You merely wish to find
an excuse to fob the work off on me. Well, I shan't stand
for it. Perhaps you are destined to be an old maid, but I
certainly am not! I fully intend to dance every dance this
evening."

The untrue and vastly unfair remark regarding the work
did not get the refutation it deserved, for Alissa was left
speechless while Henrietta drifted off on the hand of another
admirer. Her smug expression could not be observed by her
sister.

Elizabeth performed a reel with Duffy, her eyes sparkling
with happiness. Alissa refused to spoil her joy by calling upon
her to assist.

Resolutely Alissa wove her way through the hall to where
refreshments were set out on a table. She gave a puzzled look
around. It seemed to her that everything was well under
control. Meeting Parsons' gaze, she motioned him to her
side. "Is all going well?"

Having some notion of how Miss Alissa felt regarding
crowds, the butler nodded. "Indeed. There is no need for
you to fret about one thing. All is in hand here."

Alissa nodded, wondering what had prompted Henrietta's
request. Turning from the tables, she made her way through
the laughing, chattering throng with admirable calm. Odd,
it became easier each time she went through the clusters of
visitors. They were merely people she knew for the most
part, only clumped together. She smiled at the thought of
the guests like so many rosebuds on a stem.

A footman moved through the crowd, offering glasses of
champagne, lemonade, and claret. Alissa observed Lord Ives
accept a glass of claret, then sip from it while he talked with
Duffy and Elizabeth. Drawn by some inexplicable need to
be near him, Alissa wound her way past the lady in the violent

purple dress, the woman wearing an excessive amount of plumes, and Barrett with Selina's cousin.

"I trust you are enjoying yourselves?" she said, mostly to Elizabeth, but to the others too. Alissa's eyes sparkled with her newfound confidence.

Lord Ives gestured with his nearly full glass. "Delightful. Your family certainly knows how to entertain."

His words of praise gratified Alissa, as she was the one who had done most of the planning with Cook and Parsons, regardless of what her mother and Henrietta said.

Elizabeth grinned at Duffy and said, "Alissa is excessively clever at so many things. She designed the flower arrangements and the tables as well."

"I would like to try one of those tidbits I saw on that table over there." Christopher bestowed a twinkling smile on Alissa. Really, her poise quite delighted him.

"Best not try to find your way to the table with a full glass in your hand," she warned. " 'Twould be a dangerous mission. Would you permit me to select a few things for you? A sort of reversal of roles, as it were?" She chuckled so softly that only he heard it.

He bent his head to reply. "That would be most appealing."

Feeling more assured than ever before in her life, Alissa made her way to the table. It took her but a few minutes to fill a plate with her favorites. She headed back to his side with a feeling of pleasure. Suddenly it happened. Her leg, which had been so good all evening, buckled slightly under her, causing her to pitch forward . . . right into the tall form of Lord Ives!

Before her horrified eyes, claret splashed down the front of that magnificent waistcoat. The pristine white was now splotched with an ugly red stain. She dropped the plate and covered her mouth as she cried in dismay, "I knew it!"

Turning, she dashed across the hall, pushing aside those in her path, then fled up the stairs to her room, while Elizabeth hastened to blot the wine from the ruined waistcoat. Shocked faces looked first at the fleeing Alissa, then at the elegant London Lord with his wine-spattered waistcoat.

Christopher brushed aside Elizabeth's well-intentioned help, murmuring something before he followed Alissa up the stairs.

Behind them, a vexed Henrietta tightened her mouth. Stamping her foot in anger, she held out her hand to the nearest beau, demanding he see to her wants. How fortunate that she concealed her wrath before she gazed up at him.

Upstairs, the door slammed shut at the end of the hall. Christopher ran to it, pounding on the heavy oak panel with his fist. "Alissa! Open this door. I want to speak to you. The waistcoat isn't important—you are."

"Oh, go away!" came the muffled reply from the other side of the door. The click of a key in the lock was followed by anguished sobbing.

# 12

Christopher pounded on the door one more time, then, hearing nothing in response, gave up for the moment and rubbed his chin while trying to figure out what to do next. In his room across the hall, he changed his waistcoat, giving a rueful look at what had been a favorite—and rather expensive—piece of clothing. When he left the room, he met Elizabeth and Duffy in the hall. Duffy had a knowing expression on his face.

"He goeth after her straightaway, as an ox goeth to the slaughter," quoted Duffy in a lugubrious voice, first darting a sly glance at Lord Ives, then at Alissa's closed door.

"I'm surprised you are not quoting. 'The way of a fool is right in his own eyes' at me." Lord Ives ran a hand through the hair his valet had so carefully arranged, then gave Elizabeth a frustrated look. "I would not have had this happen for the world."

" 'Tis an unfortunate accident. I cannot think why she was in the thick of the crowd like that."

Lord Ives gave a disgusted sigh. "My fault. I let her go off to get me a plate of something to eat. Something I really didn't care whether I had or not. She looked so sweet in that blue thing she was wearing. I totally forgot she had any problem. She seemed so relaxed, so at ease."

Elizabeth could have told him that Alissa behaved that way only around him, but felt it was not her place to reveal that interesting little truth. She glanced at Duffy for guidance.

"We had best go back to the dance. It will appear more the thing if only one of us is missing rather than all four." Duffy's soft words were met with nods of agreement.

Lord Ives tilted his mouth in a half-grin. "But then, on the other hand, it might give the tongues something else to wag about."

Duffy and Elizabeth shared uneasy laughter as the three sauntered down the stairs, quite in harmony with one another.

Seeing the impeccable white waistcoat (though not embroidered) on his lordship, some decided they had not seen right the first time, while others thought his lordship a fine sport about the accident.

Henrietta fumed. Following the incident of the ruined waistcoat, she failed to garner another dance with Lord Ives for the remainder of the evening. She had watched as he chatted with Elizabeth, wondering what he and Duffy could possibly find to say to her dab of a sister. Henrietta had hoped that eliminating Alissa might aid in capturing Lord Ives. She didn't wish to marry him, just claim him as part of her court. Counting on disaster hadn't done the thing.

Determined to enjoy herself in spite of his lordship's defection, she abandoned herself to her party and to her many beaux. Surely no one as beautiful as she need worry about a shy fawn of a sister like Alissa. But Henrietta intended to keep a watchful eye.

In the soft light of the candles on her dresser, Alissa gave her mirrored reflection a woebegone look, then scolded herself. "Don't be a ninny." She wiped the tears from her face and gave a determined glare at her likeness. The people who lived in the area all knew the difficulty she had with being in crowds. Goodness knew, Henrietta talked about it often enough. Those from farther away who were in attendance didn't really matter, did they?

Idly she stirred the bowl of potpourri on her muslin-draped dressing table with one finger while she considered what had happened. She had fallen against Lord Ives, spilling the claret on that beautiful waistcoat. Unpardonable? "No," she answered her image. "Unpleasant, perhaps, but not unforgivable."

Rising from the padded bench, she walked toward the window. Catching sight of her drawing pad on the small table next to the chaise longue, she paused. Rather than stare out at the stars, she picked up the pad and thoughtfully slid down onto the chaise.

He had said it didn't matter. That was kind of him. If only it didn't matter so much to her. Alissa felt so utterly gauche. How far removed she was from the graceful, polished woman Lord Ives needed as wife and hostess.

A pencil tucked in the pad fell to the chaise as she held it in a loose clasp. She picked it up, weighing the slim piece of wood in her hand. Smoothing the paper, she slowly began to draw. The face that took form under her clever fingers was that of the Earl of Ives. It was a remarkable likeness, especially considering that he was nowhere near to sit for the portrait.

He had a well-modeled head, she recalled. With a noble forehead, a rather straight nose, and the most beautiful eyes—even though she couldn't always decipher the expression in them. Sometimes they laughed at her, other times they held a different, more elusive aspect. His mouth, she decided as she sketched in that feature, revealed firmness and decision in his character. No trace of weakness could be found anywhere in his face. Handsome, resolute, and . . . incredibly forbearing, she added. Under other circumstances he was her ideal choice for a husband.

As she drew, an idea came to her. She would do his head in clay. Surely he would leave here with a disgust of her after the debacle of this evening. Henrietta would undoubtedly enjoy his attentions for the rest of the dance. How she would puff and preen at that! Alissa felt a twinge of yearning.

But if Alissa made this small sculpture of Christopher, she would have it to remember forever, her gallant, charming, and most courageous gentleman. She finished the sketch, then sat back to study it while she listened to the strains of music, tapping her foot to the rhythm of a particularly pretty tune.

Was she even more foolish to remain here? Silly to permit the disaster to cloud what pleasure she might get from the music? She ought to apologize to Christopher . . . Lord Ives—she had best think of him that way, she admonished herself.

Going to the mirror, Alissa patted her hair into place, dusted a bit of fine powder on her nose and cheeks, then added a faint hint of rouge to her cheekbones. Normally she would never resort to cosmetics, but tonight it seemed a definite improvement on her pale features. She, as did any lady of refinement, aimed for a look of natural beauty. If upon occasion that natural beauty needed a bit of assistance, who could know?

Once in the hall, she was relieved to discover that no one was abroad. Quickly walking to the stairs before she could lose her courage, she watched a few moments before going down, one step at a time. She trailed her hand along the banister, ensuring she would have a support should her leg play her false once again.

Christopher saw her when she was about halfway down the stairs. He excused himself from the squire who had been diverting him with a tale of last year's Salisbury sheep fair. Threading his way through the crowd, he reached her side about the same moment her foot touched the floor.

Alissa gave him an apprehensive look. "I must apologize to you, Lord Ives. I fear my temporary weakness quite ruined that beautiful waistcoat." She extended her slim, capable hand to his and added, "Forgive me?"

Christopher clasped her hand, took one look around, then whisked her off to the terrace, where they might have some chance to talk. If this brave young woman had the courage to face the crowd by returning to the scene of the accident, he certainly didn't want anyone to endanger her newfound pluck by some thoughtless remark. He was delighted with her composure. He felt certain he'd contributed to this improvement. She definitely seemed more at ease.

"First of all, explain what happened."

"My, er, leg gave way as I returned to you. How absurd of me to forget. I ought to have remembered it is not to be trusted." She might have spared the hint of rouge. Her cheeks felt as pink as a rose under his questioning. Yet she stood tall, head up, a smile pinned to her lips.

"I didn't know anything about this problem. You failed to tell me," he accused, somehow feeling responsible for this latest development, though how he could be was more than he could say.

"Please, it is very difficult for me to talk about my impediment. Indeed, I cannot believe I did so now."

He gave her a most warm, approving smile. "Well, I am glad you saw fit to return. I know you desire anything but to enter the drawing room. Could we not simply walk along the terrace and converse—in an unexceptionable way, of course?"

Bestowing a grateful look on him, Alissa accepted his proffered arm, and strolled beside him in the pleasant night. It was a bit chilly, but she never noticed it in the least. As far as Alissa was concerned, the most beautiful evening of her entire life unfolded around her. Not only had she managed to commit the most awful faux pas she could imagine, she had survived and found the courage to come back down. That Lord Ives not only forgave her, but actually appeared to welcome her, was a bonus she certainly had not expected. *That* had seemed quite beyond hope.

"Pity we could not organize a game of blindman's buff. I believe I might find that rather entertaining." Lord Ives slanted a look at his companion, highly pleased to note the half-smile on her lips.

"I think you are a wicked man, Lord Ives," she scolded. "Do you know, I suspect that you were quite able to see who I was from beneath that blindfold you wore."

"The question then becomes, why?" He observed her rise in color with amusement. She never disappointed him.

"Could it be that you are a tease?" she ventured slyly.

He merely laughed in reply and they continued to walk.

They were fortunate to evade the others for the rest of the party. Henrietta missed the earl, but never thought he might be strolling with Alissa. Indeed, it never occurred to Henrietta that Alissa would have the termerity to return to the scene of the disaster. Henrietta was glad to be rid of her for the nonce.

Elizabeth and Duffy caught a glimpse of the two parading along the south terrace deep in conversation, and hoped Henrietta never thought to hunt in that direction.

At long last the guests began to drift homeward, a few at a time. From the safety of a sheltering statue, Alissa and the earl watched one after another carriage depart from the manor house.

"I feel delightfully wicked, somehow, like a naughty child peeping on a grown-up party," Alissa whispered. She gave him an engaging smile and tried in vain to suppress a giggle.

"May I assure you that I feel it is quite otherwise. You in no way resemble any child I have seen. Did I tell you that you look very lovely this evening? If I was so remiss, allow me to make up for it now."

He reached out one hand to lightly touch her chin, but at that moment a carriage rumbled by rather noisily, and Alissa withdrew into the shadows, away from him and that disturbing sensation caused by the touch of his hand. She dared not permit another kiss. Life would be difficult enough without the additional memory of what she could not claim as her own. She waved a hand in the direction of the rear entry to the house. "I suspect we had better return before someone decides to come looking for one of us." They retraced their steps to the conservatory door, slipping inside with great care. Alissa gave him a heartfelt smile. "I am exceedingly grateful to you for your gracious forbearance. Tomorrow we go to the fair. Then Sunday all will be quiet again. What a pity the fair is but one day here instead of many days, as in other towns."

"They would not permit it on a Sunday anyway, would they?"

"True." She nodded, wishing she might return to the moment when he touched her chin, perhaps changing her mind. Now she suspected he would leave her without another word.

Before parting from her agreeable companion, Alissa again apologized. "It was too bad of me to keep you from the others. I fear I am a terrible hostess, reserving the company of the guest of honor to myself."

"You have the perfect excuse . . . I did not realize I had been so designated." He bent over to lightly kiss the hand he held, then added in a whisper, "Besides, if you whisk yourself up the back stairs, who is to know where you have been this past hour or more?"

Grateful again to this most understanding of gentlemen, Alissa slipped away, winding up the steps in hasty silence until she reached the bedroom floor. Peeking from the door, she saw no one about, then scurried to th safety of her room.

"It is about time, dear sister!" Elizabeth sat on the chaise longue, giving Alissa a mock frown.

"Oh, dear," replied a very dismayed Alissa, stripping off her gloves as she crossed the room. She tossed them on the dressing table, then turned to face Elizabeth.

"You might very well say that. Papa has been asking what happened to you and Mama was about as annoyed as she ever gets. Henrietta told all, you know. How she happened to observe the catastrophe is more than I can figure out. But you know Henrietta. She couldn't wait to run to Mama and fill her ear with exaggerations of your wrongdoing." Elizabeth's expression revealed precisely what she thought of such sneaky behavior.

"He forgave me. I was crushed that my misfortune should ruin such an exquisite waistcoat. If I had any talent in that line, I would embroider him a new one. Alas, *that* would never do." Alissa threw an amused glance at her sister, walking over to stand by the chaise.

Elizabeth chuckled, sobering as the rest of her message came to mind. "There is more."

"Not the birds?" Alissa knew that her mother's mind easily could be changed by Henrietta. As her sister despised the falcon and the goshawk, it would not be surprising if she contrived to banish them from the property.

"Worse than that!"

Alissa dropped to sit beside Elizabeth, both her legs weakening as she feared what might be worse than eliminating her birds.

"Papa said he felt it was time to take you in hand and see to your future. He said no more than that, but I thought you ought to be prepared." Elizabeth gave Alissa an anxious look. "What do you suppose he intends to do?" Whenever Papa took it into his head to act the father, it was time for caution.

Alissa shook her head, wondering if it was to be London or something different. What could be more threatening than London? The two girls shared a worried look.

The household woke early the next morning. A few of the inhabitants had never achieved sleep, in spite of the fact that the guests had departed quite early by London standards. It was the day of the fair, and not one soul in the house wished to miss a moment of the glorious attractions to be seen. Matty had determined she would enter the sack race this year. She had heard they were presenting a rather fetching prize, a straw bonnet of elegant design in place of the usual shift.

Up in Alissa's room, that young lady sipped her chocolate and studied a nosegay of flowers that had come with her tray. Matty whispered as how the gentleman across the hall had begged leave to put the posy on the tray before she came into the bedroom.

Once alone, Alissa smiled happily to herself. A nosegay. That meant gallantry in the language of flowers. Did he know that? she wondered.

Elizabeth rapped softly on the door, then slipped inside. "I see someone has been at Mama's flowers. Goodness, I hope he didn't touch any of her favorites."

"I suspect he had the gardener cut them, as I notice sweet william in abundance, and Mama cares naught for that."

"Did you come to any conclusion regarding Papa's plans?" Elizabeth crossed to the window, her hands clasped anxiously before her as she considered her sister's probable fate. She paused by the draperies, turning to study Alissa. "If only Henrietta had kept her mouth shut."

"All I can think is that Papa means to send me to London *with* Henrietta! He knows full well what punishment that would be for me. I had best get dressed immediately. He will not be pleased if I delay."

Alissa set the flowers aside with her tray and slid from the bed. She pulled her favorite green sprigged India mull from the wardrobe, then allowed Elizabeth to brush and arrange her long hair in a becoming fashion.

Alissa was more worried that she wished Elizabeth to see. Alissa had always feared her father's anger, but what she faced now was not a birching for being disobedient. It was his disposal of her future.

"I vow I do not wish to go down to breakfast this morning. I do not have the least appetite." Alissa tucked the sketchbook safely away from prying eyes before leaving the room. It would not do to have anyone, especially Henrietta, see that drawing.

"Think of the fair! Do not worry so about what Papa says. Nothing can happen overnight. No matter what he says, surely it will take time to fulfill. We can find a way out of almost any predicament. I know Duffy will help if he can. Perhaps Lord Ives? Surely Papa would defer to so noble a gentleman?" Elizabeth sought to give Alissa hope, but she knew their father. He was capable of anything if angered. She had little expectation he would look favorably on Duffy if furious with Alissa.

"I do not feel we can look in that direction, no matter how kind he is. This is a perfect bundle of thorns; we don't know where to begin or how to act. Best find out what faces us. Dear Elizabeth, how glad I am that you are my friend as well as my sister." Alissa thrust her nosegay into the carafe of water that sat on her dressing table, pleased with the splash of color as well as the consideration of the man who had sent it. If only she could find a husband to wed that had the same manner of courtesy and kindness revealed by Lord Ives.

Elizabeth walked with Alissa down to the breakfast room, where they found everyone assembled. This astounding circumstance was easily explained by the fair. Henrietta sat next to Lord Ives with a sweet expression, one that bordered on a smirk, to Alissa's thinking. Those demure-looking eyes held a trace of malice. Why couldn't Henrietta accept she was not only the pronounced beauty of the family, but likely to go to London as desired?

A warning touch of Alissa's hand kept Elizabeth silent as Henrietta greeted them. "Sleepyheads. Surely you have not forgotten 'tis the day of the Salisbury sheep fair. Why, just think of twelve and a half acres covered with wonderful delights.''

"You include sheep in those delights? Why is it you never go near the sheep pens at home?'' Barrett gave Henrietta a disgusted look, then excused himself to see to the preparations for the day.

"Of course I do not mean the sheep. I spoke of the endless pleasures. There will be hot gingerbread and trinkets for sale, the ups and downs, conjurers, and fortune-telling.'' She shivered with anticipation at the very thought of all that delicious fun.

Baron ffolkes cleared his throat. "I feel those ups and downs are dangerous, they go to painful heights. I do not want to see any of you girls near them.'' His stern glance went from girl to girl, resting on Elizabeth's face a little longer, as though he could tell the rebellious thoughts in her mind.

"Yes, Papa,'' replied Elizabeth for them all. Though one never knew about Henrietta. That young miss managed to get what she wished most times, and doubtless would now too. "The puppet shows are quite harmless and I always enjoy them. I heard tell there is to be a display of foreign animals this year. Do you know anything about this, Papa?'' Elizabeth felt that by keeping her father talking, he might forget to speak to Alissa about whatever maggoty notion he had acquired after listening to Henrietta. It could quite ruin the day for Alissa, and simply was not just.

"Not a word,'' he replied, rising from the table with ceremony. "If you will excuse me, I would like to speak with Alissa in the library as soon as she finishes her meal.''

Her appetite having flown at these words, Alissa rose to follow him. She gave Elizabeth a wan smile, ignoring the sympathetic look from Lord Ives as she quit the room.

"I would hear you now, Papa. What is it you wished to say to me?'' She entered the library after him and braced herself against the desk while awaiting his answer.

"Your sister brought to our attention your disgraceful behavior of last evening. It caps your many other failings by far. As a result I feel it would be pointless to send you to London for a second Season.''

Alissa breathed a sigh of relief. Perhaps this was not to be bad news, but good?

He continued. ''On that regard, I feel it is necessary to tell you I have decided to find a husband for you. I will determine who will be the most likely man to approach and try to reach an understanding. I simply hope that your, ah, difficulty does not put him off.''

Alissa swallowed with care. ''Very well, Papa. Is that all?'' She had to get out of this room before she gave way to tears. At his brisk nod, she walked from the room, closing the door behind her with a muted click.

''It is not as bad as I feared,'' she said to Elizabeth, who waited in the hall, mangling her handkerchief. ''I do not have to travel to London for the Season.'' Alissa gripped her hands tightly before her, adding in a rueful voice, ''However, it seems Papa has decided to find me a husband. One he hopes has not heard of my 'difficulty.' ''

Near the door to the breakfast room, and close to where the two girls stood in soft conversation, Lord Ives heard the words and frowned.

# 13

"Do hurry. We shall miss the opening ceremonies as it is." Lady ffolkes gave an impatient look at her dearest of daughters. "I so enjoy all that festive display."

Henrietta studied the landau with a jaundiced eye. Her dear papa and Barrett had left an hour ago. Mama and Elizabeth were waiting patiently in the carriage. Lord Duffus rode his horse close to where Elizabeth sat. Not for Henrietta the insipid family vehicle. Lord Ives stood next to his curricle, and *that* was the vehicle Henrietta intended to ride in to the fair. Of course, there was room for two more in the family landau, but what young woman would not prefer to ride with this handsome lord?

The difficulty occurred with the handsome lord. So far he had not invited her to ride with him, and Henrietta was infuriated, to put it mildly. She coquettishly tilted her head so charmingly covered with the little chip hat tied round with blue riband. Fluttering her eyelashes at Lord Ives, she said in an admiring voice, "La, sir, such a lovely curricle. I vow there will not be another like it at the fair."

Bestowing a rather cool smile upon her, Lord Ives bowed (rather distantly, Elizabeth thought from where she sat), replying, "I am charmed by your approval, Miss Henrietta."

Alissa hurried breathlessly from the manor house, holding up the reticule that she unaccountably hadn't been able to locate. "Here it is. I am so sorry to keep you waiting."

Henrietta gave Alissa an incensed look as Lord Iveds offered her his hand, helping her up into the curricle with a deference Henrietta found most annoying. She snapped, "Another minute and we would have gone without you." The disgruntled young lady marched to the landau and plumped herself down across from Elizabeth, bonnet ribands

168

bouncing with her ire as she smoothed out her dress of pale blue jaconet.

The roads to Salisbury were clogged with carriages and men on horseback, even at this early hour. The dust threatened to cover everyone with a gray film in spite of the rain shower that had dampened the road during the night. Henrietta fretted, brushing the dust with an impatient hand.

Once through town, the carriages stopped at the fairgrounds, with the grooms drawing lots to see who would stand which portion of duty with the horses. The chattering, laughing group descended upon the fair with great cheer.

Lord Ives lifted Alissa from the curricle, then placed her hand on his arm, thus effectively holding her close to his side. "I suspect you had better remain near me. Your brother and father are probably to be found in the direction of the sheep pens. You undoubtedly won't see them for the remainder of the day."

Alissa blushed and shook her head. "I would not desire to have any ill befall you, given my penchant for accidents. Besides, with my height, I am not likely to become lost."

"Actually, I hoped to talk with you." Lord Ives drew her out of the way of a band of jolly youths intent on finding the raree-shows.

She laughed at the notion of conversation. " 'Shout' is more like it. The noise will become worse as the day grows long." Her leg twinged, causing her to lean on his arm with gratitude. Perhaps she had best depend on his strong support after all.

"Nevertheless, I would have you safe at my side."

"I doubt I am in danger, Lord Ives." Her grave words concealed the hammering heart caused by his nearness.

Christopher glanced over her head to where Henrietta gave them a malevolent look from where she stood with the ever-faithful Algernon Smythe-Pipkin. The beauty *might* not harm her sister, but she wouldn't lift a finger to help her either. If Alissa experienced a weakening of her leg today, Christopher wanted to be at hand to assist.

Alissa gave him a happy smile as they began to stroll

toward the center of the fair. "I must thank you for the nosegay. 'Twas most delightful. And I confess that an escort would be appreciated today."

"Does your, ah, are you bothered by any pain or discomfort this morning?" His look of concern was balm to one who was often ignored.

She shook her head, not wishing to reveal that momentary stab of pain. "I cannot predict when it will trouble me, which is why I accept your generous offer. I made sure you would desire to see the sheep pens." Even if Henrietta forgot, Alissa clearly recalled that the main reason for Christopher's attendance at the fair was to buy a flock of sheep.

"Would you mind if we stopped by there first? My steward is here and I wish to give him final instructions. There is a ram I particulary wish to purchase." His chagrin at her motive for remaining by his side was well-concealed. For a gentleman much sought after, it was a distinct novelty to be treated so casually. He decided he would make a special effort to beguile the lady.

She gave a little skip to keep up with his long stride. Though her own legs were long, the narrow skirt of her dress hampered her walk. How lovely it might be if she were able to stride through the crowd in fawn pantaloons such as Lord Ives now wore. Even her mother would swoon at the sight of that!

For attending a mere country fair, Ives looked quite elegant with that well-fitting dark brown coat and tasteful green waistcoat. His fawn beaver tilted at just the precise angle to let the viewer know this man was no local lad.

Alissa felt she barely did him justice in her green sprigged Indian mull, but she had an attachment to the dress. Fond memories. Never could she play blindman's buff without recalling this dress and Lord Ives. She peeped at his face from beneath the short brim of her cottage bonnet of green twilled sarcenet, wondering if the fat green bow under her chin might not get a bit warm as the day progressed. Then she thought of the roundabout she dearly loved to ride, not to mention the ups and downs, which she intended to patronize in spite of what her father said. It would be a shocking thing to have her bonnet go sailing off her head in such a crowd.

They managed to locate the steward, and Lord Ives gave him a string of instructions, which the man appeared to take in stride. It would have daunted Alissa to have all that flung at her in one swallow.

Nearby a drover stood, ever-watchful eyes on the sheep. He was colorfully dressed in a white coat and yellow waistcoat, a bright red-and-yellow-spotted handkerchief around his neck, and blue-and-white-striped stockings above stout shoes. A badge on his left arm proclaimed his status, as did the crook he held firmly in his right hand. Once the purchase was made, he and that frisky dog at his feet would see to it the sheep were safely moved to Lord Ives's estate, a journey of many days. Traveling at eight to ten miles per day, the sheep would make slow progress.

Lord Ives and Alissa stood for a few moments looking over the milling animals, the din of thousands of sheep nearly obliterating conversation. Then Lord Ives moved away, and as her hand was still firmly tucked next to that warm, comforting body, Alissa hastily moved along with him. It was a relief to leave the bleating sheep far behind them, though the raucous sounds of the rest of the fair were not exactly gentle to the ears.

"What do you wish to see first? The stalls with all the things for sale, or the booths with shows and amazing animals? Or do I detect a wanton desire to have a go at the ups and downs?"

"You are laughing at me," she protested, knowing full well she must have the wondrous look of a child of ten in her eyes.

"I spent a bit of time in your father's library this morning—after you had your visit with him. I found a book of poems by Wordsworth. A line or two stuck in my mind."

She glanced at him, a sparkle lending her eyes great depth. "And what would that be?" she asked obediently.

"Minx. Let me see, it had to do with daisies, a subject you profess to be familiar with. Ah, yes:

"Thou unassuming Common-place

Of Nature with that homely face,
And yet with something of a grace,
Which Love makes for thee! . . .
A nun demure of lowly port;
Or sprightly maiden of Love's court,
In thy simplicity the sport
Of all temptations.

"You see? The poet felt that daisies were tempting, made for love, I believe. At the very least, a maiden of love's court. How does that meet with innocence?" He kept his face straight with difficulty at the expression on her face. It was half chagrined young lady and half imp.

"Well," she said, far louder than she would have wished, given the subject, but necessary because of the crowd, "I expect it refers to the days of chivalry, when a lady gave permission for her knight to wear her double daisy on his shield as a sign that his affections were returned."

"I see. Shall I request a double daisy from you, Miss Alissa?"

His voice came from a point dangerously close to her ear. That was the trouble with being so tall, it left one open to all manner of strange things, like having a gentleman whisper ridiculous remarks to you. Not that he could whisper in this crowd, mind you.

She pretended not to hear the question that she was sure was utter nonsense. He could not be interested in bearing her "daisy" on his "shield" as proof she returned an affection that she doubted existed in the first place.

Elizabeth danced up to them holding a small parcel. "Oh, Alissa, do look at this. Duffy insisted upon buying me a remembrance of the fair. Is it not the most dear little music box you ever saw?"

A warning glance at Elizabeth reminded her that it was not strictly proper to be accepting gifts from gentlemen. But one look at the dainty music box in question revealed why it had been irresistible. The domed lid was inlaid with a pretty design of a lute with ribands and flowers. When the lid was lifted the delicate sound of "Under the Greenwood Tree" came tinkling out with charming clarity, in spite of the throng about them. Alissa closed the lid and handed the fruitwood box to Elizabeth.

"Quite the loveliest I have ever seen. I can see what made you succumb." She gave Duffy an understanding smile.

The four wandered along the booths displaying the multitude of wares carried from fair to fair by the itinerant merchants. China, ironmongery, and Woodstock gloves vied with fruit, sweetmeats, and cakes. Everywhere people thronged about, looking, testing the merchandise. Dealers inspected great heaps of cheese before buying and sending their purchases to their wagons. To their right Alissa observed a lady with a length of veiling preen before a mirror, while a farmer several feet away chuckled at the vanity displayed. Little boys daringly darted in and out of the crowd, followed by devoted dogs, their wagging tails causing havoc when they came too close to the stalls. Bonneted little girls squealed and clung to their mothers' skirts.

Alissa cast a longing look at the nearest gingerbread stand. She had money of her own to spend. She desired a tasty slab of gingerbread more than anything. Was it proper to hint, or should she merely walk over to purchase what she desired? The difficulty lay with her arm so firmly tucked close to Christopher's side. It appeared nigh unto impossible to extricate herself from his hold. Then again, when she considered the rowdy boys, she was glad enough for his protection.

"I am perishing for some gingerbread," bubbled Elizabeth. "Do say we may have some, Alissa."

Reaching for her reticule with distinct relief, Alissa found herself thwarted by the determined gentleman at her side. He stepped forward, purse at the ready, to buy the treat. Still-warm pieces of delicious-smelling gingerbread were soon in their hands. Not caring a farthing for propriety while here at the fair, Alissa tucked her York tan gloves in her reticule. Now she could enjoy the treat with no worry for her new gloves.

"You would not deny me the pleasure of providing you with gingerbread, surely?" Ives watched with amusement as she daintily nibbled the cooling bread while they strolled along the booths.

Mouth full of gingerbread, Alissa gave him a twinkling glance. When she could speak, she said, "You make it difficult to be independent, sir."

She was jostled by a youth intent on getting to the area where the games were going on, judging by his conversation with his friend. They were set on competing in the wheelbarrow race. Alissa once again had cause to be grateful for the protecting arm offered by Lord Ives.

"Shall we follow them?"

Alissa nodded. "In a minute. I see something I wish to buy." She had spotted a display of bells from India, perfect for her hawks. Hurrying over to the booth, she examined the various bells, looked yearningly at a pair much chased and delicately made, then decided on plainer, cheaper ones. Lord Ives took them from her hand, replaced them, and picked up the more beautiful bells.

"I think Princess deserves these, don't you?" The gleam in those dark eyes dared her to contradict him.

How could she possibly reply to that? "But . . ."

"If Duffy can buy a trinket for Elizabeth, how can you deny me the same privilege? And these aren't for you, they are for your hawks."

As logic went, it was irrefutable. She thanked him warmly, tucking the little packet into her reticule with great care.

Henrietta and Algernon had joined the group in time to see Lord Ives hand the small packet to Alissa. Henrietta's eyes flared with fury and not a little jealousy. That was a distinctly new emotion for the beauty. In her spoiled and pampered life she had always been the recipient of pretty gifts. It was the outside of enough to see her plain sister receiving something. And from Lord Ives to boot! She dragged the hapless Algernon along toward the portion of the field where the wheelbarrow race was set to begin, an unpleasant pout on her face.

Several flags waved in the welcome breeze while the competitors were blindfolded and led to their wheelbarrows. It was great fun to see the men running awkwardly across the field, frequently crashing into each other, overturning, even occasionally injuring others. Alissa turned away when an accident happened, unable to see the joy in that.

"Amazing to see what can be accomplished while wearing a blindfold," commented Lord Ives in the most bland of voices.

Darting a dubious look at the elegant lord at her side, Alissa made no reply to that leading remark. Instead she gestured to where a group of young women clustered about the far end of the field. Each was stepping into a coarse hemp sack and soon struggling across the field in ungainly jumps in an attempt to secure the pretty straw bonnet displayed at the judges' stand.

"Come on, Matty!" Alissa cried softly, not wishing to call attention to herself. "Oh, I hope she wins, she has had her heart set on that bonnet for such a long time."

"Your maid, I take it."

"Not precisely. The upstairs maid. She took care of me following the accident." Alissa jumped up and down with excitement as Matty passed her nearest rival and tumbled across the finish line with a joyful shout of glee.

"I am so glad," Alissa pronounced with great satisfaction. "It is ever so much better than my simply giving her the bonnet. There is something to be said for the pleasure of achieving a thing on your own merits."

Elizabeth towed a cheerful Duffy to the roundabout, and shortly they were all (even Henrietta, who could not resist the lures of the fair for long) enjoying a ride. From here Elizabeth demurely led them to where the ups and downs stood, her eyes twinkling with naughtiness. She looked to Alissa, pleading most politely. "I do wish we could."

Desiring nothing more than a ride herself, Alissa gave a considering look at the attraction. Papa could not have been serious in his refusal of the treat, undoubtedly said in a fit of pique. Surely he would not deny them this treat? "This appears to be sturdy enough. I vote we go."

Henrietta experienced a feeling akin to war as she debated between enjoying a ride and telling her parents of the disobedience. She had no choice in the matter when Lord Ives

and Algernon whisked her into one of the partially enclosed
seats. Algernon seated himself beside her and dropped the
board down, effectively ending her deliberation.

It was a thrill reminding Alissa of sailing over a fence on
Fancy or watching Princess reach the top of a climb and
prepare to plummet to earth once more. Though the small
wooden cages moved at a somewhat slow pace, they climbed
high in the air, and her stomach lurched as she and
Christopher attained the peak.

Far across the grounds of the fair she espied the figure
of her father. She hoped he could not see her in the forbidden
treat. He was talking to a distant neighbor, Lord Quarley.
How Alissa detested the man, so foppish in his dress. What
on earth could her father, who utterly despised the exquisite
Quarley, have to say to him?

"Is something the matter, Miss Alissa?" Christopher noted
the frown that had settled on Alissa's brow, wondering what
could mar her pleasure of the ride. Following her fixed stare,
he picked out her father with an amusingly dressed pink of
the *ton*. What the devil was old Quarley doing at the fair?
Christopher would have bet a goodly sum that nothing might
have induced the baron to come within a mile of it.

"No, er, that is, yes." Alissa gasped as a sudden thought
struck her. "He would not serve me such a turn."

Jumping to conclusions, Ives inquired, "I trust the visit
with your father this morning was not a dreadful one?"

Without consideration of her choice of confidant, she said
faintly, "Papa mentioned that he intended to see me wed.
Lord Quarley is a noted hater of hawks; he claims one killed
a pet of his. And I doubt if he would tolerate a woman who
dabbled in clay—such dirty stuff. Since my father cannot
abide the man, I can only conclude Papa means to follow
up on his promise to me this morning."

Normally she would have bitten her tongue rather than
reveal this news. But if her father indeed intended to match
her with the elegant London dandy—who undoubtedly would
welcome her dowry with open arms—she must think of her
birds.

Turning to Lord Ives, she was about to request he take

her hawks when they came to a bouncing halt and had to hurriedly exit the ride.

Earnestly she clasped his arm, forgetting the bustle and noise about her in her desire to protect her birds. She again opened her mouth to beseech Ives to accept her birds, when she was once more interrupted.

Henrietta walked up to them, annoyed at the closeness of Alissa and Lord Ives, who *must* be getting a bit weary of tending to her sister. "Why do we not all go to the booths? I declare it would be vastly amusing to see the Italian lady walk the high rope. Can it be true she performs tricks on it?" She sought Lord Ives's attention, but found it directed elsewhere.

Giving Henrietta an impatient glance, Lord Ives turned to Algernon and motioned to him. "You four go ahead. We will follow right behind you. I fear Alissa is getting tired with all this rushing about." It was the best he could do for an excuse on such short notice.

Henrietta cast a narrow-eyed stare at Alissa that, if seen, would have warned of impending danger.

"Now," Christopher said when the others had drifted in the direction of the sideshows, where a drum could be heard, inviting attention to the attractions inside, "tell me again what this business is about."

"My wits are scattered. Forgive me. Papa said he intends to see me wed and out of his hair. He was most angry with me for something." She prudently omitted the reason, not wishing Lord Ives to feel in any way responsible. "I fear he intends me to wed Lord Quarley. I would that you take my hawks. I cannot see them destroyed, and either Papa or Lord Quarley would manage to accomplish that, I expect."

Her eyes searched his face, wondering if he had truly meant his promise to care for her beloved birds if the necessity should arise. Her fears subsided as his dark eyes snapped with anger and he nodded curtly. "But, of course. However, it may not come to that. It is possible you might be able to avoid marriage to Lord Quarley. And it is no certainty that he will fall in with your father's wishes."

"When I was in London I heard rumors that Lord Quarley

was a shocking gamester. I suspect that my healthy dowry
would be more than welcome to one of his ilk. Do not men
in that position traditionally look for well-dowered
spinsters?'' She could not conceal the hint of anger in her
voice. To think her father would sell her thus simply to punish
her for something she could not help. How frustrating the
life of a woman was, even in the enlightened age of 1812.

"You are not to be considered a spinster at your tender
years. Naturally I will take the hawks if it comes to that.
But perhaps I will think of something.''

Alissa supposed he meant to comfort her, but there was
little doubt in her mind that she would be forced to wed the
man she despised if what she suspected were true. "Let us
rejoin the others. I would not have anyone asking questions.''
She refrained from mentioning Henrietta, but Alissa strongly
suspected her hand in the matter. Henrietta knew full well
how Alissa loathed Lord Quarley. She could have suggested
to Papa last night that Lord Quarley would be a most suitable
groom. Alissa's heart sank at the very thought. She clung
to Lord Ives, determined she would do something to prevent
that marriage.

They caught sight of Elizabeth and Duffy standing by the
entrance to the puppet show. Elizabeth stood enthralled with
the promised treat, much given to clever things to be done
with her hands. She had confided to Alissa that when she
had children, she intended to make a puppet show for them.
Now she planned to watch with care, storing up useful
knowledge for her future.

"I know not where Henrietta and Algernon went. I suspect
Henrietta desired to look at the trinkets once again.'' She
exchanged a look with Alissa. Algernon might not be of the
peerage, but he was excessively plump in the pocket, and
that helped considerably in Henrietta's eyes. Once Henrietta
had observed the gifts each of her sisters had acquired, she
was most likely determined to outshine them.

Alissa gave a discreet nod and the four entered the puppet
booth with varied smiles on their faces.

Although the production was humorous, with Punch his
usual outrageous self, Alissa could not pay it much heed.

In the dim light of the interior of the tent, she sat and worried.

Could she remind Lord Ives that he had suggested his Aunt Catherine as a refuge for her? Perhaps Alissa had truly given him a disgust of herself, and now he was merely masking his thoughts, doing the civil? She was distracted as they left the booth.

Elizabeth wanted to head for the swingboats once they left the puppet show. "Even Henrietta cannot complain about that. Papa has not said a word about it."

"Most unexceptional," proferred Duffy as he tucked Elizabeth's hand into the crook of his arm and led her toward the enormous swingboats, not very far from the ups and downs. A smug Henrietta and a thoughtful-looking Algernon stood near the attraction.

Alissa happily joined the others as they entered the ride, and settled down next to Christopher. Henrietta flashed a look of dislike at Alissa, which she quite missed. Here was Alissa, thought Henrietta, again thrusting herself at his poor lordship. The dear man was most put upon.

A few good pulls on the ropes, and shortly the six found themselves rising higher and higher in the air. Henrietta began to look slightly green. Elizabeth and Alissa giggled, while Duffy and Christopher saw to it that the swing went as high as could go.

Alissa suddenly took note of Henrietta's tinge and clutched at Lord Ives. He mistook her touch for that horrified delight one knows on amusement rides, and signaled the ropes be pulled harder.

Alissa struggled to her feet, calling to Lord Ives, "Henrietta does not feel well. I fear we ought to stop the swingboat." Her message delivered, she turned to sit down. Then it happened. Alissa lost her balance and fell. Right upon Lord Ives! In an incredible tangle of legs and arms, her skirts and bonnet awry!

Never in her life had she heard such guffaws of laughter as she did when the swingboat hastily came to a halt. Her skirt had flown up to reveal an inordinate amount of fine white cambric petticoat. And she was flat upon Lord Ives's chest—once again! He was as she remembered, with that long-limbed body, so firmly muscled and very enticing. She looked up to his face and saw the laughter lurking in his eyes as he placed his hands at her waist. Oh, double drat!

Red-cheeked with embarrassment, she clambered from the boat-shaped ride to stalk away with wounded dignity. Elizabeth rushed to her side with soothing words.

Henrietta began her customary recital of dire predictions. She was utterly furious that Alissa had disgraced them with her foolish action. Worse yet, Alissa had gained the attention of Lord Ives. Henrietta had decided *she* would have him. Oh, Alissa would pay dearly for this insult.

With the assistance of Duffy and Algernon, everything managed to get sorted out.

Lord Ives walked them away from the scene, watching the color in Alissa's cheek fade as the laughter dissipated.

"Now the fat is in the fire, for certain," muttered a distressed Alissa. "Papa will be sure to hear of this disaster. I shall likely find myself wed to Lord Quarley before a cat could wipe its ear."

"You mustn't brood on the thing, you know." Lord Ives would have cheerfully thrashed Baron ffolkes at the moment. That the man could treat so fine a young woman as Alissa in such a manner was not to be endured. He suspected the wrongdoing that had brought the matter to a head was the incident of the wine on the waistcoat. In a way, he felt as though he might be responsible. He ought never to have allowed Alissa to fetch him a plate, wine or no wine. If only he had paid attention to her in the swingboat. Guilt stung his sense of honor. He would contrive something to save her. He must.

Alissa blindly turned to where Wombwell's Menagerie display proclaimed the wonders to be seen inside. "I rather think I might prefer to see the Russian eagle," she said in a strained voice. "Can it be as black as they paint it? And of course the other wild animals." If they went inside, they would be out of view for a time. It would be preferable to the sniggers and leers coming her way at the moment.

Falling in with her suggestion, and suspecting the motive behind it, he added, "A panther and a hare that plays the pipes! Let us not delay.'' He courteously conducted her to the menagerie booth.

Not far away, Henrietta stared at Alissa and Lord Ives as they disappeared into the wild-animal booth. Her wrath boiled over and she wheeled about, searching the crowd for one particular person.

When Alissa and Christopher later returned to the throng of the fair, they were not long in spying Henrietta and Algernon. The two stood with Lady ffolkes. Algernon wore a disgusted expression on his face. Lord Ives wondered if the long-suffering swain had at last seen the light in regard to the beautiful but spoiled blond.

Lady ffolkes was not best pleased, from the face she presented to the group that joined her.

Elizabeth danced up to her mother, placing a hand upon her arm, crying delightedly, ''Is this not remarkable, Mama? The fair is so full of marvelous sights. We must see as much as possible before we head for home.'' The half-wreath of roses that ornamented Elizabeth's chip bonnet flounced about in her enthusiasm.

''I understand Alissa has again disgraced herself by unseemly behavior. While I will not mar the pleasure of the day for the rest of you, I wish to say that your father is correct, Alissa. Something will be done, and soon.''

Henrietta darted a pleased smile toward Lord Ives before turning her triumphant gaze upon Alissa. That would teach her sister a thing or two.

Behind them the naphtha flares were lit, flaming up into the dusky night, promising, enticing.

# 14

"Her ways are ways of pleasantness, and all her paths are peace," quoted Duffy as he lounged in the one decent chair in Christopher's room. "I believe that in spite of her youth, Miss Elizabeth is the girl I have searched for these years. Now, if her father can be persuaded to part with her company, I shall look forward to a household of great harmony and pleasure."

"Is there any doubt he might refuse your suit? He seems anxious enough to get his females off his hands." The words were snapped out while Lord Ives changed from the dusty clothes worn to the fair. "I believe there is a proverb that applies to Lord ffolkes and his children, at least one daughter, rather well."

Duffy nodded, giving his irate friend a sage look. "I believe I recollect what you mean . . . the one regarding he that spareth his rod hateth his son, or daughter, as the case might be."

"Henrietta ought to be punished at the very least. I believe it is her doing, in great part, that Alissa is to be driven into the bed of a man she despises." Christopher found he disliked that bit about the bed above all.

"We must do a bit of thinking," Duffy replied blandly. "I've no doubt we can find a solution, if we but try." It was almost amusing to see Ives in such a bother. The poor devil didn't know quite how to respond, so accustomed was he to thinking of marriage for anyone but himself.

"Aunt Catherine, I suppose," concluded Ives.

Duffy gave a resigned sigh, shaking his head at his friend. "There are none so blind . . ." he muttered to the chair arms.

Baron ffolkes was a happy man that evening, in spite of

the problems with his eldest daughter that continued to plague him like a swarm of bees that refuse to leave the hive. His sale of sheep had gone well. He confided to Ives over the after-dinner port, "Got a fair price today. Sheep brought between fifty-five and seventy-two shillings per, depending. Good results, if I do say so. You were satisfied with the fair?" He studied the well-set lord down from London. Seemed as though he had no intention of offering for Henrietta, peculiar as that might be. Perhaps he was one of those men who had to have a title. Pity, that. Well, if things went right tomorrow, and Quarley was pleased with the sight of Alissa, one of his girls would be off his hands. Lord ffolkes doubted if Henrietta would be any problem to launch. Still . . . firing her off now would have saved him the cost of a Season in London.

Lord Ives smiled politely. "My steward sought me out before departing for my estate. We did well enough; bargaining is something at which Banks excels." Christopher rotated the fine crystal glass between his fingers before looking at Lord ffolkes. "I was surprised to see you chatting with Lord Quarley today. I understand he has an estate not far from here. Sadly encumbered, if my memory serves me right."

Shifting as though uncomfortable in his large chair at the head of the table, Lord ffolkes failed to meet the disconcerting gaze directed at him. "Fine young man."

"Not so young, four-and-thirty if a day," Ives denied. "I recall he was several years ahead of me at Eton." And had managed to make everyone's life as miserable as he could.

Lord ffolkes did not wish to discuss his plans regarding Lord Quarley the coming day, so he simply replied, "I expect we shall see him after services tomorrow."

Duffy exchanged a questioning look with Ives as they rose and followed their host from the dining room to where the ladies waited for them.

Henrietta was feeling in a musical mood and demanded that Alissa play for her. The knowledge that Alissa must feel less than enthusiastic about playing some joyful tunes this evening concerned her not one whit.

Duffy consented to sing for them, and Alissa played for both while planning furiously. Tomorrow. The very thought loomed like a specter before her. She must find a means to avert this disaster if she could.

Lady ffolkes sat with a book by the fireside while Lord ffolkes watched the young people, wearing a pleased expression until his eyes happened to fall on Alissa. He frowned, causing her to miss a few notes when she observed his look.

Duffy caught the appeal in Christopher's eyes and suggested a rousing game of whist. Lord ffolkes and Henrietta played against Duffy and Elizabeth, much to Henrietta's annoyance.

Alissa escaped from the drawing room out to the terrace before her mother could command her to continue playing. She folded her shawl about her against the slight nip in the air.

" 'Tis a bit crisp this evening. Perhaps it signals a change in the weather. This has been a lovely day.'' The sharp clicks of his boots on the brick drew her up abruptly.

Turning to face Lord Ives, Alissa said, "Mayhap for you. And for me,'' she confessed, as she remembered the delightful parts of the day, before her disaster and the confrontation with her mother. "Though I could do without the continual difficulties that seem to beset me. Elizabeth's guardian angels let me down today.''

"And you feel there will be a decision to face soon? Your father mentioned something about seeing Lord Quarley tomorrow after services.'' Christopher peered down at her in the gloom, wondering if those words had meant what he thought they might.

"After services?'' she echoed with dismay. So soon? When her father had taken the notion to dispose of her, it seemed he did not waste time. What a blessing that he had apparently decided Lord Ives would not be interested in her. She could not have tolerated the kind of bargaining her father would most likely conduct with that distinguished gentleman.

Lady ffolkes came out on the terrace just then, pointing out to Lord Ives the splendid pear orchard to be glimpsed off to the east, near the artificial lake Lord ffolkes had created for her pleasure years ago. "Alissa," she said, guiding her daughter toward the drawing room again, "do go out in the morning and pick a few ripe pears for breakfast. Cook will be wanting some as well, so do not stint on the number." She studied the wan face at her side. "I imagine you must be tired after such a busy day."

Feeling that perhaps there was an implied criticism in those words, Alissa assured her, "I shall remember to pick the pears, Mama. I confess I am a wee bit tired. I had best get to bed now. Good night, all."

Her voice reached Lord Ives where he stood in the doorway. He remained lost in thought, watching her march up the broad stairs to her room, firmly holding her night-candle in one hand, the other trailing along the banister. Later, when he also walked up, he found Lady sprawled outside the door opposite his. The dog raised her head in puzzled greeting, looking like she'd lost her last friend. "You too, eh, Lady?" There was no sound from within the room.

The house was barely stirring when Alissa rose in the morning. Dressing sensibly and wrapping a warm shawl about her shoulders, she tiptoed down the stairs, through the hall, and used the conservatory exit from the house. Lady trotted along behind, a hopeful wag of her tail bringing a smile from her mistress.

The crisp air was a sharp contrast to the humid fragrance of the conservatory. Alissa gathered up a basket from the gardening shed and continued her way toward the pear orchard.

It was a fine morning in which to think. The sun had risen, sending soft golden rays over the heavy dew that had formed during the night. Diamond dewdrops winked at her from the petals of late-blooming asters and hydrangeas. Each step she took left a mark on the damp grass until she reached the neat graveled path.

What manner of barrier might she throw up to prevent the marriage her father desired? From what she knew of Quarley, he demanded perfection, no matter that his purse was often too small to pay for such. Her dowry would scarce last long in his hands. What might possibly give him a disgust of her?

Setting down her basket beneath the first of the trees, she began to select the best of the pears. Many were fit only for baking, but there seemed a goodly number to grace the table as well.

"Very nice."

Alissa jumped as the voice reached out from the early-morning quiet. She dropped the pears in her hands, whirling about in sudden confusion. She had thought herself to be alone. "Lord Ives," she whispered. She ought not to be surprised; the man seemed to turn up at the oddest moments.

He gathered up the fallen fruit, placing it carefully in the wicker basket, then faced her. "I want to talk with you. We were interrupted last evening. I suspect your mother did not wish us to converse in privacy."

"You must admit that it might be considered unseemly." The small grin she'd been holding back had escaped at the sight of him picking up the fallen pears.

Christopher leaned against one of the limbs of the pear tree, surveying the area. "Let's take a boat out on the lake," he said impulsively.

"At this hour of the morning? You must be daft!"

"It's one way to assure we get privacy." He was piqued at her lack of regard for him. His address must be in need of polishing. Not so much as a blush or a flutter of an eyelash did he merit this morning.

She gave him a curious look, permitted him to set the full basket of pears on the pathway, then escort her to the edge of the lake, where a neat little rowboat was pulled up by the shore. "I fail to see why it is so important we be alone. If all you wish to do is to talk . . ." Her brows raised in question as a few rather dubious thoughts drifted through her mind. She gave a glance to where Lady sprawled on the grass in a patch of sun, watching carefully through half-raised lids.

"I hoped that perhaps I might try the hypnotism once more." He casually checked the boat over to assure himself of its lake-worthiness.

"I don't mean to cast aspersions on your ability, but it

does not seem to have done me much good so far.'' What a curious man. He obviously had no interest in Henrietta. Alissa had quite decided upon that point. But what *did* he want?

Ives picked her up, setting her firmly on one of the two broad boards which served as seats in the small boat, then placed the oars in the locks. He pushed out before jumping in to sit opposite her on the remaining board.

The gentle splash of the oars in the water mingled with the song of the birds hidden in the trees along the shore. Alissa leaned back, resting her elbows on the high frame of the boat, enjoying the light warmth of the morning sun on her face.

Ives felt certain she'd improved. He desired to strengthen her further. Toward the center of the small lake, he paused, allowing the oars to rest on the surface of the water. ''Trust me to try once again?''

Sighing, she shrugged. ''I suppose it can do no harm. It cannot, I gather?'' She gave him a sharp look before resuming a relaxed pose against the curved back of the boat.

Christopher once again spoke in his soft, soothing manner, reassuring the slim girl across from him that she was lovely, capable, able to cope, that she need not fear others, who were quite as likely to fear her censure in return. She had appeared to drift into a light sleep, her eyes opening with reluctance when he finished.

She blinked, then gave him a slow look. She really could not detect any change within her, save her growing love for this man. Although Elizabeth *had* mentioned that Alissa seemed more at ease with others lately. If it gave him pleasure to think he was helping her, she could go along with this silliness. Actually, his caring might do more than this hypnosis business.

''I doubt it will help in the least, if what I suspect is true. If my father intends me to wed Baron Quarley, I believe his reference to 'after the morning service' has something to do with an agreement they have reached. Perhaps I must pass an inspection first? It seems Lord Quarley does not remember me, either.'' Her hint of a smile was rueful as she thought how forgettable she was. "I respect the gentleman for not wishing to buy a pig in a poke."

Christopher's anger flared. He longed to shake her. He stretched out a hand as though to do just that. "How dare you refer to yourself in that manner!"

"Have you given any more consideration to your Aunt Catherine?" It had taken daring to ask him that. He had said nothing these past days, perhaps having second thoughts as he saw what a bumbler she had turned out to be.

"Yes," he replied absently, studying the charming face across from him. Whatever had possessed him to think Henrietta was such a beauty? There was no character revealed in the vapid blond. Alissa exhibited all the traits of real beauty, inward as well as outward.

"And?" Alissa leaned forward in her urgency. She must find a place to which she might flee if necessary. She had no intention of marrying Baron Quarley!

Christopher began to row them slowly back to shore.

"Oh," he replied absently, "I sent off a note the other day. Should get some sort of reply by tomorrow. She lives not too far from here. Has a place that marches with mine. I think you will like her. I do."

A loud splash brought both heads about.

"Oh, drat," said Alissa, observing with dismay Lady paddling through the chilly water toward the boat. If that silly dog took a notion to try to climb into the boat, it might get a bit difficult, to put it mildly.

Not aware of the dog's fondness for a boat ride, Christopher encouraged her.

Alissa was about to remonstrate with him regarding that particular inclination when Lady reached them and put a dripping paw up on the side of the boat. "Good dog," said Christopher with approval, bending over to pat the black-and-white head.

Suddenly the boat gave a wild rock as the dog made a concerted effort to climb inside . . . with disastrous results. The cold water was not welcome as a bath, Alissa decided as they sailed over the side of the boat and into the lake.

She floundered about in the waist-deep water, her long skirts hampering her attempts to move.

"Sorry . . ." she gasped. "I neglected to tell you she likes a ride."

"Are you all right? Other than wet, that is?" Christopher found a footing on the sandy lake bottom and stood, wondering what Roberts would say about his clothes this time. "We had best make for shore. Come, let me help you."

"Lady is seldom far from my side when I am to home. She thought she ought to join us." Alissa glared at the unrepentant dog, who now seemed to be laughing at them from the bank of the lake.

Lord Ives picked pond weeds off his elegant waistcoat and held a hand toward Alissa. "My tailor is indebted to the dog," he murmured as they slogged toward the shore. Alissa most fortunately failed to hear the remark.

They collapsed on the bank in the shelter of a mass of hydrangeas. Alissa looked at the earl, stifling a desire to giggle at the sight of his dripping clothes. Wringing out the hem of her dress, she shook her head, saying ruefully, "It has happened again. I vow I am like a figure in a Greek tragedy, with awful things occurring whenever I appear. They seem to be getting worse rather than better. I am responsible for the ruination of two of your waistcoats. I must apologize for that, Christopher," she offered softly. Then, looking back at the house, she added, " 'Tis a fine kettle of fish we are in. 'Twill be a wonder if we do not catch some dire ailment from this dousing."

"A devil of a mess, I'll agree, but you can hardly say 'tis your fault, when it was the dog who precipitated our morning plunge-bath." He pulled off both boots, dumping a minnow from one of them.

"I do hope your Roberts can salvage those fine boots," she observed as she rose to her feet. "We had better play least in sight until we reach the safety of our rooms. I will order you some water for a hot soak. 'Tis as well you are soon leaving." She held out her hand for the basket of pears he had picked up. "You would not have a garment left in condition to be worn, at the rate I manage to ruin them. Now, go ahead and I will leave this fruit at the kitchen. I shall see you later, most likely before we go to church. Papa wants to attend the cathedral this morning, probably to impress our fine visitors.''

They walked a short distance together, then parted, Alissa going to the kitchen, where the cook exclaimed over the condition of her favorite.

After quietly ordering that hot water be taken up to the earl, Alissa slipped up the back stairs to her room. There she removed her clothes, rubbing her skin briskly until she was pink from neck to toes. A slathering of rose-scented lotion, dry clothing, and she felt no worse for the dunking. She could only hope that his lordship took no ill. She had distinctly heard a sneeze as he rounded the corner to the conservatory door.

At the breakfast table, no mention was made of the early-morning rendezvous or of the catastrophic results. Alissa meekly slid to her chair at the table under her father's narrow gaze.

Lady ffolkes neatly cut up a pear, nodding approval at the perfect ripeness of the fruit. ''I see you were up early this morning, Alissa. Good girl. Lovely fruit, this. Do you not agree, Lord Duffus?'' She gestured to the pear that sat on Duffy's plate. For some peculiar reason, Lord Ives had ignored the lovely autumn offering.

''To be sure, Lady ffolkes.'' Duffy looked at his friend, who promptly sneezed. Duffy wondered what in the world had been going on this morning while all the house was sound asleep. The *rest* of the house, he amended, as he caught the guarded look exchanged between Alissa and Christopher.

Following the hasty breakfast, the family gathered for the drive to Salisbury to attend the morning service in the cathedral, as Alissa had foretold. Rather than create a scene, Alissa hurriedly joined her mother in the landau. Duffy sat with Elizabeth on the opposite side, while her father rode up in front with Barrett, who had elected to drive.

Henrietta twirled her new pagoda parasol in blue sarcenet with white fringe, and sauntered to the curricle, batting her eyelashes at Lord Ives before a groom stepped forward to assist her into the vehicle. "Lovely day, is it not, Lord Ives?" She seated herself with a flourish, careful to reveal her reticule, which modishly matched the dashing parasol. It was plain to see that Miss Henrietta was as up to snuff as could be for a young lady who had not the advantage of a trip to a London modiste.

His lordship sneezed.

Henrietta drew away in dismay. Lord Ives was not looking at her with admiration. Rather, his poor eyes seemed to hold the sort of glazed expression she had noticed when one was coming down with a nasty cold. Henrietta edged away from the silent lord whose curricle she insisted was to be her transport, and wondered if she ought to switch with Alissa. Then a happy thought popped into her head. She was never ill, so why worry?

The carriages set off for Salisbury at a smart clip. Henrietta regaled Lord Ives with her triumphs (for he surely would want to know such things) at the Salisbury assemblies and various country balls she had attended. Even a few she hadn't attended, for, she reasoned, he would never know the difference. She was quite certain she had impressed him, for he murmured approving noises at all the right moments. In between sneezes, that is.

At the church, Duffy joined Ives after they left the carriages in care of a young lad. The ladies all walked ahead. Lord ffolkes and Barrett were in a discussion of some problem with one of their horses. Ives looked at Duffy and sighed.

"Do you have any notion of what I have endured this past thirty minutes? I suspect I am coming down with some nasty ailment. At least I feel not in plump current for a number of reasons, and that . . . that bird-witted girl nigh talked my head off. She is an aggravating wigeon if ever I heard one."

Duffy cleared his throat, making a cautionary gesture to where the others walked ahead of them—unnecessary, as Lord Ives had dropped his voice to a near-whisper.

"I cannot wait to get clear of this place. S'help me, if I have to listen to more of the same going home, I shall do violence." He gave Duffy an assessing look, then said in an offhand way, "Why don't you give Miss Elizabeth a treat going back? You take the curricle and I'll take your place in the landau. At least I can look at Alissa that way, and ignore the pratings of that bumptious miss."

"You were quite taken with the lass at one time, as I recall," ventured Duffy.

"Never!" replied Ives in his most lordly manner.

The service was well-attended. Many had stayed over following the fair and wished to take in the service before returning to their respective villages. The ffolkes family took their seats, and if few of them actually listened to the sermon of the day, it was understandable.

Henrietta was lost in dreams of glory: she would stroll into Almack's and the entire male population of the rooms would be at her feet.

Elizabeth darted thoughtful glances at Duffy, wondering if he actually would ask for her hand as he had implied. If he did, would her father permit the marriage?

Alissa possessed the most sober of faces, thinking as she did of Lord Quarley and what her future most likely held. While riding in the carriage, she had considered a few desperate plans. She could not disgrace her family and guests by anything extreme. No, it must be something that would possibly give Lord Quarley a disgust of her, yet not unduly upset her mother and father. Not that their feelings must be her first consideration. Her situation was most desperate. She had no doubt she could be wed by special license to Lord Quarley before the week was out, given her father's temper.

Just as they reached the church, a rather splendid idea popped into her mind. She had paused to consider it, acted upon it accordingly, and now she waited in suspense to see if her bold scheme might work. If ever she had need of a thespian ability, it was today.

At the conclusion of the service, during which Lord Ives sneezed at least twenty times, the group filed out, shaking hands with the canon before strolling into the pale sunshine.

Alissa paused, falling behind the others as she bent to the ground to adjust her slipper. Her heart was ticking away at a furious pace, her mouth dry, hands clammy. She fumbled, shaking her head in frustration at the delay. Her father must not suspect anything until too late.

Henrietta observed Lord Quarley's approach, giving Alissa a triumphant smirk before turning to answer a question from Algernon, who had joined her.

Ahead of Alissa, Lord ffolkes met Lord Quarley near the area where the carriages stood waiting. Ignoring the notion that ffolkes might wish to be alone with Quarley, Ives and Duffy followed behind, exchanging meaningful looks. Lord Quarley was arrayed in great splendor this morning. A lilac waistcoat embroidered with butterflies topped a pair of pale cream pantaloons over which he wore a long-tailed coat of dove gray. His cravat was a towering monument to the efficacy of starch.

"Blasted twiddle-poop looks like a bouquet of spring posies," Duffy muttered. He got a nudge in the ribs to achieve silence as the two neared the pair in bargaining session.

Lord Quarley appeared not best pleased to see his acquaintances from London strolling toward him. He nodded in a polite greeting before turning aside to what he had obviously hoped would be a private conversation with Baron ffolkes. The terms had been set forth the day before. Now he wanted to see the girl.

As though summoned, Alissa limped toward them with a sweetly somber expression on her face. While she traversed the graveled path, four pairs of eyes watched her halting progress with varied expressions. Lord Quarley looked horrified, an expression of distaste crossing his face.

When she neared the men, Alissa realized that in the past she would never have attempted so bold a scheme to defeat her father's plans. She came to stand before them, drawing a sad little breath as she smiled wanly and said, "Good day, Lord Quarley."

"What on earth!" blurted her father.

"Are you all right, Miss Alissa?" offered Lord Ives, his tone most sympathetic.

Alissa shot him a suspicious glance before turning to her father. "You wished to see me?"

"I say, ffolkes, you didn't tell me the chit was crippled." Lord Quarley was clearly most affronted at the sight of his nearly-betrothed limping. Even a comfortable dowry didn't help in this case. It was a distinct incivility to imagine that a man of Quarley's position in the *ton* would consent to a marriage, however needed, to a woman less than perfect.

Duffy cleared his throat, then said with admiration, "Fine man you are to take a bride to wed like this. Fine man."

"Most noble of you, Quarley. Didn't expect you to react in this manner. Fine chap, as Duffy says." Lord Ives rolled pious eyes toward the heavens and added, "When you think it might get worse . . . well, most noble of you, is all I can say. Dashed if I could be as magnanimous." Ives wondered if he ought to suggest Henrietta, then decided even she didn't deserve such a fate.

Lord ffolkes appeared to be on the verge of apoplexy. His prim mouth compressed itself into a thin line. "But she ain't crippled. Are you, gel?" He glared at his innocent-looking daughter as though she had just absconded with the crown jewels.

"Of course not, Father," came the obedient reply. Alissa wished she might cross her eyes at the noxious lord, but decided it would be going a bit too far.

Lord Quarley narrowed his gaze as though he felt that reply was a shade too pat. He appeared puzzled at this turn of events. What did a man do when confronted with such a thing? While not the brightest individual, Lord Quarley was not stupid either. Obviously Lord ffolkes was trying to put one over on him, fobbing off his crippled chit in this shabby manner.

Duffy and Ives exchanged looks. "Fine girl," Ives said a degree too heartily. "She is great at hawking. Of course, she can do that while seated. And she does a lovely bit of sculpture," he added in a hopeful voice. "Though it *is* a bit messy." He bestowed a benign smile on Alissa, as though she were a child of about two-and-ten.

Instead of taking umbrage, Alissa gave the gentlemen each a demure smile, mentally promising Lord Ives she would deal with him later.

Lord Quarley made up his mind. "Sorry, ffolkes. Like to oblige. Nothing signed, you know. Suddenly remembered I'm expected to home." He swept a proper bow before hurrying away toward a natty curricle at the far end of the close.

"I shall speak to you later, Alissa, my dear." Lord ffolkes shot a malevolent glance at the two London gentlemen before going off to talk with his wife.

Alissa reached down to remove her slipper. She dumped a shower of pebbles onto the path, then calmly replaced it. Straightening, she attempted to glare at Duffy and Lord Ives. As a glare it failed rather badly. She covered her mouth with a dainty scrap of white linen and tried for serenity.

"I had not expected help this morning. For that I thank you. Tell me," she said idly, "just how did you *know* I did not wish to wed Lord Quarley?"

The gentlemen had no need to exchange looks at this question. " 'Twas simple," answered Lord Ives. "We could not imagine a lively young woman like you married to such a fop."

"Butterflies on his lilac waistcoat, indeed," murmured Duffy as he sought Elizabeth to explain they were to have the privilege of sharing the curricle on the way home. "The blasted twiddle-poop."

Lord Ives sneezed.

# 15

"Oh, Matty, will he be all right?" Alissa stood in the center of the hall staring at the closed door behind which she knew lay a very ill Lord Ives.

"Aye, Miss Alissa. 'Twill take a bit of time, that's all," said the somber maid before bustling off.

Alissa clasped her hands before her in worried silence, deeply in thought.

By the time they had reached the manor house after leaving the cathedral in Salisbury, it was evident that Lord Ives was not merely not in plump current, he was downright unwell. Lady ffolkes had whisked him up to his bedroom, ordered Matty and Roberts to see to his wants, then disappeared in the direction of the stillroom.

It was up to Alissa to see to it that Lord Ives took his medicine, her mother informed her some time later. "I have made several for him. Let me see, here is a decoction of feverfew and honey for the aching, and a syrup of cherry bark for his chest. This decoction of yarrow will relieve his nose. Oh, and give his man this bottle." She handed Alissa a stoppered glass bottle of evil-looking liquid. "You know what this is. It ought to help him. Poor man, I cannot think how he came to be ill. If he is so inclined, perhaps it is as well Henrietta is not to wed him. I would not like to think of her a widow so early in life."

"Yes, Mama." Alissa set up a tray, refraining from any comment on Lord Ives or the state of his health. She returned to the upper hall, taking a deep breath before knocking gently on his slightly open door. She could see his large frame outlined beneath the pile of covers. Cautiously she entered the room.

Lord Ives turned red-rimmed eyes toward Alissa, gave her a bleary look, then sneezed. "What is it you have there?"

He cast a suspicious glance at the contents of the tray and rolled to his other side in the great bed, his broad back to Alissa.

She took one look at his linen-covered frame and swallowed carefully. She hadn't anticipated these flutterings inside her at the mere sight of him, especially when he was ill.

"These potions are to help you feel better. My mother is skilled at making decoctions and syrups." Alissa could not help but feel nervous at being so near him. His illness was all her fault.

He turned fretfully and studied the bottle of dark liquid. "That looks deadly enough to wipe out half the population of this house. What is it?"

She placed the tray on the table next to his bedside. "You are not required to drink it, milord. Roberts can bathe your aching, ah, self with it. It contains mullein leaves, sage, marjoram, and chamomile flowers."

"The others?" He shuddered at the sight of the bottles of medicines, all looking so ominous.

"Cherry-bark syrup, feverfew with honey, plus a decoction of yarrow if you need it. Mama is prepared for any eventuality. I cannot tell you how sorry I am that you have fallen ill." Alissa bravely met those dark eyes. "I feel it is somehow my fault. Had you not been seeking to help me, you would now be well . . . and your clothes in far better condition. And it *was* my dog."

She poured out a spoonful of the cherry-bark syrup and popped it into his mouth when he opened it to speak.

He glared at her, his gaze softening as he observed her distress. "Roberts has assured me that Matty has been most generous with her help. My clothes have been restored to excellent condition."

"But for that beautiful waistcoat that I spilled claret over." Yet she could not resist a final excuse of sorts. "You *would* interfere." He appeared to ignore her righteous defense.

"Can you draw up a chair? I feel better when talking to you, and 'tis your duty to see me well." He attempted a smile before he gave another rousing sneeze. He accepted a large square of soft linen from her and blew his nose, wishing he felt more like himself. He ached like the very devil and wanted nothing more than to sleep. But as long as Alissa was here, he had something to say to her.

"About my Aunt Catherine . . . you can go to her if needs be. Though her letter has not come, I know she will not refuse me." Watery eyes carefully monitored Alissa's expressive face. What he saw satisfied him.

"Horrid man, to be so sure of yourself." With great difficulty, she quelled the spate of emotions that threatened her. Lord Ives dressed in all his elegance was one thing. Lord Ives in a fine linen nightshirt and appealingly vulnerable was quite another matter entirely. The sight stirred emotions within that she simply could not identify, but that seemed deliciously wicked to her innocent mind.

"You seem to be progressing in that direction." He blew his nose, then studied her with a disconcerting gaze. Alissa dropped her eyes before his penetrating look. "You are sure you are not sorry about Quarley?"

Shaking her head with amusement, Alissa replied, "That I am not." If he but knew what thoughts swam about in her foolish head. "I confess I had a few trepidations, but that awful fate awaiting me gave me the strength to proceed."

"I trust the experience has not put you off the institution of marriage forever." He sneezed again, thus missing her look of dismay. "I am proud of your improvement. I daresay you might not have attempted to thwart your father in the past."

She shifted as though uncomfortable. "It remains to be seen how much I benefit." She had no desire to tell him she feared the next candidate her father might produce.

"Think you that Elizabeth will accept Duffy, or ought I say 'David' now? He intends to ask for her hand. I cannot believe he is getting leg-shackled at long last."

"First of all, he is not so very old." She gave Ives a reproving look which seemed not to affect him in the least. "And second, though I cannot speak for Elizabeth, I know she cares for him. I imagine it depends on how Papa reacts. He once expected me to marry first. Who knows if he will permit Elizabeth to be wed before Henrietta and me." Alissa neatly folded a stack of soft old linen squares, experience telling her he would have need of every one of them before the day was gone.

"Could Elizabeth be feigning interest in him? I would not have my friend deceived." He blew his nose again and wondered if the contents of one of those bottles on the tray would help him sleep. He felt as though the oblivion of Morpheus would be most welcome.

"It is not in Elizabeth to be devious. In spite of the difference in ages, they ought to get along well—between his proverbs and her guardian angels." She gave him an amused smile, then dropped the last of the squares to offer him another spoon of medicine, the yarrow decoction. There was enough sugar to make it palatable, and sufficient laudanum with the yarrow leaves in it to ease the stuffiness of his nose and help Lord Ives get needed sleep. Satisfied with his apparent tractability, she prepared to quit the room.

"You are feeling well?" he suddenly asked, forestalling her departure.

"Well enough. My greatest concern is that you rest and recover." She felt considerably stronger at this safe distance. Heavens, the man exerted the most tempting charm without trying in the least.

"You are no doubt wishing us to perdition." He gave an enormous sigh, looking helpless and susceptible.

Alissa wagered he had captured every heart around when he was a lad. She shook her head, soft curls threatening to tumble from beneath the dainty linen cap she wore this afternoon. "I suspect it is quite the opposite. Lady is properly chastised. I doubt she will so much as look at a rowboat again. I daresay I am the same. Neither swing nor boat carries much appeal for me now." She noted his drooping lids and added, "You had best get some sleep. There's a bell on the table that someone is bound to hear should you desire anything. Roberts ought to be lurking about close by."

With those words, she slipped from the room, ignoring his protest. Matty was just leaving Henrietta's room. The maid had a guilty grin on her face.

"Problems, Matty?"

"My new bonnet is much too like Miss Henrietta's. She be unhappy. No matter, when my Jeb saw me in the bonnet, he was proper impressed."

Alissa nodded. "I should hate to lose you, but I know how much you wish to wed Jeb." She touched Matty on the hand, wondering how they would get on without the kindly maid. If Alissa ever married, she would cease the practice of firing a maid simply because she wed. It was a great deal of bother to train a new maid. Fortunately Jeb had a good position with promise of advancement, so Matty would not feel hardship at the loss of her income.

Everyone was thinking marriage this autumn, it seemed. Lord Duffus wished to wed Elizabeth, and the girl most certainly felt the same toward him. Henrietta wanted to marry any handsome, well-set-up lord—the more impressive, the better. Barrett had quiet glances for Selina's cousin from Bath. Only Alissa held no illusions about her future. Her father, now thwarted in his plans with Baron Quarley, would seek another man for her to wed, most likely a rustic squire. Sooner or later she would be unable to prevent a betrothal. Lord Ives's Aunt Catherine might be her only alternative.

The conservatory beckoned. Alissa welcomed the peace after the bustle of the household. Lord Duffus, Alissa had been informed by Parsons, was in conference with Lord ffolkes.

Out in the peace of the plant room, Alissa was ignored. Pulling the drawing of Lord Ives from where she had concealed it, she first studied it. She then located a well-protected mound of clay and set to work.

An hour later a breathless Elizabeth dashed around the corner with Duffy in tow. "Papa agreed! Is that not splendid?" She bestowed a loving look at her dear David, as she had begun to call him, and continued. "David is going to his home to get the betrothal ring that has been in his family for simply ages, and when he returns, we are to be wed. Six weeks or thereabouts."

"That is little enough time to prepare. You are certain?" Alissa searched Elizabeth's face for reassurance that the girl truly loved her betrothed and wasn't simply opting for a way out of a household she feared more than loved.

"Indeed!" A glowing Elizabeth drew Duffy after her to the terrace, leaving Alissa to stare after them in thoughtful contemplation. Henrietta would not be pleased at this turn of events. When Alissa had failed to snare a husband in London, Henrietta had vowed to be the first to marry. She must needs work quickly to manage that. And one didn't find husbands growing on trees in the wilds of Wiltshire.

Looking at the mass of clay on the table before her, Alissa had very private wishes that she knew not even Elizabeth's guardian angels might fulfill.

The days fell into a pattern of sorts. Lord Ives was a terrible patient—for he wasn't. Patient, that is.

"You must be the grumpiest mulligrubs I have ever seen," Alissa scolded. "You are not the first person to have a nasty cold. Permit me to offer my small efforts at entertaining you, now that you feel up to living once again." She daringly lifted the pillows from behind his back, shook them, then replaced them carefully.

"Roberts will no doubt thank you for your sacrifice." He blew his nose and settled against the smooth pillows, scented faintly with lavender. He could smell again, which indicated to him he was quite on the mend.

"Oh," she replied airily, "I sit up with sick dogs and birds as well. You needn't feel particularly flattered." She produced the backgammon board, men, and dice she judged Lord Ives to be able to handle at this point.

"I fully intend to wipe you out in backgammon." His growl might be intended to sound fierce, but it made her chuckle. He wished she *would* flatter him. Never once did she flirt or lead him on. It made her a challenge.

Alissa set out the board, offering him his two dice and dice box. Then she sat back to watch him.

He won the first move and the game was on. Alissa surprised herself with the determination she felt to beat this utterly odious man. Goodness, but he had been such a bear the past days. Not that he didn't have some reason. But now that he was better, no quarter would be spared.

He won the game, though it was hard fought, and with a bare margin of victory. She had two men left on the board when he removed his last.

"I see you don't feel the need to pamper me anymore." His tone was wistful, indicative that he knew his stay was drawing to a close.

"Indeed," she said, rising to place the board on the far table. "You can be up and about any day you please."

"I think that medicine your mother gave me has permanently addled my brain. I doubt I can move." In truth, he was in no rush. Once he got up from his bed, he would be obliged to leave for his home. "Alissa . . ."

"Yes?" She paused near the open door. All proprieties had been observed during his illness. She wanted no opportunity for her scheming father to claim that Lord Ives must do the civil and wed someone he felt pity for, no more.

Henrietta could be heard in the hall approaching rapidly, if Alissa was correct. She shared a rueful smile with Lord Ives as he sighed, then turned away from the door, pretending to be asleep.

"Pst! Alissa, come here." Henrietta beckoned imperiously. She had assiduously avoided the sickroom.

Casting a glance at the recumbent figure draped in fine linen, Alissa carefully closed his bedroom door, then followed her sister down the hall and into her room. "What is it? Judging from your agitation, I would say it is rather serious."

"I have heard such news. Only fancy this: Algernon has inherited a fortune from an uncle. A fortune!"

"We always knew he was well-connected. What meaning has this for you?" Alissa leaned against the open door, folding her arms while she watched her sister.

Henrietta paced back and forth in her beautifully decorated room. The largest of the bedrooms given to the girls, it was a delicate blue and gold, complimenting the young woman who claimed it as her own. "I fear Papa will insist I accept him. You know he offered forme some time ago? Papa postponed any answer, telling Algernon I ought to have a Season in London before I settle down. Now I fear that when Papa hears of this, he will hand me over to Algernon immediately.''

''Doubtless Papa fears some other girl will grasp Algernon when she learns he not only has money, but is nice as well.'' Alissa had little sympathy for her sister on this point. Algernon doted on Henrietta and would be a kind husband. He wasn't given to gaming excesses. Nor did he fail to show an interest in managing his family estate. Henrietta had led him on most shamelessly. Perhaps it was time for her dear sister to learn a few lessons of life.

Henrietta rounded on Alissa, her wrath awesome to see. ''How like you to defend him. I cannot abide him! I deserve an earl at the very least, a man like Lord Ives. Papa said so. Algernon is such a nothing. Though lately,'' she amended consideringly, ''he has changed. He actually gave me a scolding when we were at the fair. Imagine! Scolding me for doing my duty as a daughter. You know I had to tell Mother that you had had an accident.''

''Did you? Was it so necessary, Henrietta? It seems to me that Mama could have managed to live without that particular bit of information. And did you have to urge Papa to seek out Lord Quarley? Oh, yes, I deduced your hand in that business. I agree with Algernon. You have done naught but make life difficult for me, and now I cannot feel but that you deserve to reap what you have sowed.'' Amazed at her own temerity, Alissa forged on. ''It seems only just that you be required to marry when you would rather not. You were quite happy to see me in a similar position not so very long ago.''

''But it was for your own good! With your being crippled, you will never get a husband if left to your own devices!'' Henrietta glared at Alissa, hands on her hips, fury at her sister's obtuseness flashing from her eyes.

''I need not listen to you, and I won't.'' For once Alissa glared back at her sister, then turned to flounce out the door, slamming it behind her with no regard for the patient next door.

Left alone in her room, Henrietta threw herself across her bed and wept bitter tears. Surely her dear papa would not serve her such a turn! He had promised her a Season in London. Pretty dresses. Adoring beaux. Rides in the park. Her aunt had guaranteed vouchers for Almack's for such a beauty as Henrietta. Oh, the thought of being wed before she could taste these delights was not to be borne.

Alissa ignored the rage she could hear, even from the hallway, and calmly slipped down to the conservatory. Here her pounding heart returned to normal while she concentrated on shaping the clay head she had so lovingly created.

Duffy, who had stopped by to bid Christopher farewell, gave him a curious look while the histrionics from the next room were clearly overheard. "Whoso findeth a wife findeth a good thing," he mused.

"Not in this case. It seems Henrietta has a temper as great as her beauty. I don't envy poor Smythe-Pipkin if he has to contend with that." Their eyes met in mutual agreement.

"Aye. If the lad is wise, he'll begin as he means to go on, and I wonder if he knows how to cope with the lass." Duffy gathered up his many-caped greatcoat and prepared to leave the room. His future father-in-law was to drive with him to Salisbury, where Duffy would pick up a post chaise to carry him north.

"And you do?" Christopher slid from his bed, testing his legs on a trip to the better chair near the window.

"Oh, aye. Be firm with her. Give her orders and mayhap threaten a paddling if need be." Duffy pulled on his gloves, making it clear he would have no hesitation to administer such a thing if it were necessary.

"A paddling? I'd give a monkey to see that! Though it does seem a bit harsh . . . for anyone but the miss next door. Perhaps I ought to pass along your advice."

He chuckled at the notion, then said an affectionate farewell to his best of friends. "Take care. We shall see each other before long. Of course, I'll return here for the wedding. It won't be many days before I can quit this room."

Christopher then stared out the window at the falling rain,

not envying Duffy his trip, yet in a way envious of the quiet joy he saw reflected in his old friend's eyes. Duffy had asked him to be his groomsman, and it was expected Alissa would attend Elizabeth. Knowing what a skinflint the old man was regarding his daughters, Ives suspected the marriage would be by special license, thus saving the expense of an elaborate ceremony in the cathedral and all that it entailed.

Ives anticipated it would be lonely after Duffy left. Alissa took great care when she came to see him. The door always remained open; she whisked in and out of the room as though afraid of him. Or perhaps it was herself she feared? Christopher had long hours in which to consider those stolen kisses. Miss Alissa was not unshaken by them. She had responded so beautifully for an untutored woman. He spent quite a number of contemplative minutes reflecting on how it would be to tutor her further.

Suddenly impatient with his enforced isolation, he put on his dressing gown over the breeches and shirt normally worn for lounging. He found his cane and, with the help of a strongly disapproving Roberts, made his way down the stairs and out to the conservatory. He figured this was where he might find Alissa on such a gloomy day. He was right. She sat at a table working on some clay thing while the seemingly unrepentant Lady sprawled at her feet.

Alissa glanced up at the shuffling sound, to find Lord Ives on the arm of his valet. Horrified that he might see her portrait sculpture of him, she hastily covered up the head and rose from the table, quickly placing the mound of modeled clay behind her. Lady rose and walked over to reacquaint herself with the gentleman.

"Good morning, Lord Ives. Please—rest in this chair. You look a trifle down-pin as yet. I cannot approve your venturing so far from your bed," she scolded. She glanced to where the valet stood with a stern expression on his normally bland facade. "By the looks he is giving you, I believe Roberts agrees with me." She hurried to place the most comfortable chair in the room at an angle from which her sculpture, even though concealed, could not easily be seen.

Glad to find a reasonably adequate seat in this house that

seemed to favor hard chairs, Lord Ives sank down, a little
more abruptly than usual. He dismissed Roberts, who left
the room, his back stiff with disapproval.

"I shall ring for tea," she blurted in her desire to take
his mind away from her work.

"Do that," he sighed. The trip had been more tiring than
he expected. "Duffy has gone. I expect Elizabeth will be
busy getting her bride clothes ready. What about Henrietta?"

"Oh, dear." Alissa placed an embarrassed hand to her
mouth, giving him a most rueful look. "I quite forgot you
were in the next room. You could scarcely fail to overhear
that horrid conversation. I am utterly ashamed of my speech
to my own sister." She turned to pull the bell rope, and Ives
had a fine view of that tall, slender form, very well-shaped
as he recalled from when he carried her. Pretty ankles, too.

"Well, you cannot deny she deserved what you said, for
it was naught but the truth." He reached out to fondle the
dog's silky ears, earning a blissful look and a sleek head
thrust on his lap.

Pulling her chair away from the table—and the mound of
clay—Alissa cautiously seated herself, giving him a wary
look. "That does not give me the right to say such things.
Are you sure you feel well enough to be here? I vow I thought
you would not be up and around for a day or two at the
earliest." She would have welcomed the advance notice. Yet
she hadn't expected to entertain him in the conservatory. In
fact, she hadn't expected to entertain him at all.

"I must be leaving as soon as I can. A good deal of
business awaits me." He slyly peeked to see how she
accepted the news. It was lowering to see how eager she
seemed to be rid of his presence.

Alissa welcomed a footman bearing a tray. He set it on
the corner of her table before discreetly leaving, his eyes
busily taking in the elegantly casual dress of the London
gentleman so he could repeat the details belowstairs.

"I imagine that is so. I can only say again how sorry I
am." Her hands were unsteady as she poured the tea.

He shook his head. "I think it did you good, though."
Accepting the steaming cup of tea laced with lemon and sugar

the way he preferred it, he added, "Look how well you stood up to Henrietta. Could you have done that a month ago?"

After a considering look out the window at the downpour of rain, she nodded agreement. "I am certain you have the right of it. That still does not excuse my behavior."

"You *can* see you don't have to be, indeed you don't *want* to be, like Henrietta. You are such a charming young woman. You have a native wit and intelligence Henrietta quite lacks. In short, you ought to like what you see in the mirror." He sipped at his tea, wondering how much of what he said would be believed. "You mentioned Henrietta as being so perfect. Underneath that facade of beauty is a lady not too agreeable. Much better to be you."

"But Henrietta does not have the accidents I do. You would never find her spilling claret down a waistcoat." She set her cup on the tray and moved restlessly on her chair.

"She might if she thought it would gain her an advantage." He cursed his impetuous words as he saw the horrified expression leap into her eyes.

"Surely you don't think I did it deliberately!" She rose from her chair in agitation. Hands clasped before her, she strolled to the window, looking back at Lord Ives with distress. What a lovely, vital woman posed tautly against the gray of the sky and dark green of the plants. Those turbulent eyes reflected the deep blue of a stormy sea. Lord Ives knew a desire to look at them much closer.

He used his gold-handled cane to assist him from the chair and walked to stand at her side. "I know you did no such thing. There isn't a devious bone in your body." His free hand reached up to touch her chin lightly.

Alissa trembled at that touch, as gentle as it might be. No deviousness? How surprised he might be if he knew her thoughts this very moment. If she could do as she wished, she would throw her arms about that tall man and kiss him with all the love she knew in her heart.

"Henrietta was wrong, my dear. You are not crippled. And there is no reason in the world why a man would not ask you to marry him." He drew her closer, wanting to hold her close once again.

He bent forward, capturing her lips with an ease that jolted Alissa to her inner being. His touch was magical, trailing sparks of heat wherever his hand strayed. Feelings akin to the flutter of alarm she'd experienced when faced with crowds now spread through her—but it was enchantment that followed, not fear. She slipped her hands up to shyly touch his shoulders, his neck, then his head, caressing it beneath her fingers as she might model her sculpture, knowing every curve, memorizing every line.

When he released her to gaze down at those enchanting features that had haunted his nights, he said impulsively, "Marry me, Alissa."

"Marry you?" she echoed. For one delirious moment she contemplated the idea of marriage to this man. He was kind and probably would be most loving. She liked being with him and his droll sense of humor. Not the least of all, she loved him most desperately. Then she recalled his manner of living. She could never be his countess. Never. Even with her changed spirit, he deserved better.

"You do me great honor, my lord. I cannot accept, however. I fear we would not suit." She dropped her gaze to the rain-swept grounds beyond the snug conservatory. He must not see the lie in her eyes.

Inside her, she felt that newfound spirit wilt more than a little. How could she face losing the man she loved? Yet she had valid reasons for her refusal. Three, to be precise. The first two consisted of her unreliable leg and her far-from-strong self-confidence. The third remained sadly true: she feared he did not love her as she loved him. His proposal had sounded spontaneous, not the kind well-thought-out in advance. Pity? Perhaps.

Ives had the oddest feeling she meant every word she said. There was no artifice or coyness to her reply. It would take some time to unravel what lay behind her words.

His hand dropped away from her as he turned aside to also contemplate the dismal scene from the window. The sky to the west held a gleam of light. The rain would be gone before long.

"I shall leave once the rain stops. You can see it would

not do for me to remain. I am well enough and my home is not that far from here." Besides, his spirits had taken a drubbing.

"But," she sputtered, concerned yet relieved, "you have but the curricle. It has turned chilly; you might get worse."

"Would that you truly cared, my dear." He moved from her side, pausing as he reached the doorway, more sure on his feet now, and feeling as though he might do well to be apart from her. "Just remember . . . I intend to return."

# 16

"Have you heard the latest, my dear? Quite the most delicious news." Elizabeth plopped herself down on the chair in the conservatory to have a comfortable rainy-day coze with Alissa. "Selina Hardwick is to marry with Sir William before Christmas! Is not that delightful? *And* he has asked Barrett to be his groomsman! She is to have her cousin from Bath as her bridesmaid." The girls exchanged significant looks. "Selina is all aflutter, choosing bride clothes and helping to oversee the renovations at Sir William's neat little estate."

"So many weddings. I wonder how Henrietta will take this bit of news?" Alissa had discreetly dropped a cloth over her head sculpture when she heard Elizabeth's approach. Now she took another chunk of clay to pretend a different interest. She began to shape a falcon, wishing it would stop raining so she might go out with the hawks.

"She was not pleased. And all this talk of Algernon's great good fortune, well!" Elizabeth studied Alissa before speaking again. "You have been very withdrawn since Lord Ives left. Are you so unhappy?"

"Me?" Alissa croaked in alarm. "I have been tired, that is all. Mama left the supervision of the cleaning to me. This is the first opportunity I have had to sit for a bit without feeling as though I was neglecting something."

"I hate to leave you here. How will you manage with Henrietta?" Elizabeth rose to pace restlessly back and forth. Fortunately she took little interest in the project sitting on the table where Alissa worked. Her mind was on Duffy, or David as she now called him, and her pretty new clothes.

"Papa was good to let me buy so many lovely things. I vow, I am so excited I scarce can sleep a wink."

"It would be a shame if he did not provide you with all

you need—considering you are being married in the chapel
by special license. For all the money he is saving by being
spared a huge wedding and feast, he can well afford to be
generous,'' Alissa declared.

"All the same, I imagine Henrietta would wheedle more
out of him.'' Elizabeth sighed, drawing flowers on the
windowpane she had steamed up with her breath. "I wish
I could like our sister better. She has been impossible these
past few days.''

"You know how she looks forward to her Season. She
fears Papa . . .'' Alissa looked up to see the object of their
discussion standing in the doorway, her face extremely pale.
"What has happened?''

"He did it! After I begged him not to.'' Henrietta drifted
across the room in the way only she could manage, like a
floating bit of thistledown. At the moment, dressed in her
many-tucked white muslin gown, she resembled Alissa's
vision of the tragic Ophelia.

"Did what?'' demanded Elizabeth, impatient with
Henrietta's dramatics. "And who, more to the point?''

Henrietta arrayed herself against the bank of greenery,
lifted a lily-white hand to her brow, and sniffed—once.
Dabbing a delicate lace handkerchief to her rosebud mouth,
she sighed, turning mournful eyes on her sisters.

"Well?'' Alissa had lost what patience she had with
Henrietta. The girl really overdid the theatrical gestures.

"Papa consented to my marriage with Algernon! Even now
he is meeting with Algernon to inform him of the agreement.
My name is to be plain Smythe-Pipkin! Oh''—the word was
wrung from her soul—"it is simply too much! Papa said he
could not allow this advantageous match to slip through my
fingers. He said''—she paused for effect—"I might not do
half so well in London. 'Tis all your fault, Alissa. Had you
made a good match of it, I would not be so plagued now!''

Elizabeth advanced on Henrietta, fists at her sides. "Don't
you dare scold Alissa for your own troubles. If you had not
flirted with Algernon so in the first place, he would never
have given you a look.''

"Well!'' Henrietta dropped her hand to glare at Elizabeth.

Any further words were lost as Algernon entered the conservatory, obviously looking for Henrietta.

Alissa quietly studied Algernon, noting he seemed taller, more sure of himself. He possessed an air of confidence hitherto lacking.

Facing Henrietta, he announced, "Your father has done me the honor of accepting my suit. We will be wed immediately. I have waited for you long enough; I need a wife now." Henrietta sputtered, preparing to launch a counterattack, when he continued. Rubbing his chin in contemplation, he said, "The first thing you will do is to wear a plain cap on your head. There will be none of this folderol business. I have no intention of catering to you like your papa has in the past." He glanced at Alissa, giving her a faint wink.

Henrietta gasped like a beached flounder while Algernon gave her a cool look, then went on. "Your father will put it about that we have been betrothed these many weeks and now we shall wed promptly due to my inheritance, which is no less than the truth. There will be no Season for you, my dear. I fear you have a few things to learn before we venture into society. For one, you will learn to be a good wife."

He moved to stand close to Henrietta. She stared at him as though he was an awful apparition, not the boy she had flirted with these past years, nor the man she was now to wed. He nodded. "Quite so, my dear, and don't you forget it. Prepare yourself for a quiet wedding by special license at our local church." With that, he took her by the arm and the two walked from the room. Henrietta appeared to be in a state of shock, Algernon quite in charge.

Alissa and Elizabeth looked at each other in amazement.

"Will you fancy that? If Duffy were here, he would say that 'Pride goeth before destruction and a haughty spirit before a fall.' I cannot believe my own eyes." Elizabeth wandered about the conservatory, picked a leaf off one of the plants, and twiddled it between her fingers.

"At least she will get her wish to be married before the rest of us." Alissa set aside her little falcon, to join her sister by the window, her soft muslin skirts rustling in the silence of the room. They gazed out across the garden, blessed by a gentle rain. Alissa turned to face Elizabeth. "That leaves me. Perhaps with you two fired off and Barrett looking April and May with Selina's cousin from Bath, I shall be left in peace."

"True. Even Papa must realize the household needs guidance. Mama is too occupied with her gardening to bother much about the interior. Were it not for you, the manor would be in sad condition."

Alissa shook her head in denial. "I have had your help as well. You go well-prepared to manage Duffy's castle in the wilds of Scotland." She reached out to touch Elizabeth lightly. "You have no doubts?"

"Duffy said we need not spend very much time up there. He raises cattle for market in Yorkshire and has able men to handle that business." She smiled with the happy memories of her beloved. "He has a lovely house in Edinburgh; we will have the winters in that erudite society. It shall please me above all things. Duffy is well-acquainted with Sir Walter Scott, and I am to meet him. Oh, I can scarce wait."

A wistful look of longing on her sweet face, Alissa watched Elizabeth drift from the conservatory. It was impossible to return to the work on the sculpture. Rather, she energetically began to turn out a cupboard in the downstairs hall. This type of busywork was her salvation during the following days. When she was not employed in this manner, she helped her sisters go over their clothes, the bride chests, and endless arrangements. For even simple weddings required a certain amount of planning.

Henrietta's wedding was the first. Algernon had surprised them all by turning into a sure-minded young man with a strong will. He confided to Alissa that he had taken her advice to heart and acted accordingly. He knew what he wanted. Henrietta. But it was to be a strangely subdued Henrietta, who would know her place and position.

Alissa quite astonished herself. She managed the wedding breakfast Henrietta insisted upon with discreet aplomb.

Though a fair number of guests came from beyond the surrounding neighborhood, Alissa felt little of her former panic. She wondered how much of her newfound confidence was due to Lord Ives and his hypnotic whatever-it-was, and how much to his warm, caring attitude.

The Smythe-Pipkins were gracious and charming, though perhaps not all that pleased to see their only son wed the fluttery beauty. How lowering for Henrietta to discover that it was her generous dowry that made her acceptable to her in-laws.

Once Henrietta was gone, the manor grew more silent. With October winds whirling about the house, Lady ffolkes spent more time in the conservatory and the little room she used as an office of sorts, planning her gardens for the coming year, writing orders for bulbs and plants.

Alissa took to long walks in the misty rain, her oiled-silk umbrella a constant companion. In her hooded cloak, she resembled a spectral apparition. She was always alone, but for the companionship of Lady at her side. The hawks didn't like being out in the rain. And in truth, Alissa feared they might catch a fatal ailment if exposed to inclement weather.

Birds sought shelter in bad weather, and she supposed she was a fool to risk an inflammation of the lungs in this manner. But she could not abide remaining in the house, where her parents seemed to pop up all too frequently, a considering reflection in their eyes as they looked at her. She truly feared their designs. If Lord Quarley was the first, who might be the second? Last Sunday she had caught her father studying a neighboring squire with a speculative look. The squire was short, grossly fat, and possessed an enormous nose—and was single.

Alissa spent considerable time on these lonely walks formulating what she must do to avoid a marriage planned by her father. She had a feeling that although he was much occupied at the moment with the upcoming marriage of his youngest daughter, he was merely biding his time with her. One of these autumn days he would pounce on her like a cat on a mouse. She shuddered with very real dread at the prospect of any husband her papa might present to her after she had thwarted his scheme with Lord Quarley.

At last she settled upon a plan of action. She would send her hawks to Lord Ives with Thomas to watch after them. He could be depended upon to care for them properly. And she would attain her own refuge.

She sought out her father in his room.

"Papa, I have a matter I wish to discuss with you." Alissa waited politely by the door to his library, where most of his business was planned.

His lips compressed into a thin line, Lord ffolkes beckoned her into his room. "Well?"

Not intimidated by this cold reception as she once might have been, Alissa stepped to the desk, placing her hands on the polished mahogany surface. "I have been giving a good deal of thought to my future, and 'tis clear I must do something to make my way in this world. I cannot remain a burden here. If Barrett weds, he will be close by to assist you." She took a deep, cautious breath. "Therefore I have decided to accept a position with Lady Catherine Ivesleigh."

"Never say so! I'll not have my daughter working like some commoner." Baron ffolkes rose from his chair, his unprepossessing height not helping him to intimidate his tall daughter as he did the others. He sputtered with anger as he recalled the various men he had been considering as a potential match for Alissa. Ungrateful chit.

" 'Tis merely a position as companion. I received a lovely letter from her. It seems she never married and lives alone on her small estate in Richmond. Her nephew has seen to her comforts."

"And he is . . . ?" Lord ffolkes had subsided onto his cushioned chair. Though he knew the answer to this question, he was curious as to what explanation his most undutiful daughter might give him. The memory of her treacherous behavior regarding Lord Quarley never completely left his mind.

"Lord Ives."

"Hmm." Lord ffolkes mulled over the situation being

offered. While both Henrietta and Elizabeth were settling in to fine estates with men who had money and position to offer, Alissa had nothing. This lowly position would serve her right. His mouth quirked upward in a semblance of a smile. "Indeed. A companion. When would you be required by Lady Catherine? You know your mother will need your help with Elizabeth's wedding. Though we wish a quiet celebration, there are certain amenities that must be observed."

Hopeful that her suggestion might actually be accepted by her father without any argument, Alissa shrugged. "She states 'tis no problem when I come. Certainly after Elizabeth's wedding, since I wish to remain here for that."

He toyed with a quill pen, eyes shifting about while he thought. "I shall consider it. Must talk about it with your mother first. 'Tis an admission to all and sundry that our crippled daughter cannot get herself wed."

She flinched only slightly from the unkind words. "I am not crippled now, Papa. My leg cannot always be trusted, but it does me well enough most of the time. And if I take after Grandmama, 'tis not my fault." She could almost hear Duffy telling her that "a soft answer turneth away wrath." "I promise to try to please the Lady Catherine, and you shall be spared my presence."

He waved his hand in a gesture of denial. "You know we do not hold you in contempt, child. 'Tis merely that your mother and my mother did not get on well. As you just said, you resemble her."

Alissa kept her thoughts well-concealed. She doubted if there were many women who could be charmed by Lady ffolkes unless they were mad about gardening to the exclusion of all else. Leaving her father's library on quiet feet, she began to hope for her future . . . just a little.

And so the days flowed by. Alissa dwelt on Elizabeth's upcoming wedding with a mixture of fear and nervous anticipation. The last she had seen of Lord Ives was the day he proposed to wed her. She had sensed it a spontaneous offering, not one from the heart. She would have no man's pity. Especially not Lord Ives's. Besides, he needed a whole woman, not someone whose leg failed at awkward moments, who was too shy to entertain as he must desire. But how she missed him.

She had no idea when he might arrive for Elizabeth's wedding, and took to absenting herself from the house, edgy at the mere thought of his appearance. Weather permitting, she rode out with her hawks. On inclement days she wandered off on thoughtful walks, her cloak tangling about her feet as the wind playfully tugged at the heavy wool.

The sculpture completed, she glazed and fired it, then tucked it back on the shelf by her worktable. It was one item that would make the journey to Lady Catherine's home along with Alissa's most treasured belongings.

Christopher Ivesleigh glanced across the dinner table at his Aunt Catherine with apprehension. As darling a woman as might be, she still had her odd moments and starts. Right now she sat exquisitely dressed in silver lace and lavender silk, a delicate confection of the same stuff on her white-threaded dark hair. She appeared like a delectable comfit rather than the usual proper aunt.

"You look at me as though you expect me to go into some manner of distempered freak. I never do such a thing." She fluttered a disparaging hand in the air. "However, I certainly observe a change in you, dear boy. Most beloved of all my relations, tell me what is troubling you. I gather it is a woman. No other matter can put a man into such a fit of the dismals."

He shook his head in amusement. "I suppose you have the right of it. It is the girl I wrote to you about, the one I asked you to make your companion. You know I shall pay her way."

"I don't really need a companion, my dear. But I would do anything within reason to please you." She gave him a shrewd look from beneath lowered lashes, then popped a bite of roasted guinea hen into her mouth. "So . . . what is the problem? I take it there is one."

"I asked her to marry me and she rejected me."

Christopher had little appetite for dinner, as elegant as it might be. He toyed with the delicate crystal wine goblet before him, taking a sip of claret and thinking of the time Alissa had fallen against him, spilling the damn wine down his waistcoat.

"What? Refused the hand of the most promising young parliamentarian of the century? A woman who does not seek to be the reigning hostess of London? Fiddle. Count on it, there is some strange reason behind her answer. I take it she does not hold you in aversion?"

A memory of the tumble by the stream, the dash through the rain to the conservatory, and their final kiss in that secluded room brought a fond smile to his lips. "I believe I can safely discount that for a cause." No, she had responded most satisfactorily.

His aunt noted that euphoric expression, taking hope that her dear nephew had at last found a girl he could love. For obviously he loved the sweet creature, having such a silly, moonstruck gaze in his eyes. "Then what else might be the problem?" Catherine probed gently.

"She is quite shy. I tried to help her, and fear I did not succeed. At least she said I didn't. Her sister confides to me that Alissa fears those very dinners of which you speak. Though Elizabeth hints that she feels if I am by Alissa's side, she will do well enough. Apparently Alissa did famously during the recent breakfast given for Henrietta's marriage." That his aunt might be confused by all these names escaped him at the moment.

"You travel there shortly to attend yet another wedding of the ffolkes daughters, do you not?" At his musing nod, she continued, "Seek your girl out, try again. Remember the old saying: faint heart ne'er won fair lady."

Christopher bestowed a patient look on his aunt before a slow gleam lit his eyes. "I shall leave in the morning."

Lady Catherine gave a pleased, rather feline smile of satisfaction, thinking with relief that she could well be spared another female in the house to censure her rather singular mode of living.

* * *

Dawn crept over the downs as Christopher cantered along the well-traveled route toward Salisbury. Close by, his groom tooled the curricle. Christopher intended to be prepared for any event, and he did not relish using one of Lord ffolkes's high-bred horses for a possible hunt to locate his beloved. If the weather remained fine, Alissa would likely be out on the downs. He frowned at the gathering clouds, willing them to go away.

The air was redolent with the scent of thyme and burnet. A stray goldfinch attacked the seeds of a thistle along the roadside, oblivious of the passage of men and cattle. Though a gray day, and windy, yet flashes of autumnal colors blossomed red and gold like concealed gems amidst the green of the hills. The golden-russet of the beech leaves brought Alissa to mind, though she was never far from his thoughts.

His groom caught his attention, and noting the threat of the heavens, they decided to pause at the Pheasant Inn for the night. On the morrow he should see Alissa. With that in mind, he spent a restless evening, wondering how his suit would prosper this time. He had discovered during his absence from High ffolkes that he could not survive without his dear girl.

"Did not the cathedral look lovely midst the golden foliage? I vow 'twas a sight to gladden the heart." Alissa dumped her parcels on Elizabeth's bed, hoping she might slip out to her hawks once again. "Do you need me anymore this day?"

Taking pity on her patient and dear sister, Elizabeth shooed her from the room. "I shall pack such things in my trunk that I do not need. 'Twill be no problem at all. I suspect this will be our last trip to Salisbury. I cannot believe there are no shops in Edinburgh worth patronizing, despite what Henrietta says."

Alissa paused by the door, glancing back at Elizabeth with concern. "She has a hard time of it, does she not? Perhaps when she stops fighting Algernon on every little point she will get on better. Poor foolish girl."

"One can only hope for her. How do you feel about seeing

Lord Ives once again?'' Elizabeth observed the shadow that
crept into her sister's eyes at the mention of the man Elizabeth
was certain Alissa loved.

"He has never communicated . . . as was only proper,
mind you. I do not know how I feel. I confess I have missed
him dreadfully.'' Then, lest she say more, Alissa gave a tiny
wave of her hand and slipped from the room.

It took but a brief time to change into her teal-blue habit.
It was becoming shabby with frequent wearing. But Alissa
retained such fond memories that she could not bear to part
with it. Since her mother never seemed to notice what she
wore, and her father was only too happy not to be plagued
with another bill, she continued to jaunt from the house
clothed in teal.

Princess chortled with pleasure at being taken from the
mews. Together they rode out to the very same area where
Alissa had first sighted Lord Ives riding across the meadow
from the woods. He had stared at her with a near-frightening
intensity until she felt almost weak.

How much she had changed since that day. She had been
most pleased with herself at Henrietta's wedding, handling
all those people with little difficulty. How proud Lord Ives,
her dear Christopher, would be of her if he could have but
seen her. His plan to help her had succeeded fairly well, if
he but knew it.

Her sorrow at losing him had not left her. He would attend
the wedding, then be gone. She would not see him again.
How difficult it would be to look at him and conceal her love.
But she must, she sighed. He deserved better.

Tossing Princess into the air, Alissa watched with great
pleasure as the falcon soared high into the sky. Yesterday
had been so rainy and nasty out. Today the cobalt heavens
were all one could ask. Of sky. Lady dashed madly about,
then slunk down the hill toward where a covey of partridge
might lurk.

Seated on Fancy, Alissa mulled over the past weeks. The
sun warmed her back and a gentle wind tugged at the curls
peeping from beneath her hat. Far across the valley the colors

of the mountains blended into a tapestry of greens and golds and reds, soft and rich. Such timeless beauty.

At the manor house Christopher asked for Alissa and was informed she was out. Without so much as a by-your-leave, he marched to the conservatory. A large bundle on the shelf where she kept her sculptures caught his eye, and he paused, pulling off the cloth. He was dumbfounded to see his own likeness staring back at him.

The head was carved and molded with loving care, sending his spirits rising as he realized the implications of this small sculpture. She *must* love him to create such an affectionate portrait, far more handsome than life. Carefully he replaced the object, new eagerness giving a spring to his step as he then headed for the mews.

Alissa slid from the mare and walked to a high point, watching Princess as she hovered in the heavens, preparing to swoop to earth at the covey.

The snap and crackle of twigs on the ground of the woods alerted her to the approach of someone, even as Fancy turned skittish and danced around in a very feminine manner.

Alissa turned, staring at the man who rode across the rock-strewn meadow. "Christopher," she whispered.

Below, in the vale, Lady flushed the covey and Princess shot to the ground, a puff of feathers signaling a kill. Alissa waited, her heart pounding so hard she thought it like to burst from her bosom. Princess returned to her perch, noisily reminding Alissa of the treat she was due.

Alissa absently fed the bird, placed the partridge in her bag, then put Princess on a nearby limb. The bird sat as though puzzled at this odd behavior, casting a canny eye on the dog's activity below.

On the far side of the meadow, Christopher reined in his horse. He sat there in silence, watching, waiting for some mark of welcome.

Alissa wondered what had brought him here to this lonely spot. She raised a hand in greeting.

Christopher slid from his horse, tying him to a branch of a convenient tree. He took a step forward, hoping she had changed her mind, praying she would not reject him this time. Then he lifted his arms, hands out in a gesture of supplication. Would she come to him? Or had he lost?

In the grass below, Lady froze in her familiar position, and Princess, her keen eyes taking note of this action, took wing, ringing heavenward in a flash of gray.

Heedless of the hawk or dog or, indeed, anything else on this planet, Alissa stared at Christopher's outstretched hands. Could she? Dared she take that risk? She knew what he asked; love communicated his message as clearly as if he had shouted it to her. She took a faltering step and her leg gave way as she placed her weight on it. She fell heavily to the ground. Christopher started forward.

From her place on the soft turf, she shook her head at him, intending him to remain where he stood. Determined, she scrambled slowly, awkwardly to her feet and took another step, a little prayer winging to her guardian angel to help her, keep her from falling again.

Tears of joy slowly running down her cheeks, she again set forth, this time with success. Each step went faster. At last she ran, haltingly, with great courage, across the meadow until she reached those welcoming arms.

He hugged her to him with a fierce exaltation. "My own, my love!"

She lifted her face to receive his kiss, knowing that for all time he was hers, she his. What else could matter?

Above the two figures so closely entwined, a peregrine falcon, her wings curved like a bow, hurtled across the sky. The song of a skylark echoed over the downs.